The whole city seemed to be rocking heavily, like a ship in a storm. At one instant, the street ended in nothing but sky; at the next, Chris was staring at a wall of sheared earth, its rim looming clifflike, fifty feet or more above the new margin of the city; and then the blank sky was back again—

These huge pitching movements should have brought the whole city down in a roaring avalanche of steel and stone. Instead, only these vague twitchings and shuddering of the ground came through, and even those seemed to be fading away. Now the city was level again, amidst an immense cloud of dust, through which Chris could see the landscape begin to move solemnly past him. There was no longer even the slightest sensation of movement; the illusion that it was the valley that was revolving around the city was irresistible and more than a little dizzying.

But now the high rim of the valley was sinking. In a breath, the distant roadbed of the railroad embankment was level with the end of the street; then the lip of the street was at the brow of the mountain; then with the treetops . . . and then there was nothing but blue sky, becoming rapidly darker; and even as Chris looked up the stars became visible—at first only a few of the brightest, but the others came out steadily in their glorious hundreds.

Oddly, the sunshine was still as intense as ever. From now on, "day" and "night" would be wholly arbitrary terms aboard the city; Scranton had emerged into the realm of Eternal Daylight-Saving Time.

VOLUME 1

JAMES BLISH

CITIES IN FLIGHT, VOL. I

Copyright © 1991 by James Blish

They Shall Have Stars copyright © 1957 by James Blish. Originally published under the title Year 2018!
A Life for the Stars copyright © 1962 by James Blish.

A Baen Book

Baen Publishing Enterprises
P.O. Box 1403
Riverdale, N.Y. 10471

ISBN: 0-671-72050-3

Cover art by David Mattingly

First printing, April 1991

Distributed by
SIMON & SCHUSTER
1230 Avenue of the Americas
New York, N.Y. 10020

Printed in the United States of America

CONTENTS

THEY SHALL
HAVE STARS

And death shall have no dominion
Dead men naked they shall be one
With the man in the wind and the west moon;
When their bones are picked clean and the
    clean bones gone,
They shall have stars at elbow and foot . . .
DYLAN THOMAS

" . . . While Vegan civilization was undergoing this peculiar decline in influence, while at the height of its political and military power, the culture which was eventually to replace it was beginning to unfold. The reader should bear in mind that at that time nobody had ever heard of the Earth, and the planet's sun, Sol, was known only as an undistinguished type Gô star in the Draco sector. It is possible—although highly unlikely—that Vega knew that the Earth had developed space flight some time before the events we have just reviewed here. It was, however, only local interplanetary flight; up to this period, Earth had taken no part in Galactic history. It was inevitable, however, that Earth should make the two crucial discoveries which would bring it on to that starry stage. We may be very sure that Vega, had she known that Earth was to be her successor, would have exerted all of her enormous might to prevent it. That Vega failed to do so is evidence enough that she had no real idea of what was happening on Earth at this time. . . ."

ACREFF-MONALES: The Milky Way:
Five Cultural Portraits

BOOK ONE

PRELUDE: Washington

We do not believe any group of men adequate enough or wise enough to operate without scrutiny or without criticism. We know that the only way to avoid error is to detect it, that the only way to detect it is to be free to inquire. We know that in secrecy error undetected will flourish and subvert.
—J. ROBERT OPPENHEIMER

The shadows flickered on the walls to his left and right, just inside the edges of his vision, like shapes stepping quickly back into invisible doorways. Despite his bone-deep weariness, they made him nervous, almost made him wish that Dr. Corsi would put out the fire. Nevertheless, he remained staring into the leaping orange light, feeling the heat tightening his cheeks and the skin around his eyes, and soaking into his chest.

Corsi stirred a little beside him, but Senator Wagoner's own weight on the sofa seemed to have been increasing ever since he had first sat down. He felt drained, lethargic, as old and heavy as a stone de-

3

spite his forty-eight years; it had been a bad day in a long succession of bad days. Good days in Washington were the ones you slept through.

Next to him Corsi, for all that he was twenty years older, formerly Director of the Bureau of Standards, formerly Director of the World Health Organization, and presently head man of the American Association for the Advancement of Science (usually referred to in Washington as "the left-wing Triple A-S"), felt as light and restless and quick as a chameleon.

"I suppose you know what a chance you're taking, coming to see me," Corsi said in his dry, whispery voice. "I wouldn't be in Washington at all if I didn't think the interests of the AAAS required it. Not after the drubbing I've taken at MacHinery's hands. Even outside the government, it's like living in an aquarium—in a tank labeled 'Piranha.' But you know about all that."

"I know," the senator agreed. The shadows jumped forward and retreated. "I was followed here myself. MacHinery's gumshoes have been trying to get something on me for a long time. But I had to talk to you, Seppi. I've done my best to understand everything I've found in the committee's files since I was made chairman—but a nonscientist has inherent limitations. And I didn't want to ask revealing questions of any of the boys on my staff. That would be a sure way to a leak—probably straight to MacHinery."

"That's the definition of a government expert these days," Corsi said, even more dryly. "A man of whom you don't dare ask an important question."

"Or who'll give you only the answer he thinks you want to hear," Wagoner said heavily. "I've hit that too. Working for the government isn't a pink tea for a senator, either. Don't think I haven't wanted to be back in Alaska more than once; I've got a cabin on Kodiak where I can *enjoy* an open fire, without wondering if the shadows it throws carry notebooks. But that's enough self-pity. I ran for the office, and I mean to be good at it, as good as I can be, anyhow."

"Which is good enough," Corsi said unexpectedly, taking the brandy snifter out of Wagoner's lax hand and replenishing the little amber lake at the bottom of it. The vapors came welling up over his cupped hand, heavy and rich. "Bliss, when I first heard that the Joint Congressional Committee on Space Flight was going to fall into the hands of a freshman senator, one who'd been nothing but a press agent before his election—"

"Please," Wagoner said, wincing with mock tenderness. "A public relations counsel."

"As you like. Still and all, I turned the air blue. I knew it wouldn't have happened if any senator with seniority had wanted the committee, and the fact that none of them did seemed to me to be the worst indictment of the present Congress anyone could ask for. Every word I said was taken down, of course, and will be used against you, sooner or later. It's already been used against me, and thank God *that's* over. But I was wrong about you. You've done a whale of a good job; you've learned like magic. So if you want to cut your political throat by asking me for advice, then by God I'll give it to you."

Corsi thrust the snifter back into Wagoner's hand with something more than mock fury. "That goes for you, and for nobody else," he added. "I wouldn't tell anybody else in government the best way to pound sand—not unless the AAAS asked me to."

"I know you wouldn't, Seppi. That's part of our trouble. Thanks, anyhow." He swirled the brandy reflectively. "All right, then, tell me this: what's the matter with space flight?"

"The army," Corsi said promptly.

"Yes, but that's not all. Not by a long shot. Sure, the Army Space Service is graft-ridden, shot through with jealousy and gone rigid in the brains. But it was far worse back in the days when a half-dozen branches of government were working on space flight at the same time—the weather bureau, the navy, your bureau, the air force and so on. I've seen some documents dating back that far. The Earth Satellite Program was announced in 1944 by Stuart Symington; we didn't actually get a manned vehicle up there until 1962, after the army was given full jurisdiction. They couldn't even get the damned thing off the drawing boards; every rear admiral insisted that the plans include a parking place for his pet launch. At least now we *have* space flight.

"But there's something far more radically wrong now. If space flight were still a live proposition, by now some of it would have been taken away from the army again. There'd be some merchant shipping maybe; or even small passenger lines for a luxury trade, for the kind of people who'll go in uncomfortable ways to unliveable places just because it's horribly expensive." He chuckled heavily. "Like fox-hunting in England a hundred years ago; wasn't it Oscar Wilde who called it 'the pursuit of the inedible by the unspeakable'?"

"Isn't it still a little early for that?" Corsi said.

"In 2013? I don't think so. But if I'm rushing us on that one point, I can mention others. Why have there been no major exploratory expeditions for the past fifteen years? I should have thought that as soon as the tenth planet, Proserpine, was discovered some university or foundation would have wanted to go there. It has a big fat moon that would make a fine base—no weather exists at those temperatures—there's no sun in the sky out there to louse up photographic plates—it's only another zero-magnitude star—and so on. That kind of thing used to be meat and drink to private explorers. Given a millionaire with a thirst for science, like old Hale, and a sturdy organizer with a little grandstand in him—a Byrd-type—and we should have had a Proserpine Two station long ago. Yet space has been dead since Titan Station was set up in 1981. Why?"

He watched the flames for a moment.

"Then," he said, "there's the whole question of invention in the field. It's stopped, Seppi. Stopped cold."

Corsi said: "I seem to remember a paper from the boys on Titan not so long ago—"

"On xenobacteriology. Sure. That's not space flight, Seppi; space flight only made it possible; their results don't update space flight itself, don't improve it, make it more attractive. Those guys aren't even interested in it. *Nobody* is any more. That's why it's stopped changing.

"For instance: we're still using ion-rockets, driven by an atomic pile. It works, and there are a thousand minor variations on the principle; but the principle itself was described by Coupling in 1954! Think of it, Seppi—not one single new, basic engine design in *fifty years!* And what about hull design? That's still based on von Braun's work—older even than Coupling's. Is it really possible that there's nothing better than those frameworks of hitched onions? Or those powered gliders that act as ferries for them? Yet I can't find anything in the committee's files that looks any better."

"Are you sure you'd know a minor change from a major one?"

"You be the judge," Wagoner said grimly. "The hottest thing in current spaceship design is a new elliptically wound spring for acceleration couches. It drags like a leaf-spring with gravity, and pushes like a coil-spring against it. The design wastes energy in one direction, stores it in the other. At last reports, couches made with it feel like sacks stuffed with green tomatoes, but we think we'll have the bugs out of it soon. Tomato bugs, I suppose. Top Secret."

"There's one more Top Secret I'm not supposed to know," Corsi said. "Luckily it'll be no trouble to forget."

"All right, try this one. We have a new water-bottle for ships' stores. It's made of aluminum foil, to be collapsed from the bottom like a toothpaste tube to feed the water into the man's mouth."

"But a plastic membrane collapsed by air pressure is handier, weighs less—"

"Sure it does. And this foil tube is already standard for paste rations. All that's new about this thing is the proposal that we use it for water too. The proposal came to us from a lobbyist for CanAm Metals, with strong endorsements by a couple of senators from the Pacific Northwest. You can guess what we did with it."

"I am beginning to see your drift."

"Then I'll wind it up as fast as I can," Wagoner said. "What it all comes to is that the whole structure of space flight as it stands now is creaking, obsolescent, over-elaborate, decaying. The field is static; no, worse than that, it's losing ground. By this time, our ships ought to be sleeker and faster, and able to carry bigger payloads. We ought to have done away with this dichotomy between ships that can land on a planet, and ships that can fly from one planet to another.

"The whole question of *using* the planets for something—something, that is, besides research—ought to be within sight of settlement. Instead, nobody even discusses it any more. And our chances to settle it grow worse every year. Our appropriations are dwindling, as it gets harder and harder to convince the Congress that space flight is really good for anything. You can't sell the Congress on the long-range rewards of basic research, anyhow; representatives have to stand for election every two years, senators every six years; that's just about as far ahead as most of them are prepared to look. And suppose we tried to explain to them the basic research we're doing? We couldn't; it's classified!

"And above all, Seppi—this may be only my personal ignorance speaking, but if so, I'm stuck with it—above all, I think that by now we ought to have some slight clue toward an *interstellar* drive. We ought even to have a model, no matter how crude—as crude as a Fourth of July rocket compared to a Coupling engine, but with the principle visible. But we don't. As a matter of fact, we've written off the stars. Nobody I can talk to thinks we'll ever reach them."

Corsi got up and walked lightly to the window, where he stood with his back to the room, as though trying to look through the light-tight blind down on to the deserted street.

To Wagoner's fire-dazed eyes, he was scarcely more than a shadow himself. The senator found himself thinking, for perhaps the twentieth time in the past six months, that Corsi might even be glad to be out of it all, branded unreliable though he was. Then, again for at least the twentieth time, Wagoner remembered the repeated clearance hearings, the oceans of dubious testimony and gossip from witnesses with no faces or names, the clamor in the press when Corsi was found to have roomed in college with a man suspected of being an ex-YPSL member, the denunciation on the senate floor by one of MacHinery's captive solons, more hearings, the endless barrage of vilification and hatred, the letters beginning "Dear Doctor Corsets, You bum," and signed "True American." To get out of it that way was worse than enduring it, no matter how stoutly most of your fellow scholars stood by you afterwards.

"I shan't be the first to say so to you," the physicist said, turning at last. "I don't think we'll ever reach the stars either, Bliss. And I am not very conservative, as physicists go. We just don't live long enough for us to become a star-traveling race. A mortal man limited to speeds below that of light is as unsuited to interstellar travel as a moth would be to crossing the Atlantic. I'm sorry to believe that, certainly; but I do believe it."

Wagoner nodded and filed the speech away. On that subject he had expected even less than Corsi had given him.

"But," Corsi said, lifting his snifter from the table, "it isn't impossible that *interplanetary* flight could be bettered. I agree with you that it's rotting away now. I'd suspected that it might be, and your showing tonight is conclusive."

"Then why is it happening?" Wagoner demanded.

"Because scientific method doesn't work any more."

"*What!* Excuse me, Seppi, but that's sort of like hearing an archbishop say that Christianity doesn't work any more. What do you mean?"

Corsi smiled sourly. "Perhaps I was overdramatic. But it's true that, under present conditions, scientific method is a blind alley. It depends on freedom of information, and we deliberately killed that. In my bureau, when it was mine, we seldom knew who was working on what project at any given time; we seldom knew whether or not somebody else in the bureau was duplicating it; we never knew whether or not some other department might be duplicating it. All we could be sure of was that many men, working in similar fields, were stamping their results *Secret* because that was the easy way—not only to keep the work out of Russian hands, but to keep the workers in the clear if their own government should investigate them. How can you apply scientific method to a problem when you're forbidden to see the data?

"Then there's the caliber of scientist we have working for the government now. The few first-rate men we have are so harassed by the security set-up—and by the constant suspicion that's focused on them because they *are* top men in their fields, and hence anything they might leak would be particularly valuable—that it takes them years to solve what used to be very simple problems. As for the rest—well, our staff at Standards consisted almost entirely of third-raters: some of them were very dogged and patient men indeed, but low on courage and even lower on imagination. They spent all their time operating mechanically by the cookbook—the routine of scientific method—and had less to show for it every year."

"Everything you've said could be applied to the space-flight research that's going on now, without changing a comma," Wagoner said. "But, Seppi, if scientific method used to be sound, it should still be sound. It ought to work for anybody, even third-raters. Why has it suddenly turned sour now—after centuries of unbroken successes?"

"The time lapse," Corsi said somberly, "is of the first importance. Remember, Bliss, that scientific method is *not* a natural law. It doesn't exist in nature, but only in our heads; in short, it's a way of thinking about things—a way of sifting evidence. It was bound to become obsolescent sooner or later, just as sorites and paradigms and syllogisms became obsolete before it. Scientific method works fine while there are thousands of obvious facts lying about for the taking—facts as obvious and measurable as how fast a stone falls, or what the order of the colors is in a rainbow. But the more subtle the facts to be discovered become—the more they retreat into the realms of the invisible, the intangible, the unweighable, the submicroscopic, the abstract—the more expensive and timeconsuming it is to investigate them by scientific method.

"And when you reach a stage where the *only* research worth doing costs millions of dollars *per experiment*, then those experiments can be paid for only by government. Governments can make the best use only of third-rate men, men who can't leaven the instructions in the cookbook with the flashes of insight you need to make basic discoveries. The result is what you see: sterility, stasis, dry rot."

"Then what's left?" Wagoner said. "What are we going to do now? I know you well enough to suspect that you're not going to give up all hope."

"No," Corsi said, "I haven't given up, but I'm quite helpless to change the situation you're complaining about. After all, I'm on the outside. Which is probably good for me." He paused, and then said suddenly: "There's no hope of getting the government to drop the security system completely?"

"Completely?"

"Nothing else would do."

"No," Wagoner said. "Not even partially, I'm afraid. Not any longer."

Corsi sat down and leaned forward, his elbows on his knobby knees, staring into the dying coals. "Then I have two pieces of advice to give you, Bliss. Actually they're two sides of the same coin. First of all, begin by abandoning these multi-million-dollar, Manhattan-District approaches. We don't need a newer, still finer measurement of electron resonance one-tenth so badly as we need new pathways, new categories of knowledge. The colossal research project is defunct; what we need now is pure skullwork."

"From *my* staff?"

"From wherever you can get it. That's the other half of my recommendation. If I were you, I would go to the crackpots."

Wagoner waited. Corsi said these things for effect; he liked drama in small doses. He would explain in a moment.

"Of course I don't mean total crackpots," Corsi said. "But you'll have to draw the line yourself. You need marginal contributors, scientists of good reputation generally whose obsessions don't strike fire with other members of their profession. Like the Crehore atom, or old Ehrenhaft's theory of magnetic currents, or the Milne cosmology—you'll have to find the fruitful ones yourself. Look for discards, and then find out whether or not the idea deserved to be *totally* discarded. And—don't accept the first 'expert' opinion that you get."

"Winnow chaff, in other words."

"What else is there to winnow?" Corsi said. "Of course it's a long chance, but you can't turn to scientists of real stature now; it's too late for that. Now you'll have to use sports, freaks, near-misses."

"Starting where?"

"Oh," said Corsi, "how about gravity? I don't know any other subject that's attracted a greater quota of idiot speculations. Yet the acceptable theories of what gravity is are of no practical use to us. They can't be put to work to help lift a spaceship. We can't manipulate gravity as a field; we don't even have a set of equations for it that we can agree upon. No more will we find such a set by spending fortunes and decades on the project. The law of diminishing returns has washed that approach out."

Wagoner got up. "You don't leave me much," he said glumly.

"No," Corsi agreed. "I leave you only what you started with. That's more than most of us are left with, Bliss."

Wagoner grinned tightly at him and the two men shook hands. As Wagoner left, he saw Corsi silhouetted against the fire, his back to the door, his shoulders bent. While he stood there, a shot blatted not far away, and the echoes bounded back from the face of the embassy across the street. It was not a common sound in Washington, but neither was it unusual: it was almost surely one of the city's thousands of anonymous snoopers firing at a counter-agent, a cop, or a shadow.

Corsi made no responding movement. The senator closed the door quietly.

He was shadowed all the way back to his own apartment, but this time he hardly noticed. He was thinking about an immortal man who flew from star to star faster than light.

CHAPTER ONE: New York

*In the newer media of communication ... the
popularization of science is confounded by rituals
of mass entertainment. One standard routine dra-
matizes science through the biography of a hero
scientist: at the denouement, he is discovered in a
lonely laboratory crying 'Eureka' at a murky test
tube held up to a bare light bulb.*

—GERARD PIEL

The Parade of celebrities, notorieties, and just plain
brass that passed through the reception room of Jno.
Pfitzner & Sons was marvelous to behold. During
the hour and a half that Colonel Paige Russell had
been cooling his heels, he had identified the following publicity-saints: Senator Bliss Wagoner (Dem.,
Alaska), chairman of the Joint Congressional Committee on Space Flight; Dr. Guiseppi Corsi, president of the American Association for the Advancement of Science, and a former Director of the World
Health Organization; and Francis Xavier MacHinery,
hereditary head of the FBI.

15

He had seen also a number of other notables, of lesser caliber, but whose business at a firm which made biologicals was an equally improper subject for guessing games. He fidgeted.

At the present moment, the girl at the desk was talking softly with a seven-star general, which was a rank nearly as high as a man could rise in the army. The general was so preoccupied that he had failed completely to recognize Paige's salute. He was passed through swiftly. One of the two swinging doors with the glass ports let into them moved outward behind the desk, and Paige caught a glimpse of a stocky, dark-haired, pleasant-faced man in a conservative grosse-pointilliste suit.

"Gen. Horsefield, glad to see you. Come in."

The door closed, leaving Paige once more with nothing to look at but the motto written over the entrance in German black-letter:

Wider den God ist kein Krautlein gewachsen!

Since he did not know the language, he had already translated this by the If-only-it-were-English system, which made it come out, "The fatter toad is waxing on the kine's cole-slaw." This did not seem to fit what little he knew about the eating habits of either animal, and it was certainly no fit admonition for workers.

Of course, Paige could always look at the receptionist—but after an hour and a half he had about plumbed the uttermost depths of that ecstasy. The girl was pretty in a way, but hardly striking, even to a recently returned spaceman. Perhaps if someone would yank those black-rimmed pixie glasses away from her and undo that bun at the back of her head, she might pass, at least in the light of a whale-oil lamp in an igloo during a record blizzard.

This too was odd now that he thought about it. A firm as large as Pfitzner could have its pick of the glossiest of office girls, especially these days. Then again, the whole of Pfitzner might well be pretty small potatoes to the parent organization, A. O. LeFevre et Cie. Certainly at least LeFevre's Consolidated Warfare Service operation was bigger than the Pfitzner division, and Peacock Camera and Chemicals probably was too; Pfitzner, which was the pharmaceuticals side of the cartel, was a recent acquisition, bought after some truly remarkable broken-field running around the diversification amendments to the anti-trust laws.

All in all, Paige was thoroughly well past mere mild annoyance with being stalled. He was, after all, here at these people's specific request, doing them a small favor which they had asked of him—and soaking up good leave-time in the process. Abruptly he got up and strode to the desk.

"Excuse me, miss," he said, "but I think you're being goddamned impolite. As a matter of fact, I'm beginning to think you people are making a fool of me. Do you want these, or don't you?"

He unbuttoned his right breast pocket and pulled out three little pliofilm packets, heat-sealed to plastic mailing tags. Each packet contained a small spoonful of dirt. The tags were addressed to Jno. Pfitzner & Sons, div. A. O. LeFevre et Cie, the Bronx 153, WPO 249920, Earth; and each card carried a $25 rocket-mail stamp for which Pfitzner had paid, still uncancelled.

"Colonel Russell, I agree with you," the girl said, looking up at him seriously. She looked even less glamorous than she had at a distance, but she did have a pert and interesting nose, and the current royal-purple lip-shade suited her better than it did most of the starlets to be seen on 3-V these days. "It's just that you've caught us on a very bad day.

We do want the samples, of course. They're very important to us, otherwise we wouldn't have put you to the trouble of collecting them for us."

"Then why can't I give them to someone?"

"You could give them to me," the girl suggested gently. "I'll pass them along faithfully, I promise you."

Paige shook his head. "Not after this run-around. I did just what your firm asked me to do, and I'm here to see the results. I picked up soils from every one of my ports of call, even when it was a nuisance to do it. I mailed in a lot of them; these are only the last of a series. Do you know where these bits of dirt came from?"

"I'm sorry, it's slipped my mind. It's been a very busy day."

"Two of them are from Ganymede; and the other one is from Jupiter V, right in the shadow of the Bridge gang's shack. The normal temperature on both satellites is about two hundred degrees below zero Fahrenheit. Ever try to swing a pick against ground frozen that solid—working inside a spacesuit? But I got the dirt for you. Now I want to see why Pfitzner wants dirt."

The girl shrugged. "I'm sure you were told why before you even left Earth."

"Supposing I was? I know that you people get drugs out of it. But aren't the guys who bring in the samples entitled to see how the process works? What if Pfitzner gets some new wonder-drug out of one of my samples—couldn't I have a sentence or two of explanation to pass on to my kids?"

The swinging doors bobbed open, and the affable face of the stocky man was thrust into the room.

"Dr. Abbott not here yet, Anne?" he said.

"Not yet, Mr. Gunn, I'll call you the minute he arrives."

"But you'll keep me sitting at least another ninety

minutes," Paige said flatly. Gunn looked him over,
staring at the colonel's eagle on his collar and stopping at the winged crescent pinned over his pocket.

"Apologies, Colonel, but we're having ourselves a
small crisis today," he said, smiling tentatively. "I
gather you've brought us some samples from space.
If you could possibly come back tomorrow, I'd be
happy to give you all the time in the world. But right
now—"

Gunn ducked his head in apology and pulled it in,
as though he had just cuckooed 2400 and had to go
somewhere and lie down until 0100. Just before the
door came to rest behind him, a faint but unmistakable
sound slipped through it.

Somewhere in the laboratories of Jno. Pfitzner &
Sons a baby was crying.

Paige listened, blinking, until the sound was damped
off. When he looked back down at the desk again,
the expression of the girl behind it seemed distinctly
warier.

"Look," he said. "I'm not asking a great favor of
you. I don't want to know anything I shouldn't know.
All I want to know is how you plan to process my
packets of soil. It's just simple curiosity—backed up
by a trip that covered a few hundred millions of
miles. Am I entitled to know for my trouble, or not?"

"You are and you aren't," the girl said steadily.
"We want your samples, and we'll agree that they're
unusually interesting to us because they came from
the Jovian system—the first such we've ever gotten.
But that's no guarantee that we'll find anything useful in them."

"It isn't?"

"No. Colonel Russell, you're not the first man to
come here with soil samples, believe me. Granted
that you're the first man to bring anything back from
outside the orbit of Mars; in fact, you're only the
sixth man to deliver samples from any place farther

away than the Moon. But evidently you have no idea of the volume of samples we get here, routinely. We've asked virtually every space pilot, every Believer missionary, every commercial traveler, every explorer, every foreign correspondent to scoop up soil samples for us, wherever they may go. Before we discovered ascomycin, we had to screen *one hundred thousand* soil samples, including several hundred from Mars and nearly five thousand from the Moon. And do you know where we found the organism that produces ascomycin? On an over-ripe peach one of our detail men picked up from a peddler's stall in Baltimore!"

"I see the point," Paige said reluctantly. "What's ascomycin, by the way?"

The girl looked down at her desk and moved a piece of paper from *here* to *there*. "It's a new antibiotic," she said. "We'll be marketing it soon. But I could tell you the same kind of story about other such drugs."

"I see." Paige was not quite sure he did see, however, after all. He had heard the name Pfitzner fall from some very unlikely lips during his many months in space. As far as he had been able to determine after he had become sensitized to the sound, about every third person on the planets was either collecting samples for the firm or knew somebody who was. The grapevine, which among spacemen was the only trusted medium of communication, had it that the company was doing important government work. That, of course, was nothing unusual in the Age of Defense, but Paige had heard enough to suspect that Pfitzner was something special—something as big, perhaps, as the historic Manhattan District and at least twice as secret.

The door opened and emitted Gunn for the second time hand-running, this time all the way.

"Not yet?" he said to the girl. "Evidently he isn't

going to make it. Unfortunate. But I've some spare time now, Colonel—"

"Russell, Paige Russell, Army Space Corps."

"Thank you. If you'll accept my apologies for our preoccupation, Colonel Russell, I'll be glad to show you around our little establishment. My name, by the way, is Harold Gunn, vice-President in charge of exports for the Pfitzner division."

"I'm importing at the moment," Paige said, holding out the soil samples. Gunn took them reverently and dropped them in a pocket of his jacket. "But I'd enjoy seeing the labs."

He nodded to the girl and the doors closed between them. He was inside.

The place was at least as fascinating as he had expected it to be. Gunn showed him, first, the rooms where the incoming samples were classified and then distributed to the laboratories proper. In the first of these, a measured fraction of a sample was dropped into a one-litre flask of sterile distilled water, swirled to distribute it evenly, and then passed through a series of dilutions. The final suspensions were then used to inoculate test-tube slants and petri plates, containing a wide variety of nutrient media, which went into the incubator.

"In the next lab here—Dr. Aquino isn't in at the moment, so we mustn't touch anything, but you can see through the glass quite clearly—we transfer from the plates and agar slants to a new set of media," Gunn explained. "But here each organism found in the sample has a set of cultures of its own, so that if it secretes anything into one of the media, that something won't be contaminated."

"If it does, the amount must be very tiny," Paige said. "How do you detect it?"

"Directly, by its action. Do you see the rows of plates with the white paper discs in their centers, and the four furrows in the agar radiating from the discs? Well, each one of those furrows is impregnated with culture medium from one of the pure cultures. If all four streaks grow thriving bacterial colonies, then the medium on the paper disc contains no antibiotic against those four germs. If one or more of the streaks fails to grow, or is retarded compared to the others, then we have hope."

In the succeeding laboratory, antibiotics which had been found by the disc method were pitted against a whole spectrum of dangerous organisms. About 90 per cent of the discoveries were eliminated here, Gunn explained, either because they were insufficiently active or because they duplicated the antibiotic spectra of already known drugs. "What we call 'insufficiently active' varies with the circumstances, however," he added. "An antibiotic which shows *any* activity against tuberculosis or against Hansen's disease—leprosy—is always of interest to us, even if it attacks no other germ at all."

A few antibiotics which passed their spectrum tests went on to a miniature pilot plant, where the organisms that produced them were set to work in a deep-aerated fermentation tank. From this bubbling liquor, comparatively large amounts of the crude drug were extracted, purified, and sent to the pharmacology lab for tests on animals.

"We lose a lot of otherwise promising antibiotics here, too," Gunn said. "Most of them turn out to be too toxic to be used in—or even on—the human body. We've had Hansen's bacillus knocked out a thousand times in the test-tube only to find here that the antibiotic is much more quickly fatal *in vivo* than is leprosy itself. But once we're sure that the drug isn't toxic, or that its toxicity is outweighed by its therapeutic efficacy, it goes out of our shop entirely, to hospitals and to individual doctors for clinical trial. We also have a virology lab in Vermont where we test our new drugs against virus diseases like the 'flu and the common cold—it isn't safe to operate such a lab in a heavily populated area like the Bronx."

"It's much more elaborate than I would have imagined," Paige said. "But I can see that it's well worth the trouble. Did you work out this sample-screening technique here?"

"Oh, my, no," Gunn said, smiling indulgently. "Waksman, the discoverer of streptomycin, laid down the essential procedure decades ago. We aren't even the first firm to use it on a large scale; one of our competitors did that and found a broad-spectrum antibiotic called chloramphenicol with it, scarcely a year after they'd begun. That was what convinced the rest of us that we'd better adopt the technique before we got shut out of the market entirely. A good thing, too; otherwise none of us would have discovered tetracycline, which turned out to be the most versatile antibiotic ever tested."

Farther down the corridor a door opened. The squall of a baby came out of it, much louder than before. It was not the sustained crying of a child who had had a year or so to practice, but the short-breathed "ah-la, ah-la, ah-la," of a newborn infant.

Paige raised his eyebrows. "Is that one of your experimental animals?"

"Ha, ha," Gunn said. "We're enthusiasts in this business, Colonel, but we must draw the line somewhere. No, one of our technicians has a baby-sitting problem, and so we've given her permission to bring the child to work with her, until she's worked out a better solution."

Paige had to admit that Gunn thought fast on his feet. That story had come reeling out of him like so much ticker tape without the slightest sign of a preliminary doubletake. It was not Gunn's fault that Paige, who had been through a marriage which had lasted five years before he had taken to space, could distinguish the cry of a baby old enough to be out of a hospital nursery from that of one only days old.

"Isn't this," Paige said, "a rather dangerous place to park an infant—with so many disease germs, poisonous disinfectants, and such things all around?"

"Oh, we take all proper precautions. I daresay our staff has a lower yearly sickness rate than you'll find in industrial plants of comparable size, simply because we're more aware of the problem. Now if we go through this door, Colonel Russell, we'll see the final step, the main plant where we turn out drugs in quantity after they've proved themselves."

"Yes, I'd like that. Do you have ascomycin in production now?"

This time, Gunn looked at him sharply and without any attempt to disguise his interest. "No," he said, "that's still out on clinical trial. May I ask you, Colonel Russell, just how you happened to—"

The question, which Paige realized belatedly would have been rather sticky to answer, never did get all the way asked. Over Harold Gunn's head, a squawk-box said, "Mr. Gunn, Dr. Abbott has just arrived."

Gunn turned away from the door that, he had said, led out to the main plant, with just the proper modicum of polite regret. "There's my man," he said. "I'm afraid I'm going to have to cut this tour short, Colonel Russell. You may have seen what a collection of important people we have in the plant today; we've been waiting only for Dr. Abbott to begin a very important meeting. If you'll oblige me—"

Paige could say nothing but "Certainly." After what seemed only a few seconds, Gunn deposited him smoothly in the reception room from which he had started.

"Did you see what you wanted to see?" the receptionist said.

"I think so," Paige said thoughtfully. "Except that what I wanted to see sort of changed in mid-flight.

Miss Anne, I have a petition to put before you. Would you be kind enough to have dinner with me this evening?"

"No," the girl said. "I've seen quite a few spacemen, Colonel Russell, and I'm no longer impressed. Furthermore, I shan't tell you anything you haven't heard from Mr. Gunn, so there's no need for you to spend your money or your leave-time on me. Good-bye."

"Not so fast," Paige said. "I mean business—or, if you like, I mean to make trouble. If you've met spacemen before, you know that they like to be independent—not much like the conformists who never leave the ground. I'm not after your maidenly laughter, either. I'm after information."

"Not interested," the girl said. "Save your breath."

"MacHinery is here," Paige said quietly. "So is Senator Wagoner, and some other people who have influence. Suppose I should collar any one of those people and accuse Pfitzner of conducting human vivisection?"

That told: Paige could see the girl's knuckles whitening. "You don't know what you're talking about," she said.

"That's my complaint. And I take it seriously. There were some things Mr. Gunn wasn't able to conceal from me, though he tried very hard. Now, I am going to put my suspicions through channels—and get Pfitzner investigated—or would you rather be sociable over a fine flounder broiled in paprika butter?"

The look she gave him back was one of almost pure hatred. She seemed able to muster no other answer. The expression did not at all suit her; as a matter of fact, she looked less like someone he would want to date than any other girl he could remember. Why *should* he spend his money or his leave-time on her? There were, after all, about five million surplus women in the United States by the Census of 2010, and at least 4,999,950 of them must be prettier and less recalcitrant than this one.

"All right," she said abruptly. "Your natural charm has swept me off my feet, Colonel. For the record, there's no other reason for my acceptance. It would be even funnier to call your bluff and see how far you'd get with that vivisection tale, but I don't care to tie my company up in a personal joke."

"Good enough," Paige said, uncomfortably aware that his bluff in fact *had* been called. "Suppose I pick you up—"

He broke off, suddenly noticing that voices were rising behind the double doors. An instant later, General Horsefield bulled into the reception room, closely followed by Gunn.

"I want it clearly understood, once and for all," Horsefield was rumbling, "that this entire project is going to wind up under military control unless we can show results before it's time to ask for a new appropriation. There's still a lot going on here that the Pentagon will regard as piddling inefficiency and highbrow theorizing. And if that's what the Pentagon reports, you know what the Treasury will do—or Congress will do it for them. We're going to have to cut back, Gunn. Understand? Cut right back to basics!"

"General, we're as far back to basics as we possibly can get," Harold Gunn said, placatingly enough, but with considerable firmness as well. "We're not going to put a gram of that drug into production until we're satisfied with it on all counts. Any other course would be suicide."

"You know I'm on your side," Horsefield said, his voice becoming somewhat less threatening. "So is General Alsos, for that matter. But this is a war we're fighting, whether the public understands it or not. And on as sensitive a matter as these death-dopes, we can't afford—"

Gunn, who had spotted Paige belatedly at the

conclusion of his own speech, had been signaling Horsefield ever since with his eyebrows, and suddenly it took. The general swung around and glared at Paige, who, since he was uncovered now, was relieved of the necessity for saluting. Despite the sudden freezing silence, it was evident that Gunn was trying to retain in his manner toward Paige some shreds of professional cordiality—a courtesy which Paige was not too sure he merited, considering the course his conversation with the girl had taken.

As for Horsefield, he relegated Paige to the ghetto of "unauthorized persons" with a single look. Paige had no intention of remaining in that classification for a second longer than it would take him to get out of it, preferably without having been asked his name; it was deadly dangerous. With a mumbled "—at eight, then," to the girl, Paige sidled ingloriously out of the Pfitzner reception room and beat it.

He was, he reflected later in the afternoon before his shaving mirror, subjecting himself to an extraordinary series of small humiliations, to get close to a matter which was none of his business. Worse: it was obviously Top Secret, which made it potentially lethal even for everyone authorized to know about it, let alone for rank snoopers. In the Age of Defense, to know was to be suspect, in the West as in the USSR; the two great nation-complexes had been becoming more and more alike in their treatment of "security" for the past fifty years. It had even been a mistake to mention the Bridge on Jupiter to the girl—for despite the fact that everyone knew that the Bridge existed, anyone who spoke of it with familiarity could quickly earn the label of being dangerously flap-jawed. Especially if the speaker, like Paige, had actually been stationed in the Jovian system for a while, whether he had had access to information about the Bridge or not.

And especially if the talker, like Paige, had actually spoken to the Bridge gang, worked with them on marginal projects, was known to have talked to Charity Dillon, the Bridge foreman. More especially if he held military rank, making it possible for him to sell security files to Congressmen, the traditional way of advancing a military career ahead of normal promotion schedules.

And most especially if the man was discovered nosing about a new and different classified project, one to which he hadn't even been assigned.

Why, after all, was he taking the risk? He didn't even know the substance of the matter; he was no biologist. To all outside eyes the Pfitzner project was simply another piece of research in antibiotics, and a rather routine research project at that. Why should a spaceman like Paige find himself flying so close to the candle already?

He wiped the depilatory cream off his face into a paper towel and saw his own eyes looking back at him from the concave mirror, as magnified as an owl's. The image, however, was only his own, despite the distortion. It gave him back no answer.

CHAPTER TWO: Jupiter V.

*. . . it is the plunge through the forbidden zones
that catches the heart with its sheer audacity. In
the history of life there have been few such epi-
sodes. It is that which makes us lonely. We have
entered a new corridor, the cultural corridor. There
has been nothing here before us. In it we are utterly alone. In it we are appallingly unique. We
look at each other and say, "It can never be done
again."*

—LOREN C. EISELEY

A screeching tornado was rocking the Bridge when
the alarm sounded; the whole structure shuddered
and swayed. This was normal, and Robert Helmuth
on Jupiter V barely noticed it. There was always a
tornado shaking the Bridge. The whole planet was
enswathed in tornadoes and worse.

The scanner on the foreman's board was given 114
as the sector where the trouble was. That was at the
northwestern end of the Bridge, where it broke off,
leaving nothing but the raging clouds of ammonia

29

crystals and methane, and a sheer drop thirty miles down to the invisible surface. There were no ultra-phone "eyes" at that end to show a general view of the area—in so far as any general view was possible—because both ends of the Bridge were incomplete.

With a sigh, Helmuth put the beetle into motion. The little car, as flat-bottomed and thin through as a bedbug, got slowly under way on its ball-bearing races, guided and held firmly to the surface of the Bridge by ten close-set flanged rails. Even so, the hydrogen gales made a terrific siren-like shrieking between the edge of the vehicle and the deck, and the impact of the falling drops of ammonia upon the curved roof was as heavy and deafening as a rain of cannon balls. In fact, the drops weighed almost as much as cannon balls there under Jupiter's two-and-a-half-fold gravity, although they were not much bigger than ordinary raindrops. Every so often, too, there was a blast, accompanied by a dull orange glare, which made the car, the deck, and the Bridge itself buck savagely; even a small shock wave traveled through the incredibly dense atmosphere of the planet like the armor-plate of a bursting battleship.

These blasts were below, however, on the surface. While they shook the structure of the Bridge heavily, they almost never interfered with its functioning. And they could not, in the very nature of things, do Helmuth any harm.

Helmuth, after all, was *not* on Jupiter—though that was becoming harder and harder for him to bear in mind. Nobody was on Jupiter; had any real damage ever been done to the Bridge, it probably would never have been repaired. There was nobody on Jupiter to repair it; only the machines which were themselves part of the Bridge.

The Bridge was building itself. Massive, alone, and lifeless, it grew in the black deeps of Jupiter.

It had been well planned. From Helmuth's point

of view—that of the scanners on the beetle—almost nothing could be seen of it, for the beetle tracks ran down the center of the deck, and in the darkness and perpetual storm even ultrawave-assisted vision could not penetrate more than a few hundred yards at the most. The width of the Bridge, which no one would ever see, was eleven miles; its height, as incomprehensible to the Bridge gang as a skyscraper to an ant, thirty miles; its length, deliberately unspecified in the plans, fifty-four miles at the moment and still increasing—a squat, colossal structure, built with engineering principles, methods, materials and tools never touched before now. . . .

For the very good reason that they would have been impossible anywhere else. Most of the Bridge, for instance, was made of ice: a marvelous structural material under a pressure of a million atmospheres, at a temperature of 94° below zero Fahrenheit. Under such conditions, the best structural steel is a friable, talc-like powder, and aluminum becomes a peculiar transparent substance that splits at a tap; water, on the other hand, becomes Ice IV, a dense, opaque white medium which will deform to a heavy stress, but will break only under impacts huge enough to lay whole Earthly cities to waste. Never mind that it took millions of megawatts of power to keep the Bridge up and growing every hour of the day; the winds on Jupiter blow at velocities up to twenty-five thousand miles per hour, and will never stop blowing, as they may have been blowing for more than four billion years; there is power enough.

Back home, Helmuth remembered, there had been talk of starting another Bridge on Saturn, and perhaps later still on Uranus too. But that had been politicians' talk. The Bridge was almost five thousand miles below the visible surface of Jupiter's atmosphere—luckily in a way, for at the top of that atmosphere the temperature was 76° Fahrenheit colder than it was down by the Bridge, but even with that differential the Bridge's mechanisms were just barely manageable. The bottom of Saturn's atmosphere, if the radiosonde readings could be trusted, was just 16,878 miles below the top of the Saturnian clouds one could see through the telescope, and the temperature down there was below -238° F. Under those conditions, even pressure-ice would be immovable, and could not be worked with anything softer than itself.

And as for a Bridge on Uranus. . . .

As far as Helmuth was concerned, Jupiter was quite bad enough.

The beetle crept within sight of the end of the Bridge and stopped automatically. Helmuth set the vehicle's "eyes" for highest penetration, and examined the nearby I-beams.

The great bars were as close-set as screening. They had to be, in order to support even their own weight, let alone the weight of the components of the Bridge. The gravity down here was two and a half times as great as Earth's.

Even under that load, the whole webwork of girders was flexing and fluctuating to the harpist-fingered gale. It had been designed to do that, but Helmuth could never help being alarmed by the movement. Habit alone assured him that he had nothing to fear from it.

He took the automatic cut-out of the circuit and inched the beetle forward on manual control. This was only Sector 113, and the Bridge's own Wheatstone scanning system—there was no electronic device anywhere on the Bridge, since it was impossible to maintain a vacuum on Jupiter—said that the trouble was in Sector 114. The boundary of that sector was still fully fifty feet away.

It was a bad sign. Helmuth scratched nervously in his red beard. Evidently there was cause for alarm—

real alarm, not just the deep grinding depression which he always felt while working on the Bridge. Any damage serious enough to halt the beetle a full sector short of the trouble area was bound to be major.

It might even turn out to be the disaster which he had felt lurking ahead of him ever since he had been made foreman of the Bridge—that disaster which the Bridge itself could not repair, sending a man reeling home from Jupiter in defeat.

The secondaries cut in, and the beetle hunkered down once more against the deck, the ball-bearings on which it rode frozen magnetically to the rails. Grimly, Helmuth cut the power to the magnet windings and urged the flat craft inch by inch across the danger line.

Almost at once, the car tilted just perceptibly to the left, and the screaming of the winds between its edges and the deck shot up the scale, sirening in and out of the soundless-dogwhistle range with an eeriness which set Helmuth's teeth on edge. The beetle itself fluttered and chattered like an alarm-clock hammer between the surface of the deck and the flanges of the tracks.

Ahead there was still nothing to be seen but the horizontal driving of the clouds and the hail, roaring along the length of the Bridge, out of the blackness into the beetle's fanlights, and onward into darkness again toward the horizon which, like the Bridge itself, no eye would ever see.

Thirty miles below, the fusillade of hydrogen explosions continued. Evidently something really wild was going on down on the surface. Helmuth could not remember having heard so much vulcanism in years.

There was a flat, especially heavy crash, and a long line of fuming orange fire came pouring down the seething air into the depths, feathering horizontally like the mane of a Lipizzan stallion, directly in front of Helmuth. Instinctively, he winced and drew back from the board, although that stream of flame actually was only a little less cold than the rest of the storming, streaming gases, and far too cold to injure the Bridge.

In the momentary glare, however, he saw something: an upward twisting of shadows, patterned but obviously unfinished, fluttering in silhouette against the lurid light of the hydrogen cataract.

The end of the Bridge.

Wrecked.

Helmuth grunted involuntarily and backed the beetle away. The flare dimmed; the light poured down the sky and fell away into the raging sea of liquid hydrogen thirty miles below. The scanner clucked with satisfaction as the beetle recrossed the danger line into Sector 113.

Helmuth turned the body of the vehicle 180 degrees on its chassis, presenting its back to the dying orange torrent. There was nothing further that he could do at the moment for the Bridge. He searched his control board—a ghost image of which was cast on the screen across the scene on the Bridge—for the blue button marked *Garage*, punched it savagely, and tore off his fireman's helmet.

Obediently, the Bridge vanished.

CHAPTER THREE: New York

Does it not appear as if one who lived habitually
on one side of the pain threshold might need a
different sort of religion from one who habitually
lives on the other?

WILLIAM JAMES

The girl whose full name, Paige found, was Anne
Abbott—looked moderately acceptable in her sum-
mer suit, on the left lapel of which she wore a model
of the tetracycline molecule with the atoms picked
out in tiny synthetic gems. But she was even less
inclined to talk when he picked her up than she had
been in Pfitzner's reception room. Paige himself had
never been expert at making small talk, and in the
face of her obvious, continuing resentment, his
parched spring of social invention went underground
completely.

Five minutes later, all talk became impossible anyhow. The route to the restaurant Paige had chosen
lay across Foley Square, where there turned out to
be a Believer Mission going. The Caddy that Paige

had hired—at nearly a quarter of his leave-pay, for commercial kerosene-fueled taxis were strictly a rich man's occasional luxury—was bogged down almost at once in the groaning, swaying crowd.

The main noise came from the big plastic proscenium, where one of the lay preachers was exhorting the crowd in a voice so heavily amplified as to be nearly unintelligible. Believers with portable tape recorders, bags of tracts and magazines, sandwichboards lettered with fluorescent inks, confessions for sinners to sign, and green baize pokes for collections were well scattered among the pedestrians, and the streets were crossed about every fifteen feet with the straight black snakes of compressed-air triggers.

As the Caddy pulled up for the second time, a nozzle was thrust into the rear window and a stream of iridescent bubbles poured across the back seat directly under Paige's and Anne's noses. As each bubble burst, there was a wave of perfume—evidently it was the "Celestial Joy" the Believers were using this year—and a sweet voice said:

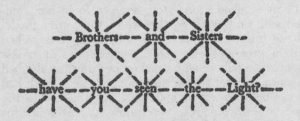

Paige fought at the bubbles with futile windmillings, while Anne Abbott leaned back against the cushions of the Caddy and watched him with a faint smile of contemptuous amusement. The last bubble contained no word, but only an overpowering burst of perfume. Despite herself, the girl's smile deepened: the perfume, in addition to being powerfully euphoric, was slightly aphrodisiac as well. This year, apparently, the Believers were readier than ever to use any means that came to hand.

The driver lurched the Caddy ahead. Then, before Paige could begin to grasp what was happening, the car stopped, the door next to the steering wheel was wrenched open, and four spidery, many-fingered arms plucked the driver neatly from his seat and deposited him on his knees on the asphalt outside.

"SHAME! SHAME!" the popai-robot thundered. "YOUR SINS HAVE FOUND YOU OUT! REPENT, AND FIND FORGIVENESS!"

A thin glass globe of some gas, evidently a narcosynthetic, broke beside the car, and not only the unfortunate chauffeur but also the part of the crowd which had begun to collect about him—mostly women, of course—began to weep convulsively.

"REPENT!" the robot intoned, over a sneaked-in-choir now singing "An-ah-ah-ah-ah-h-h-h-h" somewhere in the warm evening air. "REPENT, FOR THE TIME IS AT HAND!"

Paige, astonished to find himself choking with sourceless, maudlin self-pity, flung himself out of the Caddy in search of a nose to break. But there were no live Believers in sight. The members of the order, all of whom were charged with spreading the good word by whatever means seemed good to them, had learned decades ago that their proselytizing was often resented, and had substituted technology for personal salesmanship wherever possible.

Their machines, too, had been forced to learn. The point-of-purchase robot retreated as Paige bore down upon it. The thing had been conditioned against allowing itself to be broken.

The Caddy's driver, rescued, blew his nose resentfully and started the car again. The wordless choir,

with its eternal bridge-passage straight out of the
compositions of Dmitri Tiomkin, diminished behind
them, and the voice of the lay preacher came roaring
back through to them over the fading, characterless
music.

"I say to you," the P.A. system was moaning
unctuously, like a lady hippopotamus reading A. E.
Housman, "I say to you, the world, and the things
which are the world's come to an end and a quick
end. In his overweening pride, man has sought even
to wrest the stars from their courses, but the stars
are not man's, and he shall rue that day. Ah, vanity
of vanities, all is vanity (Preacher v: 796). Even on
mighty Jove man dared to erect a great Bridge, as
once in Babel he sought to build a tower to heaven.
But this also is vanity, it is vicious pride and defi-
ance, and it too shall bring calamity upon men. Pull
down thy vanity, I say pull down! (Ezra lxxxi: 99).
Let there be an end to pride, and there shall be
peace. Let there be love, and there shall be understanding. I say to you—"

At this point, the Believers' over-enthusiastic booby-
trapping of the square cut off whatever the preacher
was going to say next as far as the occupants of the
Caddy were concerned. The car passed over another
trigger, and there was a blinding, rose-colored flash.
When Paige could see again, the car seemed to be
floating in mid-air, and there were actual angels flap-
ping solemnly around it. The *vox humana* of a Ham-
mond organ sobbed among the clouds.

Paige supposed that the Believers had managed to
crystalize temporarily, perhaps with a supersonic pulse,
the glass of the windows, which he had rolled up to
prevent another intromission of bubbles, and to project a 3-V tape against the glass crystals with polar-
ized ultra-violet light. The random distribution of
fluorescent trace compounds in ordinary window glass

would account for the odd way the "angels" changed color as they moved.

Understanding the vision's probable *modus operandi* left Paige no less furious at the new delay, but luckily the thing turned out to be a trick, left over from last year's Revival, for which the Caddy was prepared. The driver touched something on the dash and the saccharine scene vanished, hymns and all. The car lunged abruptly through an opening in the crowd, and a moment later the square was behind them.

"Whew!" Paige said, leaning back at last. "Now I understand why taxi depots have vending machines for trip-insurance policies. The Believers weren't much in evidence the last time I was on Earth."

"Every tenth person you meet is a Believer now," Anne said. "And eight of the other nine claim that they've given up religion as a bad job. While you're caught in the middle of one of those Revivals, though, it's hard to believe the complaints you read about our times—that people have no faith and so on."

"I don't find it so," Paige said reflectively. This certainly did not strike him as light social conversation, but since it was instead a kind of talk he much more enjoyed—talk which was about something—he could only be delighted that the ice was broken. "I've no religion of my own, but I think that when the experts talk about 'faith' they mean something different than the shouting kind, the kind the Believers have. Shouting religions always strike me as essentially like pep-meetings among salesmen, their ceremonies and their manners are so aggressive because they don't really believe the code themselves. Real faith is so much a part of the world you live in that you seldom notice it, and it isn't always religious in the formal sense. Mathematics is based on faith, for instance, for those who know it."

"I should have said that it was based on the antitheesis of faith," Anne said, turning a little cooler. "Have you had any experience in the field, Colonel?"

"Some," he said, without rancor. "I'd never have been allowed to pilot a ship outside the orbit of the Moon without knowing tensors, and if I expect to get my next promotion, I'm going to have to know spinor calculus as well—which I do."

"Oh," the girl said. She sounded faintly dashed. "Go on; I'm sorry I interrupted."

"You were right to interrupt; I made my point badly. I meant to say that the mathematician's belief that there is some relationship between maths and the real world is a faith; it can't be proven, but he feels it very strongly. For that matter, the totally irreligious man's belief that there even *is* a real world, corresponding to what his senses show him, can't be proven. John Doe and the most brilliant of physicists both have to take that on faith."

"And they don't conduct ceremonies symbolizing the belief," Anne added, "and train specialists to reassure them of it every seven days."

"That's right. In the same way, John Doe used to feel that the basic religions of the West had some relationship to the real world which was valid even though it couldn't be proven. And that includes Communism, which was born in the West, after all. John Doe doesn't feel that way any more—and by my guess, neither do the Believers or they wouldn't be shouting so loud. In that sense, there's not much faith lying around loose these days anywhere, as far as I can see. None for me to pick up, that much I've found out the hard way."

"Here you are," the chauffeur said.

Paige helped the girl out of the car, trying not to notice how much fare he had to pay, and the two were shown to a table in the restaurant. Anne was silent again for a while after they were seated. Paige had about decided that she had chosen to freeze up once more and had begun to wonder if he could arrange to have the place invaded by Believers to start the conversation again when she said, "You seem to have been thinking about faith quite a bit. You talk as though the problem meant something to you. Could you tell me why?"

"I'd be glad to try," he said slowly. "The standard answer would be that while you're out in space you have lots of time to think—but people use thinking time differently. I suppose I've been looking for some frame of reference that could be mine ever since I was four, when my father and mother split up. She was a Christian Scientist and he was a Dianeticist, so they had a lot to fight about. There was a court battle over custody that lasted for nearly five years.

"I joined the army when I was seventeen, and it didn't take me very long to find out that the army is no substitute for a family, let alone a church. Then I volunteered for space service school. That was no church either. The army got jurisdiction over space travel when the whole field was just a baby, because it had a long tradition of grafting off land-grants, and it didn't want the navy or the air force to grab off the gravy from any such grants that might be made on the planets. That's one of the army's historic prerogatives; the idea is that anything that's found on an army site—diamonds, uranium, anything of value— is found money, to be lived off during peacetime when the Congress gets stingy with appropriations. I spent more time helping the army space-travel department fight unification with the space arms of the other services than I did doing real work in space. That was what I was ordered to do—but it didn't help me to think of space as the ultimate cathedral. . . .

"Somewhere along in there, I got married and we had one son; he was born the same day I entered space school. Two years later, the marriage was annulled. That sounds funny, I know, but the circumstances were unusual.

"When Pfitzner approached me and asked me to pick up soil samples for them, I suppose I saw another church with which I could identify myself—something humanitarian, long-range, impersonal. And when I found this afternoon that the new church wasn't going to welcome the convert with glad cries—well, the result is that I'm now weeping on your shoulder." He smiled. "That's hardly flattering, I know. But you've already helped me to talk myself into a spot where the only next step is to apologize, which I hereby do. I hope you'll accept it."

"I think I will," she said, and then, tentatively, she smiled back. The result made him tingle as though the air-pressure had dropped suddenly by five pounds per square inch. Anne Abbott was one of those exceedingly rare plain girls whose smiles completely transform them, as abruptly as the bursting of a star-shell. When she wore her normal, rather sullen expression, no one would ever notice her—but a man who had seen her smile might well be willing to kill himself working to make her smile again, as often as possible. A woman who was beautiful all the time, Paige thought, probably never could know the devotion Anne Abbott would be given when she found that man.

"Thank you," Paige said, rather inadequately. "Let's order, and then I'd like to hear you talk. I dumped The Story of My Life into your lap rather early in the game, I'm afraid."

"You order," she said. "You talked about flounder this afternoon, so you must know the menu here—and you handed me out of the Caddy so nicely that I'd like to preserve the illusion."

"Illusion?"

"Don't make me explain," she said, coloring faintly. "But. . . . Well, the illusion of there being one or two cavaliers in the world still. Since you haven't been a surplus woman on a planet full of lazy males, you wouldn't understand the value of a small courtesy or two. Most men I meet want to be shown my mole before they'll bother to learn my last name."

Paige's surprised shout of laughter made heads turn all over the restaurant. He throttled it hurriedly, afraid that it would embarrass the girl, but she was smiling again, making him feel instead as though he had just had three whiskies in quick succession.

"That's a quick transformation for me," he said. "This afternoon I was a blackmailer, and by my own intention, too. Very well, then, let's have the flounder; it's a specialty of the house. I had visions of it while I was on Ganymede munching my concentrates."

"I think you had the right idea about Pfitzner," Anne said slowly when the waiter had gone. "I can't tell you any secrets about it, but maybe I can tell you some bits of common knowledge that you evidently don't know. The project the plant is working on now seems to me to fit your description exactly: it's humanitarian, impersonal, and just about as long-range as any project I can imagine. I feel rather religious about it, in your sense. It's something to tie to, and it's better for me than being a Believer or a WAC. And I think you could understand why I feel that way—better than either Hal Gunn or I thought you could."

It was his turn to be embarrassed. He covered by dosing his Blue Points with Worcestershire until they flinched visibly. "I'd like to know."

"It goes like this," she said. "In between 1940 and 1960, a big change took place in Western medicine. Before 1940—in the early part of the century—the infectious diseases were major killers. By 1960 they were all but knocked out of the running. The change started with the sulfa drugs; then came Fleming and

Florey and mass production of penicillin during World War II. After that war we found a whole arsenal of new drugs against tuberculosis, which had really never been treated successfully before—streptomycin, PAS, isoniazid, viomycin, and so on, right up to Bloch's isolation of the TB toxins and the development of the metabolic blocking agents.

"Then came the broad-spectrum antibiotics, like terramycin, which attacked some virus diseases, protozoan diseases, even worm diseases; that gave us a huge clue to a whole set of tough problems. The last major infectious disease—bilharzia, or schistosomiasis —was reduced to the status of a nuisance by 1966."

"But we still have infectious diseases," Paige objected.

"Of course we do," the girl said, the little atom points in her brooch picking up the candle-light as she leaned forward. "No drug ever wipes out a disease, because it's impossible to kill all the dangerous organisms in the world just by treating the patients they invade. But you can reduce the danger. In the 1950's, for instance, malaria was the world's greatest killer. Now it's as rare as diphtheria. We still have both diseases with us—but how long has it been since you heard of a case of either?"

"You're asking the wrong man—germ diseases aren't common on space vessels. We bump any crewman who shows up with as much as a head-cold. But you win the point, all the same. Go on. What happened then?"

"Something kind of ominous. Life insurance companies, and other people who kept records, began to be alarmed at the way the degenerative diseases were coming to the fore. Those are such ailments as hardening of the arteries, coronary heart disease, embolisms, and almost all the many forms of cancer— diseases where one or another body mechanism suddenly goes haywire, without any visible cause."

"Isn't old age the cause?"

"*No*," the girl said forcefully. "Old age is just the *age*; it's not a thing in itself, it's just the time of life when most degenerative diseases strike. Some of them prefer children—leukemia or cancer of the bone marrow, for instance. When the actuaries first began to notice that the degenerative diseases were on the rise, they thought that it was just a sort of side-effect of the decline of the infectious diseases. They thought that cancer was increasing because more people were living long enough to come down with it. Also, the reporting of the degenerative diseases was improving, and so part of the rise in incidence really was an illusion—it just meant that more cases than before were being detected.

"But that wasn't all there was to it. Lung cancer and stomach cancer in particular continued to creep up the statistical tables, far beyond the point which could have been accounted for by better reporting, or by the increase in the average life-span, either. Then the same thing took place in malignant hypertension, in Parkinsonism and other failures of the central nervous system, in muscular dystrophy, and so on, and so on. It began to look very much as though we'd exchanged a devil we knew for a devil we didn't.

"So there was quite a long search for a possible infectious origin for each of the degenerative diseases. Because some animal tumors, like poultry sarcoma, are caused by viruses, a lot of people set to work hunting like mad for all kinds of cancer viruses. There was a concerted attempt to implicate a group called the pleuropneumonia-like organisms as the cause of the arthritic diseases. The vascular diseases, like hypertension and thrombosis, got blamed on everything from your diet to your grandmother.

"And it all came to very little. Oh, we did find that *some* viruses did cause *some* types of cancer, leukemia among them. The PPLO group does cause *a* type of arthritis, too, but only the type associated with a venereal disease called essential urethritis. And we found that the commonest of the three types of lung cancer was being caused by the radio-potassium content of tobacco smoke; it was the lip and mouth cancers that were caused by the tars. But for the most part, we found out just what we had known before—that the degenerative diseases weren't infectious. We'd already been down *that* dead end.

"About there was when Pfitzner got into the picture. The NHS, the National Health Service, got alarmed enough about the rising incidence-curves to call the first really major world congress on the degenerative diseases. The U.S. paid part of the bill because the armed services were getting nervous about the rising rate of draft rejections."

"I heard some talk about that part of it," Paige said. "It started right in my own service. A spaceman only has about ten years of active life; after that he's given garrison duty somewhere—so we like to catch 'em young. And even then we were turning back a huge proportion of young volunteers for 'diseases of old age'—incipient circulatory disease in most cases. The kids were shocked; most of them had never suspected any such thing, they felt as healthy as bulls, and in the usual sense I suppose they were— but not for space flight."

"Then you saw one of the key factors very early," Anne said. "But it's no longer a special problem of the Space Service alone. It's old stuff to all the armed services' medical departments now; at the time the NHS stepped in, the overall draft rejection rate for 'diseases of old age' was about 10 per cent for men in their early twenties. Anyhow, the result of the congress was that the U.S. Department of Health, Welfare and Security somehow got a billion-dollar appropriation for a real mass attack on the degenerative diseases. In case you drop zeros as easily as I do, that was about half what had been spent to produce the first atomic bomb. Since then, the appropriation has been added to once, and it's due for renewal again now.

"Pfitzner holds the major contract on that project, and we're well enough staffed and equipped to handle it so that we've had to do very little subcontracting. We simply share the appropriation with three other producers of biologicals, two of whom are producers only and so have no hand in the research; the third firm has done as much research as we have, but we know—because this is supposed to be a co-ordinated effort with sharing of knowledge among the contractors—that they're far gone down another blind alley. We would have told them so, but after one look at what *we'd* found, the government decided that the fewer people who know about it, the better. We didn't mind; after all, we're in business to make a profit, too. But that's one reason why you saw so many government people on our necks this afternoon."

The girl broke off abruptly and delved into her pocketbook, producing a flat compact which she opened and inspected intently. Since she wore almost no make-up, it was hard to imagine the reason for the sudden examination; but after a brief, odd smile at one corner of her mouth, she tucked the compact away again.

"The other reason," she said, "is even simpler, now that you have the background. *We've just found what we think may be a major key to the whole problem.*"

"Wow," Paige said, inelegantly but *affetuoso*.

"Or zowie, or biff-bam-krunk," Anne agreed calmly, "or maybe God-help-us-every-one. But so far the thing's held up. It's passed every test. If it keeps up that performance, Pfitzner will get the whole of the

new appropriation—and if it doesn't, there may not
be any appropriation at all, not only for Pfitzner, but
for the other firms that have been helping on the
project.

"The whole question of whether or not we lick the
degenerative diseases hangs on those two things: the
validity of the solution we've found and the money.
If one goes, the other goes. And we'll have to tell
Horsefield and MacHinery and the others what we've
found some time this month, because the old appropriation lapses after that."

The girl leaned back and seemed to notice for the
first time that she had finished her dinner. "And
that," she said, pushing regretfully at the sprig of
parsley with her fork, "isn't exactly public knowledge
yet! I think I'd better shut up."

"Thank you," Paige said gravely. "It's obviously
more than I deserve to know."

"Well," Anne said, "you can tell *me* something, if
you will. It's about this Bridge that's being built on
Jupiter. Is it worth all the money that they're pouring into it? Nobody seems to be able to explain what
it's good for. And now there's talk that another
Bridge'll be started on Saturn, when this one's
finished!"

"You needn't worry," Paige said. "Understand, I've
no connection with the Bridge, though I do know
some people on the Bridge gang, so I haven't any
inside information. I do have some public knowledge, just like yours—meaning knowledge that anyone can have, if he has the training to know where to
look for it. As I understand it, the Bridge on Jupiter
is a research project, designed to answer some
questions—just what questions, nobody's bothered
to tell me, and I've been careful not to ask; you can
see Francis X. MacHinery's face in the constellations
if you look carefully enough. But this much I know:
the conditions of the research demand the use of the

largest planet in the system. That's Jupiter, so it would be senseless to build another Bridge on a smaller planet, like Saturn. The Bridge gang will keep the present structure going until they've found out what they want to know. Then the project will almost surely be discontinued—not because the Bridge is 'finished,' but because it will have served its purpose."

"I suppose I'm showing my ignorance," Anne said, "but it sounds idiotic to me. All those millions and millions of dollars—that *we* could be saving lives with!"

"If the choice were mine," Paige agreed, "I'd award the money to you, not to Charity Dillon and his crew. But then, I know almost as little about the Bridge as you do, so perhaps it's just as well that I'm not allowed to route the check. Is it my turn to ask a question? I still have a small one."

"Your witness," Anne said, smiling her altogether lovely smile.

"This afternoon, while I was in the labs, I twice heard a baby crying—and I think it was actually two different babies. I asked your Mr. Gunn about it, and he told me an obvious fairy story." He paused. Anne's eyes had already begun to glitter.

"You're on dangerous ground, Colonel Russell," she said.

"I can tell. But I mean to ask my question anyhow. When I pulled my absurd vivisection threat on you later, I was out-and-out flabbergasted that it worked, but it set me to thinking. Can you explain—and if so, would you?"

Anne got out her compact again and seemed to consult it warily. At last she said: "I suppose I've forgiven you, more or less. Anyhow, I'll answer. It's very simple: the babies *are* being used as experimental animals. We have a pipeline to a local foundling home. It's all only technically legal, and had you actually brought charges of human vivisection against us, you probably could have made them stick."

His coffee cup clattered into its saucer. "Great God, Anne. Isn't it dangerous to make such a joke these days—especially with a man you've known only half a day? Or are you trying to startle me into admitting I'm a stoolie?"

"I'm not joking and I don't think you're a stoolie," she said calmly. "What I said was perfectly true—oh, I souped up the way I put it just a little, maybe because I haven't *entirely* forgiven you for that bit of successful blackmail, and I wanted to see you jump. And for other reasons. But it's true."

"But Anne—why?"

"Look, Paige," she said. "It was fifty years ago that we found that if we added minute amounts of certain antibiotics, really just traces, to animal feeds, the addition brought the critters to market months ahead of normally-fed animals. For that matter, it even provokes growth spurts in plants under special conditions; and it works for poultry, baby pigs, calves, mink cubs, a whole spectrum of animals. It was logical to suspect that it might work in newborn humans too."

"And you're trying that?" Paige leaned back and poured himself another glass of Chilean Rhine. "I'd say you souped up your revelation quite a bit, all right."

"Don't be so ready to accept the obvious, and listen to me. We are *not* doing that. It was done decades ago, regularly and above the board, by students of Paul György and half a hundred other nutrition experts. Those people used only very widely known and tested antibiotics, drugs that had already been used on literally millions of farm animals, dosages worked out to the milligram of drug per kilogram of body weight, and so on. But this particular growth-stimulating effect of antibiotics happens to be a major clue to whether or not a given drug has the kind of biological activity *we* want—and we have to know whether or not it shows that activity *in human beings*. So we screen new drugs on the kids, as fast as they're found and pass certain other tests. We have to."

"I see," Paige said. "I see."

"The children are 'volunteered' by the foundling home, and we could make a show of legality if it came to a court fight," Anne said. "The precedent was established in 1952, when Pearl River Labs used children of its own workers to test its live-virus polio vaccine—which worked, by the way. But it isn't the legality of it that's important. It's the question of how soon and how thoroughly we're going to lick the degenerative diseases."

"You seem to be defending it to me," Paige said slowly, "as though you cared what I thought about it. So I'll tell you what I think: it seems mighty damned cold-blooded to me. It's the kind of thing of which ugly myths are made. If ten years from now there's a pogrom against biologists because people think they eat babies, I'll know why."

"Nonsense," Anne said. "It takes centuries to build up that kind of myth. You're over-reacting."

"On the contrary. I'm being as honest with you as you were with me. I'm astonished and somewhat repelled by what you've told me. That's all."

The girl, her lips slightly thinned, dipped and dried her fingertips and began to draw on her gloves. "Then we'll say no more about it," she said. "I think we'd better leave now."

"Certainly, as soon as I pay the check. Which reminds me: do you have any interest in Pfitzner, Anne—a personal interest, I mean?"

"No. No more interest than any human being with a moment's understanding of the implications would have. And I think that's a rather ugly sort of question."

"I thought you might take it that way, but I really wasn't accusing you of being a profiteer. I just wondered whether or not you were related to the Dr. Abbott that Gunn and the rest were waiting for this afternoon."

She got out the compact again and looked carefully into it. "Abbott's a common enough name."

"Sure. Still, *some* Abbotts are related. And it seems to make sense."

"Let's hear you do that. I'd be interested."

"All right," he said, beginning to become angry himself. "The receptionist at Pfitzner, ideally, should know exactly what is going on in the plant at all times, so as to be able to assess accurately the intentions of every visitor—just as you did with me. But at the same time, she has to be an absolutely flawless security risk, or otherwise she couldn't be trusted with enough knowledge to be that kind of a receptioni!. The best way to make sure of the security angle is to hire someone with a blood tie to another person on the project. That adds up to *two* people who are being careful. A classical Soviet form of blackmail, as I recall.

"That much is theory. There's fact, too. You certainly explained the Pfitzner project to me this evening from a broad base of knowledge that nobody could expect to find in an ordinary receptionist. On top of that, you took policy risks that, properly, only an officer of Pfitzner should be empowered to take. I conclude that you're not *only* a receptionist; your name is Abbott; and . . . there we have it, it seems to me."

"Do we?" the girl said, standing abruptly in a white fury. "Not quite! Also, I'm not pretty, and a receptionist for a firm as big as Pfitzner is usually pretty striking. Striking enough to resist being pumped by the first man to notice her, at least. Go ahead, complete the list! Tell the whole truth!"

"How can I?" Paige said, rising also and looking squarely at her, his fingers closing slowly. "If I told you honestly just what I think of your looks—and by God I will, I think the most beautiful woman in the world would bathe every day in fuming nitric acid just to duplicate your smile—you'd hate me more than ever. You'd think I was mocking you. Now you tell me the rest of the truth. You *are* related to Dr. Abbott."

"Patly enough," the girl said, each word cut out of smoking-dry ice, "Dr. Abbott is my father. And I insist upon being allowed to go home now, Colonel Russell. Not ten seconds from now, but *now*."

CHAPTER FOUR: Jupiter V

The firm determination to submit to experiment is not enough; there are still dangerous hypotheses; first, and above all, those which are tacit and unconscious. Since we make them without knowing it, we are powerless to abandon them.

—HENRI POINCARÉ

The Bridge vanished as the connection was broken. The continuous ultronic pulses from the Jovian satellites to the selsyns and servos of the Bridge never stopped, of course; and the Bridge sent back information ceaselessly on the same sub-etheric channels to the ever-vigilant eyes and ears and hands of the Bridge gang on Jupiter V. But for the moment, the vast structure's guiding intelligence, the Bridge gang foreman, had quitted it.

Helmuth set the heavy helmet carefully in its niche and felt of his temples, feeling the blood passing under his fingertips. Then he turned.

Dillon was looking at him.

"Well?" the civil engineer said. "What's the matter, Bob? Is it bad—?"

Helmuth did not reply for a moment. The abrupt transition from the storm-ravaged deck of the Bridge to the quiet, placid air of the operations shack on Jupiter's fifth moon was always a shock. He had never been able to anticipate it, let alone become accustomed to it; it was worse each time, not better.

He pulled the jacks from the foreman's board and let them flick back into the desk on their alive, elastic cables, and then got up from the bucket seat, moving carefully upon shaky legs, feeling implicit in his own body the enormous weights and pressures his guiding intelligence had just quitted. The fact that the gravity on the foreman's deck was as weak as that of most of the habitable asteroids only made the contrast greater, and his need for caution in walking more extreme.

He went to the big porthole and looked out. The unworn, tumbled, monotonous surface of airless Jupiter V looked almost homey after the perpetual holocaust of Jupiter itself. But there was an overpowering reminder of that holocaust—for through the thick quartz of the porthole, the face of the giant planet stared at Helmuth across only 112,600 miles, less than half the distance between Earth's moon and Earth; a sphere-section occupying almost all of the sky, except the near horizon, where one could see a few first-magnitude stars. The rest of the sky was crawling with color, striped and blotched with the eternal, frigid, poisonous storming of Jupiter's atmosphere, spotted with the deep-black, planet-sized shadows of moons closer to the sun than Jupiter V.

Somewhere down there, six thousand miles below the clouds that boiled in Helmuth's face, was the Bridge. The Bridge was thirty miles high and eleven miles wide and fifty-four miles long—but it was only a sliver, an intricate and fragile arrangement of ice-crystals beneath the bulging, racing tornadoes.

On Earth, even in the West, the Bridge would

have been the mightiest engineering achievement of all history, could the Earth have borne its weight at all. But on Jupiter, the Bridge was as precarious and perishable as a snowflake.

"Bob?" Dillon's voice asked. "What is it? You seem more upset than usual. Is it serious?"

Helmuth looked up. His superior's worn, young face, lantern-jawed and crowned by black hair already beginning to gray at the temples, was alight both with love for the Bridge and with the consuming ardor of the responsibility he had to bear. As always, it touched Helmuth and reminded him that the implacable universe had, after all, provided one warm corner in which human beings might huddle together.

"Serious enough," he said, forming the words with difficulty against the frozen inarticulateness Jupiter had forced upon him. "But not fatal, as far as I could see. There's a lot of hydrogen vulcanism on the surface, especially at the northwest end, and it looks like there must have been a big blast under the cliffs. I saw what looked like the last of a series of fire-falls."

Dillon's face relaxed while Helmuth was talking, slowly, line by engraved line. "Oh. It was just a flying chunk then."

"I'm almost sure that was what it was. The cross-draughts are heavy now. The Spot and the STD are due to pass each other some time next month, aren't they? I haven't checked, but I can feel the difference in the storms."

"So the chunk got picked up and thrown through the end of the Bridge. A big piece?"

Helmuth shrugged. "That end is all twisted away to the left, and the deck is burst into matchwood. The scaffolding is all gone, too, of course. A pretty big piece, all right, Charity—two miles through at a minimum."

Dillon sighed. He, too, went to the window, and

looked out. Helmuth did not need to be a mind
reader to know what he was looking at. Out there,
across the stony waste of Jupiter V plus 112,600
miles of space, the South Tropical Disturbance was
streaming toward the great Red Spot, and would
soon overtake it. When the whirling funnel of the
STD—more than big enough to suck three Earths
into deep-freeze—passed the planetary island of
sodium-tainted ice which was the Red Spot, the Spot
would follow it for a few thousand miles, at the same
time rising closer to the surface of the atmosphere.

Then the Spot would sink again, drifting back toward
the incredible jet of stress-fluid which kept it in
being—a jet fed by no one knew what forces at
Jupiter's hot, rocky, 22,000 mile core, compacted
down there under 16,000 miles of eternal ice. During the entire passage, the storms all over Jupiter
became especially violent; and the Bridge had been
forced to locate in anything but the calmest spot on
the planet, thanks to the uneven distribution of the
few "permanent" land-masses.

But—"permanent"? The quote-marks Helmuth's
thinking always put around that word were there for
a very good reason, he knew, but he could not quite
remember the reason. It was the damned conditioning showing itself again, creating another of the thousand small irreconcilables which contributed to the
tension.

Helmuth watched Dillon with a certain compas-
sion, tempered with mild envy. Charity Dillon's unfortunate given name betrayed him as the son of a
hangover, the only male child of a Believer family
which dated back long before the current resurgence
of the Believers. He was one of the hundreds of
government-drafted experts who had planned the
Bridge, and he was as obsessed by the Bridge as
Helmuth was—but for different reasons. It was widely
believed among the Bridge gang that Dillon, alone

among them, had not been given the conditioning, but there was no way to test that.

Helmuth moved back to the port, dropping his hand gently on Dillon's shoulders. Together they looked at the screaming straw yellows, brick reds, pinks, oranges, browns, even blues and greens that Jupiter threw across the ruined stone of its inner-most satellite. On Jupiter V, even the shadows had color.

Dillon did not move. He said at last: "Are you pleased, Bob?"

"Pleased?" Helmuth said in astonishment. "No. It scares me white; you know that. I'm just glad that the whole Bridge didn't go."

"You're quite sure?" Dillon said quietly.

Helmuth took his hand from Dillon's shoulder and returned to his seat at the central desk. "You've no right to needle me for something I can't help," he said, his voice even lower than Dillon's. "I work on Jupiter four hours a day—not actually, because we can't keep a man alive for more than a split second down there—but my eyes and ears and my mind are there on the Bridge, four hours a day. Jupiter is not a nice place. I don't like it. I won't pretend I do.

"Spending four hours a day in an environment like that over a period of years—well, the human mind instinctively tries to adapt, even to the unthinkable. Sometimes I wonder how I'll behave when I'm put back in Chicago again. Sometimes I can't remember anything about Chicago except vague generalities, sometimes I can't even believe there is such a place as Earth—how could there be when the rest of the universe is like Jupiter or worse?"

"I know," Dillon said. "I've tried several times to show you that isn't a very reasonable frame of mind."

"I know it isn't. But I can't help how I feel. For all I know it isn't even my own frame of mind—though the part of my mind that keeps saying 'The Bridge *must* stand' is more likely to be the conditioned part.

No, I don't think the Bridge will last. It can't last; it's all wrong. But I don't *want* to see it go. I've just got sense enough to know that one of these days Jupiter is going to sweep it away."

He wiped an open palm across the control boards, snapping all the toggles to "Off" with a sound like the fall of a double-handful of marbles on a pane of glass. "Like that, Charity! And I work four hours a day, every day, on the Bridge. One of these days, Jupiter is going to destroy the Bridge. It'll go flying away in little flinders, into the storms. My mind will be there, supervising some puny job, and my mind will go flying away along with my mechanical eyes and ears and hands—still trying to adapt to the unthinkable, tumbling away into the winds and the flames and the rains and the darkness and the pressure and the cold—"

"Bob, you're deliberately running away with yourself. Cut it out. Cut it out, I say!"

Helmuth shrugged, putting a trembling hand on the edge of the board to steady himself. "All right, I'm all right, Charity. I'm here, aren't I? Right here on Jupiter V, in no danger, in no danger at all. The Bridge is one hundred and twelve thousand six hundred miles away from here, and I'll never be an inch closer to it. But when the day comes that the Bridge is swept away—

"Charity, sometimes I imagine you ferrying my body back to the cosy nook it came from, while my soul goes tumbling and tumbling through millions of cubic miles of poison. . . . All right, Charity, I'll be good. I won't think about it out loud, but you can't expect me to forget it. It's on my mind; I can't help it, and you should know that."

"I do," Dillon said, with a kind of eagerness. "I do, Bob. I'm only trying to help make you see the problem as it is. The Bridge isn't really that awful, it isn't worth a single nightmare."

"Oh, it isn't the Bridge that makes me yell out when I'm sleeping," Helmuth said, smiling bitterly. "I'm not that ridden by it yet. It's while I'm awake that I'm afraid the Bridge will be swept away. What I sleep with is a fear of myself."

"That's a sane fear. You're as sane as any of us," Dillon insisted, fiercely solemn. "Look, Bob. The Bridge isn't a monster. It's a way we've developed for studying the behavior of materials under specific conditions of pressure, temperature and gravity. Jupiter isn't Hell, either; it's a set of conditions. The Bridge is the laboratory we set up to work with those conditions."

"It isn't going anywhere. It's a bridge to noplace."

"There aren't many *places* on Jupiter," Dillon said, missing Helmuth's meaning entirely. "We put the Bridge on an island in the local sea because we needed solid ice we could sink the foundation in. Otherwise, it wouldn't have mattered where we put it. We could have floated the caissons on the sea itself, if we hadn't wanted a fixed point from which to measure storm velocities and such things."

"I know that," Helmuth said.

"But, Bob, you don't show any signs of understanding it. Why, for instance, should the Bridge *go* any place? It isn't even, properly speaking, a bridge at all. We only call it that because we used some bridge engineering principles in building it. Actually, it's much more like a traveling crane—an extremely heavy-duty overhead rail line. It isn't going anywhere because it hasn't any place interesting to go to, that's all. We're extending it to cover as much territory as possible, and to increase its stability, not to span the distance between places. There's no point to reproaching it because it doesn't span a real gap —between, say, Dover and Calais. It's a bridge to knowledge, and that's far more important. Why can't you see that?"

"I can see that; that's what I was talking about," Helmuth said, trying to control his impatience. "I have at present as much common sense as the average child. What I am trying to point out is that meeting colossalness with colossalness—out here—is a mug's game. It's a game Jupiter will always win without the slightest effort. What if the engineers who built the Dover-Calais bridge had been limited to broom-straws for their structural members? They could have got the bridge up somehow, sure, and made it strong enough to carry light traffic on a fair day. But what would you have had left of it after the first winter storm came down the Channel from the North Sea? The whole approach is idiotic!"

"All right," Dillon said reasonably. "You have a point. Now you're being reasonable. What better approach have you to suggest? Should we abandon Jupiter entirely because it's too big for us?"

"No," Helmuth said. "Or maybe, yes. I don't know. I don't have any easy answer. I just know that this one is no answer at all—it's just a cumbersome evasion."

Dillon smiled. "You're depressed, and no wonder. Sleep it off, Bob, if you can—you might even come up with that answer. In the meantime—well, when you stop to think about it, the surface of Jupiter isn't any more hostile, inherently, than the surface of Jupiter V, except in degree. If you stepped out of this building naked, you'd die just as fast as you would on Jupiter. Try to look at it that way."

Helmuth, looking forward into another night of dreams, said: "That's the way I look at it now."

BOOK TWO

INTERMEZZO: Washington

Finally, in semantic aphasia, the full significance of words and phrases is lost. Separately, each word or each detail of a drawing can be understood, but the general significance escapes; an act is executed on command, though the purpose of it is not understood. . . . A general conception cannot be formulated, but details can be enumerated.

—HENRI PIÉRON

We often think that when we have completed our study of one we know all about two, because 'two' is 'one and one.' We forget that we have still to make a study of 'and.'

—A. S. EDDINGTON

The report of the investigating sub-committee of the Senate Finance Committee on the Jupiter Project was a massive document, especially so in the mimeographed, uncorrected form in which it had been rushed to Wagoner's desk. In its printed form—not due for another two weeks—the report would be considerably less bulky, but it would probably be more unreadable. In addition, it would be tempered in spots by the cautious second thoughts of its seven authors; Wagoner needed to see their opinions in the raw "for colleagues only" version.

Not that the printed version would get a much wider circulation. Even the mimeographed document was stamped "Top Secret." It had been years since anything about the government's security system had amused Wagoner in the slightest, but he could not repress a wry grin now. Of course the Bridge itself was Top Secret; but had the sub-committee's report been ready only a little over a year ago, everybody in the country would have heard about it, and selected passages would have been printed in the newspapers. He could think offhand of at least ten opposition senators, and two or three more inside his own party, who had been determined to use the report to prevent his reelection—or any parts of the report that might have been turned to that purpose. Unhappily for them, the report had been still only a third finished when election day had come, and Alaska had sent Wagoner back to Washington by a very comfortable plurality.

And as he turned the stiff legal-length pages slowly, with the pleasant, smoky odor of duplicator ink rising from them as he turned, it became clear that the report would have made pretty poor campaign material anyhow. Much of it was highly technical and had obviously been written by staff advisers, not by the investigating senators themselves. The public might be impressed by, but it could not read and would not read, such a show of erudition. Besides, it was only a show; nearly all the technical discussions of the Bridge's problems petered out into meaningless generalities. In most such instances Wagoner was able to put a mental finger on the missing fact, the igno-

rance or the withholding of which had left the chain
of reasoning suspended in mid-air.

Against the actual operation of the Bridge the senators had been able to find nothing of substance to
say. Given in advance the fact that the taxpayers had
wanted to spend so much money to build a Bridge
on Jupiter—which is to say, somebody (Wagoner
himself) had decided that for them, without confusing them by bringing the proposition to their attention
—then even the opposition senators had had to agree
that it had been built as economically as possible and
was still being built that way.

Of course, there had been small grafts waiting to
be discovered, and the investigators had discovered
them. One of the supply-ship captains had been
selling cakes of soap to the crew on Ganymede at
incredible prices with the co-operation of the store
clerk there. But that was nothing more than a book-
keeper's crime on a project the size of the Bridge.
Wagoner a little admired the supply-captain's ingenuity
—or had it been the store clerk's?—in discovering an
item wanted badly enough on Ganymede, and small
enough and light enough to be worth smuggling. The
men on the Bridge gang banked most of their salaries
automatically on Earth without ever seeing them;
there was very little worth buying or selling on the
moons of Jupiter.

Of major graft, however, there had been no trace.
No steel company had sold the Bridge any sub-
standard castings, because there was no steel in the
Bridge. A Jovian might have made a good thing of
selling the Bridge sub-standard Ice IV—but as far as
anyone could know there were no Jovians, so the
Bridge got its Ice IV for nothing but the cost of
cutting it. Wagoner's office had been very strict about
the handling of the lesser contracts—for pre-fabricated
moon huts, for supply ferry fuel, for equipment—
and had policed not only its own deals, but all the

Army Space Service sub-contracts connected with the Bridge.

As for Charity Dillon and his foreman, they were rigidly efficient—partly because it was in their natures to work that way, and partly because of the intensive conditioning they had all been given before being shipped to the Jovian system. There was no waste to be found in anything that they supervised, and if they had occasionally been guilty of bad engineering judgment, no outside engineer would be likely to detect it. The engineering principles by which the Bridge operated did not hold true anywhere but on Jupiter.

The hugest loss of money the whole Jupiter Project had yet sustained had been accompanied by such carnage that it fell—in the senators' minds—in the category of warfare. When a soldier is killed by enemy action, nobody asks how much money his death cost the government through the loss of his gear. The part of the report which described the placing of the Bridge's foundation mentioned reverently the heroism of the lost two hundred and thirty-one crewmen; it said nothing about the cost of the nine specially-designed space tugs which now floated in silhouette, as flat as so many tin cut-outs under six million pounds per square inch of pressure, somewhere at the bottom of Jupiter's atmosphere—floated with eight thousand vertical miles of eternally roaring poisons between them and the eyes of the living.

Had those crewmen been heroes? They had been enlisted men and officers of the Army Space Service, acting under orders. While doing what they had been ordered to do, they had been killed. Wagoner could not remember whether or not the survivors of that operation had also been called heroes. Oh, they had certainly been decorated—the Army liked its men to wear as much fruit salad on their chests as it could possibly spoon out to them, because it was good public relations—but they were not mentioned in the report.

This much was certain: the dead men had died because of Wagoner. He had known, generally at least, that many of them would die, but he had gone ahead anyhow. He knew that there might be worse to come. Nevertheless, he would proceed, because he thought that—in the long run—it would be worth it. He knew well enough that the end cannot justify the means; but if there are *no* other means, and the end is necessary. . . .

But from time to time he thought of Dostoevski and the Grand Inquisitor. Would the Millennium be worth having, if it could be ushered in only by the torturing to death of a single child? What Wagoner foresaw and planned for was by no means the Millennium; and while the children at Jno. Pfitzner & Sons were certainly not being tortured or even harmed, their experiences there were at least not normal for children. And there were two hundred and thirty-one men frozen solid somewhere in the bottomless hell of Jupiter, men who had had to obey their orders even more helplessly than children.

Wagoner had not been cut out to be a general.

The report praised the lost men's heroism. Wagoner lifted the heavy pages one after another, looking for a word from the investigating senators about the cause those deaths had served. There was nothing but the conventional phrases, "for their country," "for the cause of peace," "for the future." High-order abstractions—blabs. The senators had no notion of what the Bridge was for. They had looked, but they hadn't seen. Even with a total of four years to think back on the experience, they hadn't seen. The very size of the Bridge evidently had convinced them that it was a form of weapons research—so much "for the cause of peace"—and that it would be better for them not to know the nature of the weapon until an official announcement was circulated to them.

They were right. The Bridge was assuredly a weapon. But in neglecting to wonder what kind of a weapon it might be, the senators had also neglected to wonder at whom it was pointed. Wagoner was glad that they had.

The report did not even touch upon those two years of exploration, of search for some project which might be worth attacking, which had preceded even the notion of the Bridge. Wagoner had had a special staff of four devoted men at work during every minute of those two years, checking patents that had been granted but not sequestered, published scientific papers containing suggestions other scientists had decided not to explore, articles in the lay press about incipient miracles which hadn't come off, science-fiction stories by practicing scientists, anything and everything that might lead somewhere. The four men had worked under orders to avoid telling anybody what they were looking for, and to stay strictly away from the main currents of modern scientific thought on the subject; but no secret is ever truly safe; no face in nature is ever truly a secret.

Somewhere, for instance, in the files of the FBI, was a tape recording of the conversation he had had with the chief of the four-man team, in his office, the day the break came. The man had said, not only to Wagoner, but to the attentive FBI microphones no senator dared to seek out and muffle: "This looks like a real line, Bliss. On Subject G." (Something on gravity, chief.)

"Keep it to the point." (A reminder: Keep it too technical to interest a casual eavesdropper—if you *have* to talk about it here, with all these bugs to pick it up.)

"Sure. It's a thing called the Blackett equation.

Deals with a possible relationship between electron-spin and magnetic moment. I understand Dirac did some work on that, too. There's a G in the equation, and with one simple algebraic manipulation you can isolate the G on one side of the equals-sign, and all the other elements on the other." (Not a crackpot notion this time. Real scientists have been interested in it. There's math to go with it.)

"Status?" (Why was it never followed, then?)

"The original equation is about status seven, but there's no way anybody knows that it could be subjected to an operational test. The manipulated equation is called the Locke Derivation, and our boys say that a little dimensional analysis will show that it's wrong; but they're not entirely sure. However, it *is* subject to an operational test if we want to pay for it, where the original Blackett formula isn't." (Nobody's sure what it means yet. It may mean nothing. It would cost a hell of a lot to find out.)

"Do we have the facilities?" (Just how much?)

"Only the beginnings." (About four billion dollars, Bliss.)

"Conservatively?" (Why so much?)

"Yes. Field strength again."

(That was shorthand for the only problem that mattered, in the long run, if you wanted to work with gravity. Whether you thought of it, like Newton, as a force, or like Faraday as a field, or like Einstein as a condition in space, gravity was incredibly weak. It was so weak that, although theoretically it was a property of every bit of matter in the universe no matter how small, it could not be worked with in the laboratory. Two magnetized needles will rush toward each other over a distance as great as an inch; so will two balls of pith as small as peas if they bear opposite electrical charges. Two ceramet magnets no bigger than doughnuts can be so strongly charged that it is impossible to push them together by hand when their like poles are opposed, and impossible for a strong man to hold them apart when their unlike poles approach each other. Two spheres of metal of any size, if they bear opposite electrical charges, will mate in a fat spark across the insulating air, if there is no other way that they can neutralize each other.

(But gravity—theoretically one in kind with electricity and magnetism—cannot be charged on to any object. It produces no sparks. There is no such thing as an insulation against it—a di-gravitic. It remains beyond detection as a force, between bodies as small as peas or doughnuts. Two objects as huge as skyscrapers and as massive as lead will take centuries to crawl into the same bed over a foot of distance, if nothing but their mutual gravitational attraction is drawing them together; even love is faster than that. Even a ball of rock eight thousand miles in diameter—the Earth—has a gravitational field too weak to prevent one single man from pole-vaulting away from it to more than four times his own height, driven by no opposing force but that of his spasming muscles.)

"Well, give me a report when you can. If necessary, we can expand." (Is it worth it?)

"I'll give you the report this week." (Yes!)

And that was how the Bridge had been born, though nobody had known it then, not even Wagoner. The senators who had investigated the Bridge still didn't know it. MacHinery's staff at the FBI evidently had been unable to penetrate the jargon on their recording of that conversation far enough to connect the conversation with the Bridge; otherwise MacHinery would have given the transcript to the investigators. MacHinery did not exactly love Wagoner; he had been unable thus far to find any handle by which he might grasp and use the Alaskan senator.

All well and good.

And yet the investigators had come perilously close,

just once. They had subpoenaed Guiseppi Corsi for
the preliminary questioning.

Committee Counsel: Now then, Dr. Corsi, according to our records, your last interview with Senator Wagoner was in the winter of 2013. Did you
discuss the Jupiter Project with him at that time?

Corsi: How could I have? It didn't exist then.

Counsel: But was it mentioned to you in any
way? Did Senator Wagoner say anything about plans
to start such a project?

Corsi: No.

Counsel: You didn't yourself suggest it to Senator Wagoner?

Corsi: Certainly not. It was a total surprise to
me, when it was announced afterwards.

Counsel: But I suppose you know what it is.

Corsi: I know only what the general public has
been told. We're building a Bridge on Jupiter. It's
very costly and ambitious. What it's for is a secret.
That's all.

Counsel: You're sure you don't know what it's
for?

Corsi: For research.

Counsel: Yes, but research for what? Surely you
have some clues.

Corsi: I don't have any clues, and Senator Wagoner didn't give me any. The only facts I have are
those I read in the press. Naturally I have some
conjectures. But all I *know* is what is indicated, or
hinted at, in the official announcements. Those seem
to convey the impression that the Bridge is for weapons research.

Counsel: But you think that maybe it isn't?

Corsi: I—I'm not in a position to discuss government projects about which I know nothing.

Counsel: You could give us your opinion.

Corsi: If you want my opinion as an expert, I'll

have my office go into the subject and let you know late what such an opinion would cost.

Senator Billings: Dr. Corsi, do we understand that you refuse to answer the question? It seems to me that in view of your past record you might be better advised—

Corsi: I haven't refused an answer, Senator. I make part of my living by consultation. If the government wishes to use me in that capacity, it's my right to ask to be paid. You have no right to deprive me of my livelihood, or any part of it.

Senator Croft: The government made up its mind about employing you some time back, Dr. Corsi. And rightly, in my opinion.

Corsi: That is the government's privilege.

Senator Croft: —but you are being questioned now by the Senate of the United States. If you refuse to answer, you may be held in contempt.

Corsi: For refusing to state an opinion?

Counsel: If you will pardon me, Senator Croft, the witness may refuse to offer an opinion—or withhold such an opinion, pending payment. He can be held in contempt only for declining to state the facts as he knows them.

Senator Croft: All right, let's get some facts, and stop the pussyfooting.

Counsel: Dr. Corsi, was anything said during your last meeting with Senator Wagoner which might have had any bearing on the Jupiter Project?

Corsi: Well, yes. But only negatively. I did counsel him against any such project. Rather emphatically, as I recall.

Counsel: I thought you said that the Bridge hadn't been mentioned.

Corsi: It hadn't. Senator Wagoner and I were discussing research methods in general. I told him that I thought research projects of the Bridge's order of magnitude were no longer fruitful.

Senator Billings: Did you charge Senator Wagoner for that opinion, Dr. Corsi?

Corsi: No, Senator. Sometimes I don't.

Senator Billings: Perhaps you should have. Wagoner didn't follow your free advice.

Senator Croft: It looks like he considered the source.

Corsi: There's nothing compulsory about advice. I gave him my best opinion at the time. What he did with it was up to him.

Counsel: Would you tell us if that is your best opinion now? That research projects the size of the Bridge are—I believe your phrase was, "no longer fruitful"?

Corsi: That is still my opinion.

Senator Billings: Which you will give us free of charge . . . ?

Corsi: It is the opinion of every scientist I know. You could get it free from those who work for you. I have better sense than to charge fees for common knowledge.

It had been a near thing. Perhaps, Wagoner thought, Corsi had after all remembered the really crucial part of that interview and had decided not to reveal it to the sub-committee. It was more likely, however, that those few words that Corsi had thrown off while standing at the blinded windows of his apartment would not have stuck in his memory as they had stuck in Wagoner's.

Yet surely Corsi knew, at least in part, what the Bridge was for. He must have remembered the part of that conversation which dealt with gravity. By now he would have reasoned his way from those words all the difficult way to the Bridge—after all, the Bridge was not a difficult object for an understanding like Corsi's.

But he had said nothing about it. That had been a crucial silence.

Wagoner wondered if it would ever be possible for him to show his gratitude to the aging physicist. Not now. Possibly never. The pain and the puzzlement in Corsi's mind stood forth in what he had said, even through the coldness of the official transcript. Wagoner badly wanted to assuage both. But he couldn't. He could only hope that Corsi would see it whole, and understand it whole, when the time came.

The page turned on Corsi. Now there was another question which had to be answered. Was there a single hint, anywhere in the sixteen hundred mimeographed pages of the report, that the Bridge was incomplete without what was going on at Jno. Pfitzner & Sons? . . .

No, there was not. Wagoner let the report fall, with a sigh of relief of which he was hardly conscious. That was that.

He filed the report, and reached into his "In" basket for the dossier on Paige Russell, Colonel, Army Space Corps, which had come in from the Pfitzner plant only a week ago. He was tired, and he did not want to perform an act of judgment on another man for the rest of his life—but he had asked for the job, and now he had to work at it.

Bliss Wagoner had not been cut out to be a general. As a god he was even more inept.

CHAPTER FIVE: New York

*The original phenomena which the soul-hypo-
thesis attempted to explain still remain.* Homo
sapiens *does have some differences from other
animal species. But when his biological distinc-
tions and their consequences are clearly described, man's 'morality,' his 'soul,' and his
'immortality' all become accessible to a purely
naturalistic formulation and understanding,* . . .
*Man's 'immortality' (in so far as it differs from
the immortality of the germ plasm of any other
animal species) consists in his time-transcending
inter-individually shared values, symbol-systems,
languages, and cultures—and in nothing else.*
— WESTON LA BARRE

It took Paige no more than Anne's mandatory ten
seconds, during breakfast of the next day in his snug-
gery at the spaceman's Haven, to decide that he was
going back to the Pfitzner plant and apologize. He
didn't quite understand why the date had ended as
catastrophically as it had, but of one thing he was
nearly certain: the fiasco had had something to do

74

with his space-rusty manners, and if it were to be
mended, he had to be the one to tool up for it.

And now that he came to think of it over his cold
egg, it seemed obvious in essence. By his last line of
questioning, Paige had broken the delicate shell of
the evening and spilled the contents all over the
restaurant table. He had left the more or less safe
womb of technicalities, and had begun, by implica-
tion at least, to call Anne's ethics into question—first
by making clear his first reaction to the business
about the experimental infants, and then by pressing
home her irregular marriage to her firm.

In this world called Earth of disintegrating faiths,
one didn't call personal ethical codes into question
without getting into trouble. Such codes, where they
could be found at all, obviously had cost their adher-
ents too much pain to be open for any new probing.
Faith had once been self-evident; now it was desperate. Those who still had it—or had made it, chunk by
fragment by shard—wanted nothing but to be allowed to hold it.

As for why he wanted to set matters right with
Anne Abbott, Paige was less clear. His leave was
passing him by rapidly, and thus far he had done
little more than stroll while it passed—especially if
he measured it against the desperate meter-stick established by his last two leaves, the two after his
marriage had shattered and he had been alone again.
After the present leave was over, there was a good
chance that he would be assigned to the Proserpine
station, which was now about finished and which had
no competitors for the title of the most forsaken
outpost of the solar system. None, at least, until
somebody should discover an 11th planet.

Nevertheless, he was going to go out to the Pfitzner
plant again, out to the scenic Bronx, to revel among
research scientists, business executives, government
brass, and a frozen-voiced girl with a figure like an

ironing-board, to kick up his heels on a reception-room rug in the sight of gay steel engravings of the founders, cheered on by a motto which might or might not be Dionysiac, if he could only read it. Great. Just great. If he played his cards right, he could go on duty at the Proserpine station with fine memories: perhaps the vice-president in charge of export would let Paige call him "Hal," or maybe even "Bubbles."

Maybe it was a matter of religion, after all. Like everyone else in the world, Paige thought, he was still looking for something bigger than himself, bigger than family, army, marriage, fatherhood, space itself, or the pub-crawls and tyrannically meaningless sexual spasms of a spaceman's leave. Quite obviously the project at Pfitzner, with its air of mystery and selflessness, had touched that very vulnerable nerve in him once more. Anne Abbott's own dedication was merely the touchstone, the key. . . . No, he hadn't the right word for it yet, but her attitude somehow fitted into an empty, jagged-edge blemish in his own soul like—like . . . yes, that was it: like a jigsaw-puzzle piece.

And besides, he wanted to see that sunburst smile again.

Because of the way her desk was placed, she was the first thing he saw as he came into Pfitzner's reception room. Her expression was even stranger than he had expected, and she seemed to be making some kind of covert gesture, as though she were flicking dust off the top of her desk toward him with the tips of all her fingers. He took several slower and slower steps into the room and stopped, finally baffled.

Someone rose from a chair which he had not been able to see from the door, and quartered down on him. The pad of the steps on the carpet and the odd crouch of the shape in the corner of Paige's eye were unpleasantly stealthy. Paige turned, unconsciously closing his hands.

"Haven't we seen this officer before, Miss Abbott? What's his business here—or has he any?"

The man in the eager semi-crouch was Francis X. MacHinery.

When he was not bent over in that absurd position, which was only his prosecutor's stance, Francis X. MacHinery looked every inch the inheritor of an unbroken line of Boston aristocrats, as in fact he was. Though he was not tall, he was very spare, and his hair had been white since he was 26 years old, giving him a look of cold wisdom which was complemented by his hawk-like nose and high cheekbones. The FBI had come down to him from his grandfather, who had somehow persuaded the then incumbent president —a stunningly popular Man-on-Horseback who dripped *charisma* but had no brains worth mentioning— that so important a directorship should not be hazarded to the appointments of his successors, but instead ought to be handed on from father to son like a corporate office.

Hereditary posts tend to become nominal with the passage of time, since it takes only one weak scion to destroy the importance of the office; but that had not happened yet to the MacHinery family. The current incumbent could, in fact, have taught his grandfather a thing or two. MacHinery was as full of cunning as a wolverine, and he had managed times without number to land on his feet regardless of what political disasters had been planned for him. And he was, as Paige was now discovering, the man for whom the metaphor "gimlet-eyed" had all unknowingly been invented.

"Well, Miss Abbott?"

"Colonel Russell was here yesterday," Anne said. "You may have seen him then."

The swinging doors opened and Horsefield and

Gunn came in. MacHinery paid no attention to them. He said, "What's your name, soldier?"

"I'm a spaceman," Paige said stiffly. "Colonel Paige Russell, Army Space Corps."

"What are you doing here?"

"I'm on leave."

"Will you answer the question?" MacHinery said. He was, Paige noticed, not looking at Paige at all, but over his shoulder, as though he were actually paying no real heed to the conversation. "What are you doing at the Pfitzner plant?"

"I happen to be in love with Miss Abbott," Paige said sharply to his own black and utter astonishment. "I came here to see her. We had a quarrel last night and I wanted to apologize. That's all."

Anne straightened behind her desk as though a curtain rod had been driven up her spine, turning toward Paige a pair of blindly blazing eyes and a rigidly unreadable expression. Even Gunn's mouth sagged slightly to one side; he looked first at Anne, then at Paige, as if he were abruptly uncertain that he had ever seen either of them before.

MacHinery, however, shot only one quick look at Anne, and his eyes seemed to turn into bottle-glass. "I'm not interested in your personal life," he said in a tone which, indeed, suggested active boredom. "I will put the question another way, so that there'll be no excuse for evading it. Why did you come to the plant in the first place? What is your *business* at Pfitzner, soldier?"

Paige tried to pick his next words carefully. Actually it would hardly matter what he said, once MacHinery developed a real interest in him; an accusation from the FBI had nearly the force of law. Everything depended upon so conducting himself as to be of no interest to MacHinery to begin with—an exercise at which, fortunately up to now, Paige had had no more practice than had any other spaceman.

He said: "I brought in some soil samples from the Jovian system. Pfitzner asked me to do it as part of their research program."

"And you brought these samples in yesterday, you told me."

"No, I didn't tell you. But as a matter of fact I did bring them in yesterday."

"And you're still bringing them in today, I see." MacHinery perked his chin over his shoulder toward Horsefield, whose face had frozen into complete tetany as soon as he had shown signs of realizing what was going on. "What about this, Horsefield? Is this one of your men that you haven't told me about?"

"No," Horsefield said, but putting a sort of a question mark into the way he spoke the word, as though he did not mean to deny anything which he might later be expected to affirm. "Saw the man yesterday, I think. For the first time to the best of my knowledge."

"I see. Would you say, General, that this man is no part of the Army's assigned complement on the project?"

"I can't say that for sure," Horsefield said, his voice sounding more positive now that he was voicing a doubt. "I'd have to consult my T.O. Perhaps he's somebody new in Alsos' group. He's not part of my staff, though—doesn't claim that he is, does he?"

"Gunn, what about this man? Did you people take him on without checking with me? Does he have security clearance?"

"Well, we did in a way, but he didn't need to be cleared," Gunn said. "He's just a field collector, hasn't any real part in the research work, no official connection. These field people are all volunteers; you know that."

MacHinery's brows were drawing closer and closer together. With only a few more of these questions, Paige knew even from the few newspapers which had reached him in space, he would have material enough for an arrest and a sensation—the kind of sensation which would pillory Pfitzner, destroy every civilian working for Pfitzner, trigger a long chain of courts martial among the military assignees, ruin the politicians who had sponsored the research, and thicken MacHinery's scrapbook of headlines about himself by at least three inches. That last outcome was the only one in which MacHinery was really interested; that the project itself would die was a side-effect which, though nearly inevitable, could hardly have interested him less.

"Excuse me, Mr. Gunn," Anne said quietly. "I don't think you're quite as familiar with Colonel Russell's status as I am. He's just come in from deep space, and his security record has been in the 'Clean and Routine' file for years; he's not one of our ordinary field collectors."

"Ah," Gunn said. "I'd forgotten, but that's quite true." Since it was both true and perfectly irrelevant, Paige could not understand why Gunn was quite so hearty about agreeing to it. Did he think Anne was stalling?

"As a matter of fact," Anne proceeded steadily, "Colonel Russell is a planetary ecologist specializing in the satellites; he's been doing important work for us. He's quite well known in space, and has many friends on the Bridge team and elsewhere. That's correct, isn't it, Colonel Russell?"

"I know most of the Bridge gang," Paige agreed, but he barely managed to make his assent audible. What the girl was saying added up to something very like a big, black lie. And lying to MacHinery was a short cut to ruin; only MacHinery had the privilege of lying, never his witnesses.

"The samples Colonel Russell brought us yesterday contained crucial material," Anne said. "That's why I asked him to come back; we needed his advice. And if his samples turn out to be as important as they seem, they'll save the taxpayers quite a lot of money—they may help us close out the project a long time in advance of the projected closing date. If that's to be possible, Colonel Russell will have to guide the last steps of the work personally; he's the only one who knows the microflora of the Jovian satellites well enough to interpret the results."

MacHinery looked dubiously over Paige's shoulder. It was hard to tell whether or not he had heard a word. Nevertheless, it was evident that Anne had chosen her final approach with great care, for if MacHinery had any weakness at all, it was the enormous cost of his continual, overlapping investigations. Lately he had begun to be nearly as sure death on "waste in government" as he was traditionally on "subversives." He said at last:

"There's obviously something irregular here. If all that's so, why did the man say what he said in the beginning?"

"Perhaps because it's also true," Paige said sharply.

MacHinery ignored him. "We'll check the records and call anyone we need. Horsefield, let's go."

The general trailed him out, his back very stiff, after a glare at Paige which failed to be in the least convincing, and an outrageously stagey wink at Anne. The moment the outer door closed behind the two, the reception-room seemed to explode. Gunn swung on Anne with a motion astonishingly tiger-like for so mild-faced a man. Anne was already rising from behind her desk, her face twisted with fear and fury. Both of them were shouting at once.

"Now see what you've done with your damned nosiness—"

"What in the world did you want to tell MacHinery a tale like that for—"

"—even a spaceman should know better than to hang around a defense area—"

"—you know as well as I do that those Ganymede samples are trash—"

"—you've probably cost us our whole appropriation with your snooping—"

"—we've never hired a 'Clean and Routine' man since the project began—"

"—I hope you're satisfied—"

"—I would have thought you'd have better sense by now—"

"Quiet!" Paige shouted over them with the authentic parade-ground blare. He had never found any use for it in deep space, but it worked now. Both of them looked at him, their mouths still incongruously half-opened, their faces white as milk. "You act like a pair of hysterical chickens, both of you! I'm sorry if I got you into trouble—but I didn't ask Anne to lie in my behalf—and I didn't ask you to go along with it, either, Gunn! Maybe you'd best stop yelling accusations and try to think the thing through. I'll try to help for whatever that's worth—but not if you're going to scream and weep at each other and at me!"

The girl bared her teeth at him in a real snarl, the first time he had ever seen a human being mount such an expression and mean it. She sat down, however, swiping at her patchily red cheeks with a piece of cleansing tissue. Gunn looked down at the carpet and just breathed noisily for a moment, putting the palms of his hands together solemnly before his white lips.

"I quite agree," Gunn said after a moment, as calmly as if nothing had happened. "We'll have to get to work and work fast. Anne, please tell me: why was it necessary for you to say that Colonel Paige was essential to the project? I'm not accusing you of anything, but we need to know the facts."

"I went to dinner with Colonel Russell last night," Anne said. "I was somewhat indiscreet about the project. At the end of the evening we had a quarrel which was probably overheard by at least two of MacHinery's amateur informers in the restaurant. I had to lie for my own protection as well as Colonel Russell's."

"But you have an Eavesdropper! If you knew that you might be overheard—"

"I knew it well enough. But I lost my temper. You know how these things go."

It all came out as emotionless as a tape recording. Told in these terms, the incident sounded to Paige like something that had happened to someone whom he had never met, whose name he could not even pronounce with certainty. Only the fact that Anne's eyes were reddened with furious tears offered any bridge between the cold narrative and the charged memory.

"Yes; nasty," Gunn said reflectively. "Colonel Russell, *do* you know the Bridge team?"

"I know some of them quite well, Charity Dillon in particular; after all, I was stationed in the Jovian system for a while. MacHinery's check will show that I've no official connection with the Bridge, however."

"Good, good," Gunn said, beginning to brighten. "That widens MacHinery's check to include the Bridge too, and dilutes it from Pfitzner's point of view— gives us more time, though I'm sorry for the Bridge men. The Bridge and the Pfitzner project both suspect—yes, that's a big mouthful even for MacHinery; it will take him months. And the Bridge is Senator Wagoner's pet project, so he'll have to go slowly; he can't assassinate Wagoner's reputation as rapidly as he could some other senator's. Hmm. The question now is, just how are we going to use the time?"

"When you calm down, you calm right down to the bottom," Paige said, grinning wryly.

"I'm a salesman," Gunn said. "Maybe more creative than some, but at heart a salesman. In that profession you have to suit the mood to the occasion, just like actors do. Now about those samples—"

"I shouldn't have thrown that in," Anne said. "I'm afraid it was one good touch too many."

"On the contrary, it may be the only out we have. MacHinery is a 'practical' man. Results are what counts with him. So suppose we take Colonel Russell's samples out of the regular testing order and run them through right now, issuing special orders to the staff that they are to find something in them—anything that looks at all decent."

"The staff won't fake," Anne said, frowning.

"My dear Anne, who said anything about faking? Nearly every batch of samples contains some organism of interest, even if it isn't good enough to wind up among our choicest cultures. You see? MacHinery will be contented by results if we can show them to him, even though the results may have been made possible by an unauthorized person; otherwise he'd have to assemble a committee of experts to assess the evidence, and that costs money. All this, of course, is predicated on whether or not we have any results by the time MacHinery finds out Colonel Russell *is* an unauthorized person."

"There's just one other thing," Anne said. "To make good on what I told MacHinery, we're going to have to turn Colonel Russell into a convincing planetary ecologist—*and* tell him just what the Pfitzner project is."

Gunn's face fell momentarily. "Anne," he said, "I want you to observe what a nasty situation that strong-arm man has gotten us into. In order to protect our legitimate interests from our own government, we're about to commit a real, serious breach of security—which would never have happened if MacHinery hadn't thrown his weight around."

"Quite true," Anne said. She looked, however, rather poker-faced, Paige thought. Possibly she was enjoying Gunn's discomfiture; he was not exactly the first man one would suspect of disloyalty or of being a security risk.

"Colonel Russell, there is no faint chance, I suppose, that you *are* a planetary ecologist? Most spacemen with ranks as high as yours are scientists of some kind."

"No, sorry," Paige said. "Ballistics is my field."

"Well, you do have to know something about the planets, at least. Anne, I suggest that you take charge now. I'll have to do some fast covering. Your father would probably be the best man to brief Colonel Russell. And, Colonel, would you bear in mind that from now on, every piece of information that you're given in our plant might have the giver jailed or even shot, if MacHinery were to find out about it?"

"I'll keep my mouth shut," Paige said. "I'm enough at fault in this mess to be willing to do all I can to help—and my curiosity has been killing me anyhow. But there's something you'd better know, too, Mr. Gunn."

"And that is—"

"That the time you're counting on just doesn't exist. My leave expires in ten days. If you think you can make a planetary ecologist out of me in that length of time, I'll do my part."

"Ulp," Gunn said. "Anne, get to work." He bolted through the swinging doors.

The two looked at each other for a starchy moment, and then Anne smiled. Paige felt like another man at once.

"Is it really true—what you said?" Anne said, almost shyly.

"Yes. I didn't know it until I said it, but it's true. I'm really sorry that I had to say it at such a spectacularly bad moment; I only came over to apologize for my part in last night's quarrel. Now it seems that I've a bigger hassle to account for."

"Your curiosity is really your major talent, do you know?" she said, smiling again. "It took you only two days to find out just what you wanted to know—even though it's about the most closely guarded secret in the world."

"But I don't know it yet. Can you tell me here—or is the place wired?"

The girl laughed. "Do you think Hal and I would have cussed each other out like that if the place were wired? No, it's clean, we inspect it daily. I'll tell you the central fact, and then my father can give you the details. The truth is that the Pfitzner project isn't out to conquer the degenerative diseases alone. It's aimed at the end-product of those diseases, too. *We're looking for the answer to death itself.*"

Paige sat down slowly in the nearest chair. "I don't believe it can be done," he whispered at last.

"That's what we all used to think, Paige. That's what that says." She pointed to the motto in German above the swinging doors. *"Wider den Tod ist kein Krautlein gewachsen."* " 'Against Death doth no simple grow.' That was a law of nature, the old German herbalists thought. But now it's only a challenge. Somewhere in nature there *are* herbs and simples against death—and we're going to find them."

Anne's father seemed both preoccupied and a little worried to be talking to Paige at all, but it nevertheless took him only one day to explain the basic reasoning behind the project vividly enough so that Paige could understand it. In another day of simple helping around the part of the Pfitzner labs which was running his soil samples—help which consisted mostly of bottle-washing and making dilutions—Paige learned the reasoning well enough to put forward a version of it himself. He practiced it on Anne over dinner.

"It all rests on our way of thinking about why antibiotics work," he said, while the girl listened with an attentiveness just this side of mockery. "What good are they to the organisms that produce them? We assumed that the organism secretes the antibiotic to kill or inhibit competing organisms, even though we were never able to show that enough antibiotic for the purpose is actually produced in the organism's natural medium, that is, the soil. In other words, we figured, the wider the range of the antibiotic, the less competition the producer had."

"Watch out for teleology," Anne warned. "That's not *why* the organism secretes it. It's just the result. Function, not purpose."

"Fair enough. But right there is the borderline in our thinking about antibiosis. What is an antibiotic to the organism it *kills?* Obviously, it's poison, a toxin. But some bacteria always are naturally resistant to a given antibiotic, and through—what did your father call it?—through clone-variation and selection, the resistant cells may take over a whole colony. Equally obviously, those resistant cells would seem to produce an antitoxin. An example would be the bacteria that secrete penicillinase, which is an enzyme that destroys penicillin. To those bacteria, penicillin is a toxin, and penicillinase is an antitoxin—isn't that right?"

"Right as rain. Go on, Paige."

"So now we add to that still another fact: that both penicillin and tetracycline are not only antibiotics—which makes them toxic to many bacteria—but *antitoxins* as well. Both of them neutralize the placental toxin that causes the eclampsia of pregnancy. Now, tetracycline is a broad-range antibiotic; is there such a thing as a broad-range antitoxin, too? Is the resistance to tetracycline that many different kinds of bacteria can develop all derived from a single counteracting substance? The answer, we know now, is Yes. We've also found another kind of broad-range antitoxin—one which protects the organism against many different kinds of antibiotics. I'm told that it's a whole new field of research and that we've just begun to scratch the surface.

"Ergo: Find the broad-range antitoxin that acts against the toxins of the human body which accumulate after growth stops—as penicillin and tetracycline act against the pregnancy toxin—and you've got your magic machine-gun against degenerative disease. Pfitzner already has found that antitoxin: its name is ascomycin. . . . How'd I do?" he added anxiously, getting his breath back.

"Beautifully. It's perhaps a little too condensed for MacHinery to follow, but maybe that's all to the good—it wouldn't sound authoritative to him if he could understand it all the way through. Still it might pay to be just a little more roundabout when you talk to him." The girl had the compact out again and was peering into it intently. "But you covered only the degenerative diseases, and that's just background material. Now tell me about the direct attack on death."

Paige looked at the compact and then at the girl, but her expression was too studied to convey much. He said slowly: "I'll go into that if you like. But your father told me that the element of the work was secret even from the government. Should I discuss it in a restaurant?"

Anne turned the small, compact-like object around, so that he could see that it was in fact a meter of some sort. Its needle was in uncertain motion, but near the zero-point. "There's no mike close enough to pick you up," Anne said, snapping the device shut and restoring it to her purse. "Go ahead."

"All right. Some day you're going to have to explain to me why you allowed yourself to get into that first fight with me here, when you had that Eavesdropper with you all the time. Right at the moment I'm too busy being a phony ecologist.

"The death end of the research began back in

1952, with an anatomist named Lansing. He was the first man to show that complex animals—it was rotifers he used—produce a definite aging toxin as a normal part of their growth, and that it gets passed on to the offspring. He bred something like fifty generations of rotifers from adolescent mothers, and got an increase in the life-span in every new generation. He ran 'em up from a natural average span of 24 days to one of 104 days. Then he reversed the process, by breeding consistently from old mothers, and cut the life-span of the final generation way *below* the natural average."

"And now," Anne said, "you know more about the babies in our labs than I told you before—or you should. The foundling home that supplies them specializes in the illegitimates of juvenile delinquents—the younger, for our purposes, the better."

"Sorry, but you can't needle me with that any longer, Anne. I know now that it's a blind alley. Breeding for longevity in humans isn't practicable; all that those infants can supply to the project is a set of comparative readings on their death-toxin blood-levels. What we want now is something much more direct: an antitoxin against the aging toxin of humans. We know that the aging toxin exists in all complex animals. We know that it's a single, specific substance, quite distinct from the poisons that cause the degenerative diseases. And we know that it can be neutralized. When your lab animals were given ascomycin, they didn't develop a single degenerative disease—but they died anyhow, at about the usual time, as if they'd been set, like a clock at birth. Which, in effect, they had, by the amount of aging toxin passed on to them by their mothers.

"So what we're looking for now is not an antibiotic —an anti-life drug—but an anti-agathic, an anti-death drug. We're running on borrowed time, because ascomycin already satisfies the condition of our development contract with the government. As soon as we get ascomycin into production, our government money will be cut down to a trickle. But if we can hold back on ascomycin long enough to keep the money coming in, we'll have our anti-agathic too."

"Bravo," Anne said. "You sound just like father. I wanted you to raise that last point in particular, Paige, because it's the most important single thing you should remember. If there's the slightest suspicion that we're systematically dragging our feet on releasing ascomycin—that we're taking money from the government to do something the government has no idea can be done—there'll be hell to pay. We're so close to running down our anti-agathic now that it would be heartbreaking to have to stop, not only heartbreaking for us, but for humanity at large."

"The end justifies the means," Paige murmured.

"It does in this case. I know secrecy's a fetish in our society these days—but here secrecy will serve everyone in the long run, and it's *got* to be maintained."

"I'll maintain it," Paige said. He had been referring, not to secrecy, but to cheating on government money; but he saw no point in bringing that up. As for secrecy, he had no practical faith in it—especially now that he had seen how well it worked.

For in the two days that he had been working inside Pfitzner, he had already found an inarguable spy at the very heart of the project.

CHAPTER SIX: Jupiter V

Yet the barbarians, who are not divided by rival traditions, fight all the more incessantly for food and space. Peoples cannot love one another unless they love the same ideas.

—GEORGE SANTAYANA

There were three yellow "Critical" signals lit on the long gangboard when Helmuth passed through the gang deck on the way back to duty. All of them, as usual, were concentrated on Panel 9, where Eva Chavez worked.

Eva, despite her Latin name—such once-valid tickets no longer meant anything among the West's uniformly mixed-race population—was a big girl, vaguely blonde, who cherished a passion for the Bridge. Unfortunately, she was apt to become enthralled by the sheer Cosmicness of It All, precisely at the moment when cold analysis and split-second decisions were most crucial.

Helmuth reached over her shoulder, cut her out of the circuit except as an observer, and donned the co-operator's helmet. The incomplete new shoals caisson sprang into being around him. Breakers of boiling hydrogen seethed seven hundred feet up along its slanted sides—breakers that never subsided, but simply were torn away into flying spray.

There was a spot of dull orange near the top of the north face of the caisson, crawling slowly toward the pediment of the nearest truss. Catalysis—

Or cancer, as Helmuth could not help but think of it. On this bitter, violent monster of a planet, even tiny specks of calcium carbide were deadly, that same calcium carbide which had produced acetylene gas for buggy lamps two centuries ago on Earth. At these wind velocities, such specks imbedded themselves deeply in anything they struck; and at fifteen million p.s.i. of pressure, under the catalysis of sodium, pressure-ice took up ammonia and carbon dioxide, building protein-like compounds in a rapid, voracious chain of decay:

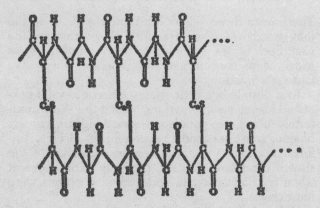

For a moment, Helmuth watched it grow. It was,

after all, one of the incredible possibilities the Bridge had been built to study. On Earth, such a compound, had it occurred at all, might have grown porous, hard, and as strong as rhinoceros-horn. Here, under nearly three times Earth's gravity, the molecules were forced to assemble in strict aliphatic order, but in cross section their arrangement was hexagonal, as though the stuff would become an aromatic compound if only it could. Even here it was moderately strong in cross section—but along the long axis it smeared like graphite, the calcium and sulphur atoms readily changing their minds as to which was to act as the metal of the pair, surrendering their pressure-driven holds on one carbon atom to grab hopefully for the next one in line, or giving up altogether to become incorporated instead in a radical with a self-contained double sulphur bond, rather like cystine. . . .

It was not too far from the truth to call it a form of cancer. The compound seemed to be as close as Jupiter came to an indigenous form of life. It grew, fed, reproduced itself, and showed something of the characteristic structure of an Earthly virus, such as tobacco-mosaic. Of course it grew from outside by accretion like any nonliving crystal, rather than from the inside, by intussusception, like a cell; but viruses grew that way too, at least in *vitro*.

It was no stuff to hold up the piers of humanity's greatest engineering project, that much was sure. Perhaps it was a suitable ground-substance for the ribs of some Jovian jellyfish; but in a Bridge-caisson, it was cancer.

There was a scraper mechanism working on the edge of the lesion, flaking away the shearing aminos and laying down new ice. In the meantime, the decay in the caissonface was working deeper. The scraper could not possibly get at the core of the trouble—which was not the calcium carbide dust,

with which the atmosphere was charged beyond re-
demption, but was instead one imbedded speck of
metallic sodium which was taking no part in the
reaction—fast enough to extirpate it. It could barely
keep pace with the surface spread of the disease.

And laying new ice over the surface of the wound
was worthless, as Eva should have known. At this
rate, the whole caisson would slough away and melt
like butter, within an hour, under the weight of the
Bridge above it.

Helmuth sent the futile scraper aloft. Drill for the
speck of metal? No—it was far too deeply buried
already, and its location was unknown.

Quickly he called two borers up from the shoals
below, where constant blasting was taking the foundation of the caisson deeper and deeper into Jupiter's
dubious "soil." He drove both blind, fire-snouted
machines down into the lesion.

The bottom of that sore turned out to be a hundred feet within the immense block of ice. Helmuth
pushed the red button all the same.

The borers blew up, with a heavy, quite invisible
blast, as they had been designed to do. A pit appeared on the face of the caisson.

The nearest truss bent upward in the wind. It
fluttered for a moment, trying to resist. It bent
farther.

Deprived of its major attachment, it tore free suddenly, and went whirling away into the blackness. A
sudden flash of lightning picked it out for a moment,
and Helmuth saw it dwindling like a bat with torn
wings being borne away by a cyclone.

The scraper scuttled down into the pit and began
to fill it with ice from the bottom. Helmuth ordered
down a new truss and a squad of scaffolders. Damage
of this order of magnitude took time to repair. He
watched the tornado tearing ragged chunks from the
edges of the pit until he was sure that the catalysis-

cancer had been stopped. Then— suddenly, prematurely, dismally tired—he took off the helmet.

He was astounded by the white fury that masked Eva's big-boned, mildly pretty face.

"You'll blow the Bridge up yet, won't you?" she said, evenly, without preamble. "Any pretext will do!"

Baffled, Helmuth turned his head helplessly away; but that was no better. The suffused face of Jupiter peered swollenly through the picture-port, just as it did on the foreman's deck.

He and Eva and Charity and the gang and the whole of satellite V were falling forward toward Jupiter; their uneventful, cooped-up lives on Jupiter V were utterly unreal compared to the four hours of each changeless day spent on Jupiter's ever-changing surface. Every new day brought their minds, like ships out of control, closer and closer to that gaudy inferno.

There was no other way for a man—or a woman—on Jupiter V to look at the giant planet. It was simple experience, shared by all of them, that planets do not occupy four-fifths of the whole sky, unless the observer is himself up there in that planet's sky, falling toward it, falling faster and faster—

"I have no intention," he said tiredly, "of blowing up the Bridge. I wish you could get it through your head that I want the Bridge to stay up—even though I'm not starry-eyed to the point of incompetence about the project. Did you think that that rotten spot was going to go away by itself after you'd painted it over? Didn't you know that—"

Several helmeted, masked heads nearby turned blindly toward the sound of his voice. Helmuth shut up. Any distracting conversation or other activity was taboo down here on the gang deck. He motioned Eva back to duty.

The girl donned her helmet obediently enough, but it was plain from the way that her normally full

lips were thinned that she thought Helmuth had
ended the argument only in order to have the last
word.

Helmuth strode to the thick pillar which ran down
the central axis of the operations shack, and mounted
the spiraling cleats toward his own foreman's cubicle.
Already he felt in anticipation the weight of the
helmet upon his own head.

Charity Dillon, however, was already wearing the
helmet. He was sitting in Helmuth's chair.

Charity was characteristically oblivious of Helmuth's
entrance. The Bridge operator must learn to ignore,
to be utterly unconscious of, anything happening
about his body except the inhuman sounds of signals;
must learn to heed only those senses which report
something going on thousands and hundreds of thousands of miles away.

Helmuth knew better than to interrupt him. Instead, he watched Dillon's white, blade-like fingers
roving with blind sureness over the controls.

Dillon, evidently, was making a complete tour of
the Bridge—not only from end to end, but up and
down, too. The tally board showed that he had already activated nearly two-thirds of the ultraphone
eyes. That meant that he had been up all night at the
job; had begun it immediately after he had last relieved Helmuth.

Why?

With a thrill of unfocused apprehension, Helmuth
looked at the foreman's jack, which allowed the operator here in the cubicle to communicate with the
gang when necessary, and which kept him aware of
anything said or done on the gang boards.

It was plugged in.

Dillon sighed suddenly, took the helmet off, and
turned.

"Hello, Bob," he said. "It's funny about this job.
You can't see, you can't hear, but when somebody's

watching you, you feel a sort of pressure on the back of your neck. Extra-sensory perception, maybe. Ever felt it?"

"Pretty often, lately. Why the grand tour, Charity?"

"There's to be an inspection," Dillon said. His eyes met Helmuth's. They were frank and transparent. "A couple of Senate sub-committee chairmen, coming to see that their eight billion dollars isn't being wasted. Naturally, I'm a little anxious to see to it that they find everything in order."

"I see," Helmuth said. "First time in five years, isn't it?"

"Just about. What was that dust-up down below just now? Somebody—you, I'm sure, from the drastic handiwork involved—bailed Eva out of a mess, and then I heard her talk about your wanting to blow up the Bridge. I checked the area when I heard the fracas start, and it did seem as if she had let things go rather far, but—What was it all about?"

Dillon ordinarily hadn't the guile for cat-and-mouse games, and he had never looked less guileful than now. Helmuth said carefully: "Eva was upset, I suppose. On the subject of Jupiter we're all of us cracked by now, in our different ways. The way she was dealing with the catalysis didn't look to me to be suitable—a difference of opinion, resolved in my favor because I had the authority. Eva didn't. That's all."

"Kind of an expensive difference, Bob. I'm not niggling by nature, you know that. But an incident like that while the sub-committees are here—"

"The point is," said Helmuth, "are we going to spend an extra ten thousand, or whatever it costs to replace a truss and reinforce a caisson, or are we to lose the whole caisson—and as much as a third of the whole Bridge along with it?"

"Yes, you're right there, of course. That could be

explained, even to a pack of senators. But—it would be difficult to have to explain it very often. Well, the board's yours, Bob; you could continue my spot-check, if you've time."

Dillon got up. Then he added suddenly, as though it were forced out of him:

"Bob, I'm trying to understand your state of mind. From what Eva said, I gather that you've made it fairly public. I . . . I don't think it's a good idea to infect your fellow workers with your own pessimism. It leads to sloppy work. I know. I know that you won't countenance sloppy work, regardless of your own feelings, but one foreman can do only so much. And you're making extra work for yourself—not for me, but for yourself—by being openly gloomy about the Bridge.

"It strikes me that maybe you could use a breather, maybe a week's junket to Ganymede or something like that. You're the best man on the Bridge, Bob, for all your grousing about the job and your assorted misgivings. I'd hate to see you replaced."

"A threat, Charity?" Helmuth said softly.

"*No.* I wouldn't replace you unless you actually went nuts, and I firmly believe that your fears in that respect are groundless. It's a commonplace that only sane men suspect their own sanity, isn't it?"

"It's a common misconception. Most psychopathic obsessions begin with a mild worry—one that can't be shaken."

Dillon made as if to brush that subject away. "Anyhow, I'm not threatening; I'd fight to keep you here. But my say-so only covers Jupiter V and the Bridge; there are people higher up on Ganymede, and people higher yet back in Washington—and in this inspecting commission.

"Why don't you try to look on the bright side for a change? Obviously the Bridge isn't ever going to inspire you. But you might at least try thinking about all those dollars piling up in your account back home, every hour you're on this job. And about the bridges and ships and who knows what-all that you'll be building, at any fee you ask, when you get back down to Earth. All under the magic words: 'One of the men who built the Bridge on Jupiter!' "

Charity was bright red with embarrassment and enthusiasm. Helmuth smiled.

"I'll try to bear it in mind, Charity," he said. "And I think I'll pass up a vacation for the time being. When is this gaggle of senators due to arrive?"

"That's hard to say. They'll be coming to Ganymede directly from Washington, without any routing, and they'll stop there for a while. I suppose they'll also make a stop at Callisto before they come here. They've got something new on their ship, I'm told, that lets them flit about more freely than the usual uphill transport can."

An icy lizard suddenly was nesting in Helmuth's stomach, coiling and coiling but never settling itself. The persistent nightmare began to seep back into his blood; it was almost engulfing him—already.

"Something . . . new?" he echoed, his voice as flat and non-committal as he could make it. "Do you know what it is?"

"Well, yes. But I think I'd better keep quiet about it until—"

"Charity, nobody on this deserted rock-heap could possibly be a Soviet spy. The whole habit of 'security' is idiotic out here. Tell me now and save me the trouble of dealing with senators; or tell me at least that you know I know. *They have antigravity!* Isn't that it?"

One word from Dillon, and the nightmare would be real.

"Yes," Dillon said. "How did you know? Of course,

it couldn't be a complete gravity screen by any means. But it seems to be a good long step toward it. We've waited a long time to see that dream come true—

"But you're the last man in the world to take pride in the achievement, so there's no sense in exulting about it to you. I'll let you know when I get a definite arrival date. In the meantime, will you think about what I said before?"

"Yes, I will." Helmuth took the seat before the board.

"Good. With you, I have to be grateful for small victories. Good trick, Bob."

"Good trick, Charity."

CHAPTER SEVEN: New York

When Nietzsche wrote down the phrase 'transvaluation of all values' for the first time, the spiritual movement of the centuries in which we are living found at last its formula. Transvaluation of all values is the most fundamental character of every civilization; for it is the beginning of a Civilization that remoulds all the forms of the Culture that went before, understands them otherwise, practises them in a different way.

—OSWALD SPENGLER

Paige's gift for putting two and two together and getting 22 was in part responsible for the discovery of the spy, but the almost incredible clumsiness of the man made the chief contribution to it. Paige could hardly believe that nobody had spotted the agent before. True, he was only one of some two dozen technicians in the processing lab where Paige had been working; but his almost open habit of slipping notes inside his lab apron, and his painful furtiveness every time he left the Pfitzner laboratory

building for the night, should have aroused someone's suspicions long before this.

It was a fine example, Paige thought, of the way
the blunderbuss investigation methods currently popular in Washington allowed the really dangerous man
a thousand opportunities to slip away unnoticed. As
was usual among groups of scientists, too, there was
an unspoken covenant among Pfitzner's technicians—
against informing on each other. It protected the
guilty as well as the innocent, but it would never
have arisen at all under any fair system of juridical
defense.

Paige had not the smallest idea what to do with his
fish once he had hooked it. He took an evening—
which he greatly begrudged—away from seeing Anne,
in order to trace the man's movements after a day
which had produced two exciting advances in the
research, on the hunch that the spy would want to
ferry the information out at once.

This hunch proved out beautifully, at least at first.
Nor was the man difficult to follow; his habit of
glancing continually over first one shoulder and then
the other, evidently to make sure that he was not
being followed, made him easy to spot over long
distances, even in a crowd. He left the city by train
to Hoboken, where he rented a motor scooter and
drove directly to the cross-roads town of Secaucus. It
was a long pull, but not at all difficult otherwise.

Outside Secaucus, however, Paige nearly lost his
man for the first and last time. The cross-roads,
which lay across U.S. 46 to the Lincoln Tunnel,
turned out also to be the site of the temporary trailer
city of the Believers—nearly 300,000 of them, or
almost half of the 700,000 who had been pouring into
town for two weeks now for the Revival. Among the
trailers Paige saw license plates from as far away as
Eritrea.

The trailer city was far bigger than any nearby

town except Passaic. It included a score of supermarkets, all going full blast even in the middle of the night, and about as many coin-in-slot laundries, equally wide open. There were at least a hundred public baths, and close to 360 public toilets. Paige counted ten cafeterias, and twice that many hamburger stands and one-arm joints, each of the stands no less than a hundred feet long; at one of these he stopped long enough to buy a "Texas wiener" nearly as long as his forearm, covered with mustard, meat sauce, sauerkraut, corn relish, and piccalilli. There were ten highly conspicuous hospital tents, too—and after eating the Texas wiener Paige thought he knew why—the smallest of them perfectly capable of housing a one-ring circus.

And, of course, there were the trailers, of which Paige guessed the number at sixty thousand, from two-wheeled jobs to Packards, in all stages of repair and shininess. Luckily, the city was well lit, and since everyone living in it was a Believer, there were no booby-traps or other forms of proselytizing. Paige's man, after a little thoroughly elementary doubling on his tracks and setting up false trails, ducked into a trailer with a Latvian license plate. After half an hour—at exactly 0200—the trailer ran up a stubby VHF radio antenna as thick through as Paige's wrist.

And the rest, Paige thought grimly, climbing back on to his own rented scooter, is up to the FBI—if I tell them.

But what would he say? He had every good reason of his own to stay as far out of sight of the FBI as possible. Furthermore, if he informed on the man now, it would mean immediate curtains on the search for the anti-agathic, and a gross betrayal of the trust, enforced though it had been, that Anne and Gunn had placed in him. On the other hand, to remain silent would give the Soviets the drug at the same time that Pfitzner found it—in other words, before the West had it as a government. And it would mean, too, that he himself would have to forego an important chance to prove that he was loyal, when the inevitable showdown with MacHinery came around.

By the next day, however, he had hit upon what should have been the obvious course in the beginning. He took a second evening to rifle his fish's laboratory bench—the incredible idiot had stuffed it to bulging with incriminating photomicrograph negatives, and with bits of paper bearing the symbols of a simple substitution code once circulated to Tom Mix's Square Shooters on behalf of Shredded Ralston—and a third to take step-by-step photos of the hegira to the Believer trailer city, and the radio-transmitter-equipped trailer with the buffer-state license. Assembling everything into a neat dossier, Paige cornered Gunn in his office and dropped the whole mess squarely in the vice-president's lap.

"My goodness," Gunn said, blinking. "Curiosity is a disease with you, isn't it, Colonel Russell? And I really doubt that even Pfitzner will ever find the antidote for that."

"Curiosity has very little to do with it. As you'll see in the folder, the man's an amateur—evidently a volunteer from the Party, Rosenberg, rather than a paid expert. He practically led me by the nose."

"Yes, I see he's clumsy," Gunn agreed. "And he's been reported to us before, Colonel Russell. As a matter of fact, on several occasions we've had to protect him from his own clumsiness."

"But why?" Paige demanded. "Why haven't you cracked down on him?"

"Because we can't afford to," Gunn said. "A spy scandal in the plant now would kill the work just where it stands. Oh, we'll report him sooner or later, and the work you've done here on him will be very useful then—to all of us, yourself included. But there's no hurry."

"No hurry!"

"No," Gunn said. "The material he's ferrying out now is of no particular consequence. When we actually have the drug—"

"But he'll already know the production method by that time. Identifying the drug is a routine job for any team of chemists—your Dr. Agnew taught me that much."

"I suppose that's so," Gunn said. "Well, I'll think it over, Colonel. Don't worry about it, we'll deal with it when the time seems ripe."

And that was every bit of satisfaction that Paige could extract from Gunn. It was small recompense for his lost sleep, his lost dates, the care he had taken to inform Pfitzner first, or the soul-searching it had cost him to put the interests of the project ahead of his officer's oath and of his own safety. That evening he said as much to Anne Abbott and with considerable force.

"Calm down," Anne said. "If you're going to mix into the politics of this work, Paige, you're going to get burned right up to the armpits. When we do find what we're looking for, it's going to create the biggest political explosion in history. I'd advise you to stand well back."

"I've been burned already," Paige said hotly. "How the hell can I stand back now? And tolerating a spy isn't just politics. It's treason, not only by rumor, but in fact. Are you deliberately putting everyone's head in the noose?"

"Quite deliberately. Paige, this project is for everyone—every man, woman and child on the Earth and in space. The fact that the West is putting up the money is incidental. What we're doing here is in every respect just as anti-West as it is anti-Soviet. We're out to lick death for human beings, not just for the armed forces of some one military coalition. What do we care who gets it first? We want everyone to have it."

"Does Gunn agree with that?"

"It's company policy. It may even have been Hal's own idea, though he has different reasons, different justifications. Have you any idea what will happen when a death-curing drug hits a totalitarian society—a drug available in limited quantities only? It won't prove fatal to the Soviets, of course, but it ought to make the struggle for succession over there considerably bloodier than it is already. That's essentially the way Hal seems to look at it."

"And you don't," Paige said grimly.

"No, Paige, I don't. I can see well enough what's going to happen right here at home when this thing gets out. Think for a moment of what it will do to the religious people alone. What happens to the after-life if you never need to leave this one? Look at the Believers. They believe in the literal truth of everything in the Bible—that's why they revise the book every year. And this story is going to break before their Jubilee year is over. Did you know that their motto is: 'Millions now living will never die'? They mean themselves, but what if it turns out to be *everybody*?

"And that's only the beginning. Think of what the insurance companies are going to say. And what's going to happen to the whole structure of compound interest. Wells's old yarn about the man who lived so long that his savings came to dominate the world's whole financial structure—*When the Sleeper Wakes*, wasn't it?—well, that's going to be theoretically possible for *everybody* with the patience and the capital to let his money sit still. Or think of the whole corpus of the inheritance laws. It's going to be the biggest, blackest social explosion the West ever had to take. We'll be much too busy digging in to care about what's happening to the Central Committee in Moscow."

"You seem to care enough to be protecting the Central Committee's interests, or at least what they probably think of as their interests," Paige said slowly. "After all, there is a possibility of keeping the secret, instead of letting it leak."

"There is no such possibility," Anne said. "Natural laws can't be kept secret. Once you give a scientist the idea that a certain goal can be reached, you've given him more than half of the information he needs. Once he gets the idea that the conquest of death is possible, no power on Earth can stop him from finding out how it's done—the 'know-how' we make so many fatuous noises about is the most minor part of research; it's even a matter of total indifference to the essence of the question."

"I don't see that."

"Then let's go back to the fission bomb again for a moment. The only way we could have kept that a secret was to have failed to drop it at all, or even test-fire it. Once the secret was out that the bomb existed—and you'll remember that we announced that before hundreds of thousands of people in Hiroshima—we had no secrets in that field worth protecting. The biggest mystery in the Smyth report was the specific method by which uranium slugs were 'canned' in a protective jacket; it was one of the toughest problems the project had to lick, but at the same time it's exactly the kind of problem you'd assign to an engineer, and confidently expect a solution within a year.

"The fact of the matter, Paige, is that you can't keep scientific matters a secret from yourself. A scientific secret is something that some other scientist can't *contribute to*, any more than he can profit by it. Contrariwise, if you arm yourself through discoveries in natural law, you also arm the other guy. Either you give him the information, or you cut your own throat; there aren't any other courses possible.

"And let me ask you this, Paige: should we give the USSR the advantage—temporary though it'll be—of having to get along *without* the anti-agathics for a while? By their very nature, the drugs will do more damage to the West than they will to the USSR. After all, in the Soviet Union one isn't permitted to inherit money, or to exercise any real control over economic forces just because one's lived a long time. If both major powers are given control over death at the same time, the West will be at a natural disadvantage. If we give control over death to the West alone, we'll be sabotaging our own civilization without putting the USSR under any comparable handicap. Is that sensible?"

The picture was staggering, to say the least. It gave Paige an impression of Gunn decidedly at variance with the mask of salesman-turned-executive which the man himself wore. But it was otherwise self-consistent; that, he knew, was supposed to be enough for him.

"How could I tell?" he said coldly. "All I can see is that every day I stick with you, I get in deeper. First I pose for the FBI as something that I'm not. Next I'm given possession of information that it's unlawful for me to have. And now I'm helping you conceal the evidence of a high crime. It looks more and more to me as though I was supposed to be involved in this thing from the beginning. I don't see how you could have done so thorough a job on me without planning it."

"You needn't deny that you asked for it, Paige."

"I don't deny that," he said. "You don't deny deliberately involving me, either, I notice."

"No. It was deliberate, all right. I thought you'd have suspected it before. And if you're planning to ask me why, save your breath. I'm not permitted to tell you. You'll find out in due course."

"You two—"

"No. Hal had nothing to do with involving you. That was my idea. He only agreed to it—and he had to be convinced from considerably higher up."

"You two," Paige said through almost motionless lips, "don't hesitate to trample on the bystanders, do you? If I didn't know before that Pfitzner was run by a pack of idealists, I'd know it now. You've got the characteristic ruthlessness."

"That," Anne said in a level voice, "is what it takes."

CHAPTER EIGHT: Jupiter V

*When new turns in behaviour cease to appear in
the life of the individual its behaviour ceases to be
intelligent.*

—C. E. COGHILL

Instead of sleeping after his trick—for now Helmuth
knew that he was really afraid—he sat up in the
reading chair in his cabin. The illuminated micro-
filmed pages of a book flicked by across the surface of
the wall opposite him, timed precisely to the reading
rate most comfortable for him, and he had several
weeks' worry-conserved alcohol and smoke rations
for ready consumption.

But Helmuth let his mix go flat and did not notice
the book, which had turned itself on, at the page
where he had abandoned it last, when he had fitted
himself into the chair. Instead, he listened to the
radio.

There was always a great deal of ham radio activity
in the Jovian system. The conditions were good for
it, since there was plenty of power available, few

110

impeding atmosphere layers and those thin, no Heaviside layers, and few official and no commercial channels with which the hams could interfere.

And there were plenty of people scattered about the satellites who needed the sound of a voice.

". . . anybody know whether or not the senators are coming here? Doc Barth put in a report a while back on a fossil plant he found here, at least he thinks it was a plant. Maybe they'd like a look at it."

"It's the Bridge team they're coming to see." A strong voice, and the impression of a strong transmitter wavering in and out to the currents of an atmosphere; that would be Sweeney, on Ganymede. "Sorry to throw the wet blanket, boys, but I don't think the senators'll be interested in our rock-balls for their own lumpy selves. They're only scheduled to stay here three days."

Helmuth thought grayly: *Then they'll stay on Callisto only one.*

"Is that you, Sweeney? Where's the Bridge tonight?"

"Dillon's on duty," a very distant transmitter said. "Try to raise Helmuth, Sweeney."

"Helmuth, Helmuth, you gloomy beetle-gooser! Come in, Helmuth!"

"Sure, Bob, come in and dampen us a little. We're feeling cheerful."

Sluggishly, Helmuth reached out to take the mike, from where it lay clipped to one arm of the chair. But before he had completed the gesture, the door to his room swung open.

Eva came in.

She said: "Bob, I want to tell you something."

"His voice is changing!" the voice of the Callisto operator said. "Sweeney, ask him what he's drinking!"

Helmuth cut the radio out. The girl was freshly dressed—in so far as anybody dressed in anything on Jupiter V—and Helmuth wondered why she was prowling the decks at this hour, half-way between

her sleep period and her trick. Her hair was hazy
against the light from the corridor, and she looked
less mannish than usual. She reminded him a little of
the way she had looked when they had been lovers,
before the Bridge had come to bestride his bed
instead. He put the memory aside.

"All right," he said. "I owe you a mix, I guess.
Citric, sugar and the other stuff are in the locker . . .
you know where it is. Shot-cans are there, too."

The girl shut the door and sat down on the bunk,
with a free litheness that was almost grace, but with
a determination which, Helmuth knew, meant that
she had just decided to do something silly for all the
right reasons.

"I don't need a drink," she said. "As a matter of
fact, I've been turning my lux-R's back to the common pool. I suppose you did that for me—by showing me what a mind looks like that's hiding from
itself."

"Evita, stop sounding like a tract. Obviously you're
advanced to a higher, more Jovian plane of existence, but won't you still need your metabolism? Or
have you decided that vitamins are all-in-the-mind?"

"Now you're being superior. Anyhow, alcohol isn't
a vitamin. And I didn't come to talk about that. I
came to tell you something I think you ought to know."

"Which is—?"

She said: "Bob, I mean to have a child here."

A bark of laughter, part sheer hysteria and part
exasperation, jack-knifed Helmuth into a sitting position. A red arrow bloomed on the far wall, obediently marking the paragraph which, supposedly, he
had reached in his reading. Eva twisted to look at it,
but the page was already dimming and vanishing.

"*Women!*" Helmuth said, when he could get his
breath back. "Really, Evita, you make me feel much
better. No environment can change a human being
much, after all."

"Why should it?" she said suspiciously, looking back at him. "I don't see the joke. Shouldn't a woman want to have a child?"

"Of course she should," he said, settling back. The pages began to flip across the wall again. "It's quite ordinary. All women want to have children. All women dream of the day they can turn a child out to play in an airless rock garden like Jupiter V, to pluck fossils and make dust-castles and get quaintly starburned. How cosy to tuck the blue little body back into its corner that night, and give it its oxygen bottle, promptly as the sound of the trick-change bell! Why it's as natural as Jupiter-light—as Western as freeze-dried apple pie."

He turned his head casually away. "Congratulations. As for me, though, Eva, I'd much prefer that you take your ghostly little pretext out of here."

Eva surged to her feet in one furious motion. Her fingers grasped him by the beard and jerked his head painfully around again.

"You reedy male platitude!" she said, in a low grinding voice. "How you could see almost the whole point, and make so little of it—*Women*, is it? So you think I came creeping in here, full of humbleness, to settle our technical differences in bed!"

He closed his hand on her wrist and twisted it away. "What else?" he demanded, trying to imagine how it would feel to stay reasonable for five minutes at a time with these Bridge-robots. "None of us need bother with games and excuses. We're here, we're isolated, we were all chosen because, among other things, we were quite incapable of forming permanent emotional attachments and capable of any alliances we liked without going unbalanced when the attraction died and the alliance came unstuck. None of us have to pretend that our living arrangements would keep us out of jail in Boston, or that they have to involve any Earth-normal excuses."

She said nothing. After a while he asked, gently: "Isn't that so?"

"Of course it's not so," Eva said. She was frowning at him; he had the absurd impression that she was pitying him. "If we were really incapable of making any permanent attachment, we'd never have been chosen. A cast of mind like that is a mental disease, Bob; it's anti-survival from the ground up. It's the conditioning that made us this way. Didn't you know?"

Helmuth hadn't known; or if he had, he had been conditioned to forget it. He gripped the arms of the chair tighter.

"Anyhow," he said, "that's the way we are."

"Yes, it is. Also it has nothing to do with the matter."

"It doesn't? How stupid do you think I am? *I* don't care whether or not you've decided to have a child here, if you really mean what you say."

She, too, seemed to be trembling. "You really don't, either. The decision means nothing to you."

"Well, if I liked children, I'd be sorry for the child. But as it happens, I can't stand children—and if that's the conditioning, too, I can't do a thing about it. In short, Eva, as far as I'm concerned you can have as many kids as you want, and to me you'll *still* be the worst operator on the Bridge."

"I'll bear that in mind," she said. At this moment she seemed to have been cut from pressure-ice. "I'll leave you something to charge your mind with, too, Robert Helmuth. I'll leave you sprawled here under your precious book . . . what is Madame Bovary to you, anyhow, you unadventurous turtle? . . . to think about a man who believes that children must always be born into warm cradles—a man who thinks that men have to huddle on warm worlds, or they won't survive. A man with no ears, no eyes, scarcely any head. A man in terror, a man crying: Mamma! *Mamma!* all the stellar days and nights long!"

"Parlor diagnosis."

"Parlor labeling! Good trick, Bob. Draw your warm woolly blanket in tight around your brains, or some little sneeze of sense might creep in, and impair your—efficiency!"

The door closed sharply after her.

A million pounds of fatigue crashed down without warning on the back of Helmuth's neck, and he fell back into the reading chair with a gasp. The roots of his beard ached, and Jupiters bloomed and wavered away before his closed eyes.

He struggled once, and fell asleep.

Instantly he was in the grip of the dream.

It started, as always, with commonplaces, almost realistic enough to be a documentary film-strip—except for the appalling sense of pressure, and the distorted emotional significance with which the least word, the smallest movement was invested.

It was the sinking of the first caisson of the Bridge. The actual event had been bad enough. The job demanded enough exactness of placement to require that manned ships enter Jupiter's atmosphere itself; a squadron of twenty of the most powerful ships ever built, with the five-million-ton asteroid, trimmed and shaped in space, slung beneath them in an immense cat's-cradle.

Four times that squadron had disappeared beneath the racing clouds; four times the tense voices of pilots and engineers had muttered in Helmuth's ears, and he had whispered back, trying to guide them by what he could see of the conflicting trade-blasts from Jupiter V; four times there were shouts and futile orders and the snapping of cables and men screaming endlessly against the eternal howl of the Jovian sky.

It had cost, altogether, nine ships, and two hundred thirty-one men, to get one of five laboriously-shaped asteroids planted in the shifting slush that was Jupiter's surface. Until that had been accomplished, the Bridge could never have been more than a dream. While the Great Red Spot had shown astronomers that some structures on Jupiter could last for long periods of time—long enough, at least, to be seen by many generations of human beings—it had been equally well known that nothing on Jupiter could be really permanent. The planet did not even have a "surface" in the usual sense; instead, the bottom of the atmosphere merged more or less smoothly into a high-pressure sludge, which in turn thickened as it went deeper into solid pressure-ice. At no point on the way down was there any interface between one layer and another, except in the rare areas where a part of the deeper, more "solid" medium had been thrust far up out of its normal level to form a continent which might last as long as two years or two hundred. It was on to one of these great ribs of bulging ice that the ships had tried to plant their asteroid—and, after four tries, had succeeded.

Helmuth had helped to supervise all five operations, counting the successful one, from his desk on Jupiter V. But in the dream he was not in the control shack, but instead on shipboard, in one of the ships that was never to come back—

Then, without transition, but without any sense of discontinuity either, he was on the Bridge itself. Not *in absentia*, as the remote guiding intelligence of a beetle but in person, in an ovular, tank-like suit the details of which would never come clear. The high brass had discovered antigravity and had asked for volunteers to man the Bridge. Helmuth had volunteered.

Looking back on it in the dream, he did not understand why he had volunteered. It had simply seemed expected of him, and he had not been able to help it, even though he had known to begin with what it would be like. He belonged on the Bridge, though he hated it—he had been doomed to go there from the first.

And there was . . . something wrong . . . with the antigravity. The high brass had asked for its volunteers before the research work had been completed. The present antigravity fields were weak, and there was some basic flaw in the theory. Generators broke down after only short periods of use; burned out, unpredictably, sometimes only moments after having passed their production tests with perfect scores. In waking life, vacuum tubes behaved in the unpredictable way; there were no vacuum tubes anywhere on Jupiter, but machines on Jupiter burned out all the same, burned out at temperatures which would freeze Helmuth solid in an instant.

That was what Helmuth's antigravity set was about to do. He crouched inside his personal womb, above the boiling sea, the clouds raging by him in little scouring crystals which wore at the chorion protecting him, lit by a plume of hydrogen flame—and waited to feel his weight suddenly become three times greater than normal, the pressure on his body go from sixteen pounds per square inch to fifteen million, the air around him take on the searing stink of poisons, the whole of Jupiter come pressing its burden upon him.

He knew what would happen to him then.

It happened.

Helmuth greeted "morning" on Jupiter V with his customary scream.

BOOK THREE

ENTR'ACTE: Washington

The layman, the "practical" man, the man in the street, says, What is that to me? The answer is positive and weighty. Our life is entirely dependent on the established doctrines of ethics, sociology, political economy, government, law, medical science, etc. This affects everyone consciously or unconsciously, the man in the street in the first place, because he is the most defenseless.

—ALFRED KORZYBSKI

4th January 2020

Dear Seppi,

Lord knows I have better sense than to mail this, send it to you by messenger, or leave it anywhere in the files—or indeed on the premises —of the Joint Committee; but if one is sensible about such matters these days, one never puts anything on paper at all, and then burns the carbons. As a bad compromise, I am filing this among my personal papers, where it will be found, opened and sent to you only after I will be beyond reprisals.

That's not meant to sound as ominous as, upon rereading, I see it does. By the time you have this letter, abundant details of what I've been up to should be available to you, not only through the usual press garble, but through verbatim testimony. You will have worked out, by now, a rational explanation of my conduct since my re-election (and before it, for that matter). At the very least, I hope you now know why I authorized such a monstrosity as the Bridge, even against your very good advice.

All that is water over the dam (or ether over the Bridge, if you boys are following Dirac's lead back to the ether these days. How do I know about that? You'll see in a moment.). I don't mean to rehash it here. What I want to do in this letter is to leave you a more specialized memo, telling you in detail just how well the research system you suggested to me worked out for us.

Despite my surface appearance of ignoring that advice, we were following your suggestion, and very closely. I took a particular interest in your hunch that there might be "crackpot" ideas on gravity which needed investigation. Frankly, I had no hope of finding anything, but that would have left me no worse off than I had been before I talked to you. And actually it wasn't very long before my research chief came up with the Locke Derivation.

The research papers which finally emerged from this particular investigation are still in the Graveyard file, and I have no hope that they'll be released to non-government physicists within the foreseeable future. If you don't get the story from me, you'll never get it from anyone; and I've enough on my conscience now to be indifferent to a small crime like breaking Security.

Besides, as usual, this particular "secret" has been available for the taking for years. A man named Schuster—you may know more about him than I do—wondered out loud about it as far back as 1891, before anybody had thought of trying to keep scientific matters a secret. He wanted to know whether or not every large rotating mass, like the Sun for instance, was a natural magnet. (That was before the sun's magnetic field had been discovered, too.) And by the 1940's it was clearly established for *small* rotating bodies like electrons—a thing called the Lande factor with which I'm sure you're familiar. I myself don't understand Word One of it. (Dirac was associated with much of that part of the work.) Finally, a man named W. H. Babcock, of Mount Wilson, pointed out in the 1940's that the Lande factor for the Earth, the Sun, and a star named 78 Virginius was identical, or damned close to it.

Now all this seemed to me to have nothing to do at all with gravity, and I said so to my team chief, who brought the thing to my attention. But I was wrong (I suppose you're already ahead of me by now). Another man, Prof. P. M. S. Blackett, whose name was even familiar to *me*, had pointed out the relationship. Suppose, Blackett said (I am copying from my notes now), we let P be magnetic moment, or what I have to think of as the leverage effect of a magnet— the product of the strength of the charge times the distance between the poles. Let U be angular momentum—rotation to a slob like me; angular speed times moment of inertia to you. Then if C is the velocity of light, and G is the acceleration of gravity (and they always are in equations like this, I'm told), then:

$$P = \frac{BG\frac{1}{2}U}{2C}$$

(B is supposed to be a constant amounting to about 0.25. Don't ask me why.) Admittedly this was all speculative; there would be no way to test it, except on another planet with a stronger magnetic field than Earth's—preferably about a hundred times as strong. The closest we could come to that would be Jupiter, where the speed of rotation is about 25,000 miles an hour at the equator—and that was obviously out of the question.

Or was it? I confess that I never thought of using Jupiter, except in wish-fulfillment daydreams, until this matter of the Locke Derivation came up. It seems that by a simple algebraic manipulation, you can stick G on one side of the equation, and all the other terms on the other, and come up with this:

$$G = \left(\frac{2PC}{BU} \right)^{.2}$$

To test that, you need a gravitational field little more than twice the strength of Earth's. And there, of course, is Jupiter again. None of my experts would give the notion a nickel—they said, among other things, that nobody even knew who Locke was, which is true, and that his algebraic trick wouldn't stand up under dimensional analysis, which turned out to be true— but irrelevant. (We *did* have to monkey with it a little after the experimental results were in.)

What counted was that we could make a practical use of this relationship.

Once we tried that, I should add, we were astonished at the accompanying effects: the abolition of the Lorentz-Fitzgerald relationship inside the field, the intolerance of the field itself to matter outside its influence, and so on; not only at their occurring at all—the formula doesn't predict them—but at their order of magnitude. I'm told that when this thing gets out, dimensional analysis isn't the only scholium that's going to have to be revamped. It's going to be the greatest headache for physicists since the Einstein theory; I don't know whether you'll relish this premonitory twinge or not.

Pretty good going for a "crackpot" notion, though.

After that, the Bridge was inevitable. As soon as it became clear that we could perform the necessary tests only on the surface of Jupiter itself, we had to have the Bridge. It also became clear that the Bridge would have to be a dynamic structure. It couldn't be built to a certain size and stopped there. The moment it was stopped, Jupiter would tear it to shreds. We had to build it to grow—to do more than just resist Jupiter—to push back against Jupiter, instead. It's double the size that it needed to be to test the Locke Derivation, now, and I still don't know how much longer we're going to have to keep it growing. Not long, I hope; the thing's a monster already.

But Seppi, let me ask you this: Does the Bridge really fall under the interdict you uttered against the gigantic research projects? It's gigantic, all right. But—is it gigantic *on Jupiter?* I say it isn't. It's peanuts. A piece of attic gadgetry and nothing more. And we couldn't have performed the necessary experiments on any other planet.

Not all the wealth of Ormus or of Ind, or of all the world down the ages, could have paid for a Manhattan District scaled to Jupiter's size.

In addition—though this was incidental—the apparent giganticism involved was a useful piece of misdirection. Elephantine research projects may be just about played out, but government budgetary agencies are used to them and think them normal. Getting the Joint Committee involved in one helped to revive the committeemen from their comatose state, as nothing else could have. It got us appropriations we never could have corralled otherwise, because people associate such projects with weapons research. And—forgive me, but there is a sort of science to politics too—it seemed to show graphically that I was *not* following the suspect advice of the suspect Dr. Corsi. I owed you that, though it's hardly as large a payment as I would like to make.

But I don't mean to talk about the politics of crackpot-mining here; only about the concrete results. You should be warned, too, that the method has its pitfalls.

You will know by now about the anti-agathic research, and what we got out of it. I talked to people who might know what the chances were, and got general agreement from them as to how we should proceed. This straight-line approach looked good to me from the beginning.

I set the Pfitzner people to work on it at once, since they already had that HWS appropriation for similar research, and HWS wouldn't be alert enough to detect the moment when Pfitzner's target changed from just plain old age to death itself. But we didn't overlook the crackpots—and before long we found a real dilly.

This was a man named Lyons, who insisted that the standard Lansing hypothesis, which postulates the existence of an aging-toxin, was exactly the opposite of the truth. (I go into this subject with a certain relish, because I suspect that you know as little about it as I do; it's not often that I find myself in that situation.) Instead, he said, what happens is that it's the *young* mothers who pass on to their offspring some substance which makes them long-lived. Lansing's notion that the old mothers were the ones who did the passing along, and that the substance passed along speeding up aging, was unproven, Lyons said.

Well, that threw us into something of a spiral. Lansing's Law—"Senescence begins when growth ends"—had been regarded as gospel in gerontology for decades. But Lyons had a good hypothetical case. He pointed out that, among other things, all of Lansing's long-lived rotifers showed characteristics in common with polyploid individuals. In addition to being hardy and long-lived, they were of unusually large size, and they were less fertile than normal rotifers. Suppose that the substance which was passed along from one generation to another was a chromosomedoubler, like colchicine?

We put that question to Lansing's only surviving student, a living crotchet named Mac-Dougal. He wouldn't hear of it; to him it was like questioning the Word of God. Besides, he said, if Lyons is right, how do you propose to test it? Rotifers are microscopic animals. Except for their eggs, their body cells are invisible even under the microscope. Technically speaking, in fact, they don't seem to have any body cells as adults—just a sort of generalized protoplasmic continuum in which the nuclei are scattered at random, rather like the plasmodium of a slime-mold. It would be quite a few months of Sundays before we ever got a look at a rotifer chromosome.

Lyons thought he had an answer for that. He proposed to develop a technique of microtome preparation which would make, not one, but several different slices through a rotifer's egg. With any sort of luck, he said, we might be able to extend the technique to rotifer spores, and maybe even to the adult critters.

We thought we ought to try it. Without telling Pfitzner about it, we gave Pearl River Labs that headache. We put Lyons himself in charge and assigned MacDougal to act as a consultant (which he did by sniping and scoffing every minute of the day, until not only Lyons, but everybody else in the plant hated him). It was awful. Rotifers, it turns out, are incredibly delicate animals, just about impossible to preserve after they're dead, no matter what stage of their development you catch them in. Time and time again, Lyons came up with microscope slides which, he said, *proved* that the long-lived rotifers were at least triploid—three labeled chromosomes per body-cell instead of two—and maybe even tetraploid. Every other expert in the Pearl River plant looked at them, and saw nothing but a blur which might have been rotifer chromosomes, and might equally well have been a newspaper halftone of a grey cat walking over a fur rug in a thick fog. The comparative tests— producing polyploid rotifers and other critters with drugs like colchicine, and comparing them with the critters produced by Lansing's and MacDougal's classical breeding methods—were just as indecisive. Lyons finally decided that what he needed to prove his case was the world's biggest and most expensive X-ray microscope, and right then we shut him down.

MacDougal had been right all the time. Lyons was a crackpot with a plausible line of chatter, enough of a technique at microdissection to compel respect, and a real and commendable eagerness to explore his idea right down to the bottom. MacDougal was a frozen-brained old man with far too much reverence for his teacher, a man far too ready to say that a respected notion was right because it was respected, and a man who had performed no actual experiments himself since his student days. But he had been right—purely intuitively—in predicting that Lyons' inversion of Lansing's Law would come to nothing. I gather that victory in the sciences doesn't always go to the most personable man, any more than it does in any other field. I'm glad to know it; I'm always glad to find some small area of human endeavor which resists the con-man and the sales-talk.

When Pfitzner discovered ascomycin, we had HWS close Pearl River out entirely.

Negative results of this kind are valuable for scientists too, I'm told. How you will evaluate your proposed research method in the light of these two experiences is unknown to me; I can only tell you what I think *I* learned. I am convinced that we must be much slower, in the future, to ignore the fringe notion and the marginal theorist. One of the virtues of these crackpots—if that is what they are—is that they tend to cling to ideas which can be tested. That's worth hanging on to, in a world where scientific ideas have become so abstract that even their originators can't suggest ways to test them. Whoever Locke was, I suppose he hadn't put a thousandth as much time into thinking about gravity as Blackett had; yet Blackett couldn't suggest a way to test his equation, whereas the Locke Derivation was testable (on Jupiter) and turned out to be right. As for Lyons, his notion was wrong; but it too fell down because it failed the operational test, the very test it proposed to pass; until we performed that test, we had no real assessment of Lansing's Law, which had been traveling for years on prestige because of the "impossibility" of weighing any contrary hypothesis. Lyons forced us to do that, and enlarged our knowledge.

And so, take it from there; I've tried to give back as good as I have gotten. I'm not going to discuss the politics of this whole conspiracy with you, nor do I want you to concern yourself with them. Politics is death. Above all, I beg you—if you're at all pleased with this report—not to be distressed over the situation I will probably be in by the time this reaches you. I've been ruthless with your reputation to advance my purposes; I've been ruthless with the careers of other people; I've been quite ruthless in sending some men—some hundreds of men—to deaths they could surely have avoided had it not been for me; I've put many others, including a number of children, into considerable jeopardy. With all this written against my name, I'd think it a monstrous injustice to get off scot-free.

And that is all I can say; I have an appointment in a few minutes. Thank you for your friendship and your help.

BLISS WAGONER

CHAPTER NINE: New York

*It is sometimes claimed that religious intolerance is
the fruit of conviction. If one can be absolutely certain
that one's faith is right and all others wrong, it
seems criminal to permit one's neighbors' obvious
error and perdition. I am tempted to think, however,
that religious fanaticism often is the result not
of conviction but rather of doubt and insecurity.*
—GEORGE SARTON

Ruthlessness, Anne had said, is what it takes. But—
Paige thought afterwards—is it?

Does faith add up to its own flat violation? It was
all well enough to have something in which you
could believe. But when a faith in humanity-in-general
automatically results in casual inhumanity toward individual people, something must have gone awry.
Should the temple bell be struck so continually that
it has to shatter—make all its worshippers ill with
terror until it is silenced?

Silence. The usual answer. Or was the fault not in
faith itself, but in the faithful? The faithful were

usually pretty frightening as people, Believers and humanitarians alike.

Paige's time to debate the point with himself had already almost run out—and with it, his time to protect himself, if he could. Nothing had emerged from his soil samples. Evidently bacterial life on the Jovian moons had never at any time been profuse and consisted now only of a few hardy spores of common species, like *Bacillus subtilis,* which occurred on every Earth-like world and sometimes even in meteors. The samples plated out sparsely and yielded nothing which had not been known for decades—as, indeed, the statistics of this kind of research had predicted from the beginning.

It was now known around the Bronx plant that some sort of investigation of the Pfitzner project was rolling, and was already moving too fast to be derailed by any method the company's executives could work out. Daily reports from Pfitzner's Washington office—actually the Washington branch of Interplanet Press, the public relations agency Pfitzner maintained —were filed in the plant, but they were apparently not very informative. Paige gathered that there was some mystery about the investigation at the source, though neither Gunn nor Anne would say so in so many words.

And, finally, Paige's leave was to be over, day after tomorrow. After that, the Proserpine station—and probably an order to follow, emerging out of the investigation, which would maroon him there for the rest of his life in the service.

And it wasn't worth it.

That realization had been staring him in the eyes all along. For Anne and Gunn, perhaps, the price was worth paying, the tricks were worth playing, the lying and the cheating and the risking of the lives of others were necessary and just to the end in view.

But when the last card was down, Paige knew that he himself lacked the necessary dedication. Like every other road toward dedication that he had assayed, this one had turned out to have been paved with pure lead—and had left him with no better emblem of conduct than the miserable one which had kept him going all the same: self-preservation.

He knew then, with cold disgust toward himself, that he was going to use what he knew to clear himself, as soon as the investigation hit the plant. Senator Wagoner, the grapevine said, would be conducting it—oddly enough, for Wagoner and Mac-Hinery were deadly political enemies; had MacHinery gotten the jump on him at last?—and would arrive tomorrow. If Paige timed himself very carefully, he could lay down the facts, leave the plant forever, and be out in space without having to face Hal Gunn or Anne Abbott at all. What would happen to the Pfitzner project thereafter would be old news by the time he landed at the Proserpine station—more than three months old.

And by that time, he told himself, he would no longer care.

Nevertheless, when the quick morrow came, he marched into Gunn's office—which Wagoner had taken over—like a man going before a firing squad.

A moment later, he felt as though he had been shot down while still crossing the door-sill. Even before he realized that Anne was already in the room, he heard Wagoner say:

"Colonel Russell, sit down. I'm glad to see you. I have a security clearance for you, and a new set of orders; you can forget Proserpine. You and Miss Abbott and I are leaving for Jupiter. Tonight."

It was like a dream after that. In the Caddy on the way to the spaceport, Wagoner said nothing. As for

Anne, she seemed to be in a state of slight shock. From what little Paige thought he had learned about her—and it was very little—he deduced that she had expected this as little as he had. Her face as he had entered Gunn's office had been guarded, eager, and slightly smug all at once, as though she had thought she'd known what Wagoner would say. But when Wagoner had mentioned Jupiter, she'd turned to look at him as though he'd been turned from a senator into a boxing kangaroo, in the plain sight of the Pfitzner Founders. Something was wrong. After the long catalog of things already visibly wrong, the statement didn't mean very much. But something had clearly gone wrong.

There were fireworks in the sky to the south, visible from the right side of the Caddy where Paige sat as the car turned east on to the parkway. They were big and spectacular, and seemed to be going up from the heart of Manhattan. Paige was puzzled until he remembered, like a fact recalled from the heart of an absurd dream, that this was the last night of the Believer Revival, being held in the stadium on Randalls Island. The fireworks celebrated the Second Coming, which the Believers were confident could not now be long delayed.

Gewiss, gewiss, es naht noch heut'
und kann nicht lang mehr säumen . . .

Paige could remember having heard his father, an ardent Wagnerian, singing that; it was from *Tristan*. But he thought instead of those frightening medieval paintings of the Second Coming, in which Christ stands ignored in a corner of the canvas while the people flock reverently to the feet of the Anti-Christ, whose face, in the dim composite of Paige's memory, was a curious mixture of Francis X. MacHinery and Bliss Wagoner.

Words began to bloom along the black sky at the hearts of starshells:

No doubt, Paige thought bleakly. The Believers also believed that the Earth was flat; but Paige was on his way to Jupiter—not exactly a round planet, but rounder than the Believers' Earth. In quest, if you please, of immortality, in which he too had believed. Tasting bile, he thought, *It takes all kinds*.

A final starshell, so brilliant even at this distance that the word inside it was almost dazzled out, burst soundlessly into blue-white fire above the city. It said:

Paige swung his head abruptly and looked at Anne. Her face, a ghostly blur in the dying light of the shell, was turned raptly toward the window; she had been watching, too. He leaned forward and kissed her slightly parted lips, gently, forgetting all about Wagoner. After a frozen moment he could feel her mouth smiling against his, the smile which had astonished him so when he had seen it first, but softened, transformed, giving. The world went away for a while.

Then she touched his cheeks with her fingertips and sank back against the cushions; the Caddy swung sharply north off the parkway; and the spark of radiance which was the last retinal image of the shell vanished into drifting purple blotches, like after-visions of the sun—or of Jupiter seen close-on. Anne had no way of knowing, of course, that he had been running away from her, toward the Proserpine station, when he had been cornered in this Caddy instead. *Anne, Anne, I believe; help me in mine unbelief*.

The Caddy was passed through the spaceport gates after a brief, whispered consultation between the chauffeur and the guards. Instead of driving directly for the Administration Building, however, it turned craftily to the left and ran along the inside of the wire fence, back toward the city and into the dark reaches of the emergency landing pits. It was not totally dark there, however; there was a pool of light on an apron some distance ahead, with a needle of glare pointing straight up from its center.

Paige leaned forward and peered through the double glass barrier—one pane between himself and the driver, the other between the driver and the world. The needle of light was a ship, but it was not one he recognized. It was a single-stage job: a ferry, designed to take them out no farther than to Satellite Vehicle One, where they would be transferred to a proper interplanetary vessel. But it was small, even for a ferry.

"How do you like her, Colonel?" Wagoner's voice said, unexpectedly, from the black corner where he sat.

"All right," Paige said. "She's a little small, isn't she?"

Wagoner chuckled. "Pretty damn small," he said,

and fell silent again. Alarmed, Paige began to wonder if the senator was feeling entirely well. He turned to look at Anne, but he could not even see her face now. He groped for her hand; she responded with a feverish, rigid grip.

The Caddy shot abruptly from the fence. It bore down on the pool of light. Paige could see several marines standing on the apron at the tail of the ship. Absurdly, the vessel looked even smaller as it came closer.

"All right," Wagoner said. "Out of here, both of you. We'll be taking off in ten minutes. The crewmen will show you your quarters."

"Crewmen?" Paige said. "Senator, that ship won't hold more than four people, and one of them has to be the tube-man. That leaves nobody to pilot her but me."

"Not this trip," Wagoner said, following him out of the car. "We're only passengers, you and I and Miss Abbott, and of course the marines. The *Per Aspera* has a separate crew of five. Let's not waste time, please."

It was impossible. On the cleats, Paige felt as though he were trying to climb into a .22 calibre long-rifle cartridge. To get ten people into this tiny shell, you'd have to turn them into some sort of human concentrate and pour them, like powdered coffee.

Nevertheless, one of the marines met him in the airlock, and within another minute he was strapping himself down inside a windowless cabin as big as any he'd ever seen on board a standard interplanetary vessel—far bigger than any ferry could accommodate. The intercom box at the head of his hammock was already calling the clearance routine.

"Dog down and make all fast. Airlock will cycle in one minute."

What had happened to Anne? She had come up the cleats after him, of that he was sure—

"All fast. Take-off in one minute. Passengers 'ware G's."

—but he'd been hustled down to this nonsensical cabin too fast to look back. There was something very wrong. Was Wagoner—

"Thirty seconds. 'Ware G's."

—making some sort of a getaway? But from what? And why did he want to take Paige and Anne with him? As hostages they were—

"Twenty seconds."

—worthless, since they were of no value to the government, had no money, knew nothing damning about Wagoner—

"Fifteen seconds."

But wait a minute. Anne knew something about Wagoner, or thought she did.

"Ten seconds. Stand by."

The call made him relax instinctively. There would be time to think about that later. At take-off—

"Five seconds."

—it didn't pay—

"Four."

—to concentrate—

"Three."

—on anything—

"Two."

—else but—

"One."

—actual—

"Zero."

—*takeoff* hit him with the abrupt, bone-cracking, gut-wrenching impact of all ferry take-offs. There was nothing you could do to ameliorate it but let the strong muscles of the arms and legs and back bear it as best they could, with the automatic tetanus of the Seyle GA reaction, and concentrate on keeping your head and your abdomen in exact neutral with the acceleration thrust. The muscles you used for that were seldom called upon on the ground, even by weight-lifters, but you learned to use them or were invalided out of the service; a trained spaceman's abdominal muscles will bounce a heavy rock, and no strong man can make him turn his head if his neck muscles say *no*.

Also, it helped a little to yell. Theoretically, the yell collapses the lungs—acceleration pneumothorax, the books call it—and keeps them collapsed until the surge of powered flight is over. By that time, the carbon dioxide level of the blood has risen so high that the breathing reflex will reassert itself with an enormous gasp, even if crucial chest muscles have been torn. The yell makes sure that when next you breathe, you *breathe*.

But more importantly for Paige and every other spaceman, the yell was the only protest he could form against that murderous nine seconds of pressure; it makes you *feel* better. Paige yelled with vigor.

He was still yelling when the ship went into free fall.

Instantly, while the yell was still dying incredulously in his throat, he was clawing at his harness. All his spaceman's reflexes had gone off at once. The powered-flight period had been too short. Even the shortest possible take-off acceleration outlasts the yell. Yet the ion-rockets were obviously silenced. The little ship's power had failed—she was falling back to the Earth—

"Attention, please," the intercom box said mildly. "We are now under way. Free fall will last only a few seconds. Stand by for restoration of normal gravity."

And then. . . . And then the hammock against which Paige was struggling was *down* again, as though the ship were still resting quietly on Earth. Impossible; she couldn't even be out of the atmosphere yet. Even if she were, free fall should last all the rest of the trip. Gravity in an interplanetary vessel—let alone a ferry—could be reestablished only by rotating the ship around its long axis; few captains bothered with the fuel-expensive maneuvre, since hardly anybody but old hands flew between the planets. Besides, this ship—the *Per Aspera*—hadn't gone through any such maneuvre, or Paige would have detected it.

Yet his body continued to press down against the hammock with an acceleration of one Earth gravity.

"Attention, please. We will be passing the Moon in one point two minutes. The observation blister is now open to passengers. Senator Wagoner requests the presence of Miss Abbott and Colonel Russell in the blister."

There was no further sound from the ion-rockets, which had inexplicably been shut off when the *Per Aspera* could have been no more than 250 miles above the surface of the Earth. Yet she was passing the Moon now, without the slightest sensation of movement, though she must still be accelerating. What was driving her? Paige could hear nothing but the small hum of the ship's electrical generator, no louder than it would have been on the ground, unburdened of the job of RF-heating the electron-ion plasma which the rockets used. Grimly, he unsnapped the last gripper from his harness, conscious of what a baby he evidently was on board this ship, and got up.

The deck felt solid and abnormal under his feet, pressing against the soles of his shoes with a smug terrestrial pressure of one unvarying gravity. Only the habits of caution of a service lifetime prevented him from running forward up the companionway to the observation blister.

Anne and Senator Wagoner were there, the dimming moonlight bathing their backs as they looked ahead into deep space. They had been more than a little shaken up by the take-off, that was obvious, but they were already almost recovered; compared to the effects of the normal ferry take-off, this could only have ruffled them; and of course the sudden transformation to the impossible one-gravity field would not have bollixed their untrained reflexes with anything like the thoroughness that it had scrambled Paige's long-conditioned reactions. Looked at this way, spaceflight like this might well be easier for civilians than it would be for spacemen, at least for some years to come.

He padded cautiously toward them, feeling disastrously humbled. Shining between them was a brilliant, hard spot of yellow-white light, glaring into the blister through the thick, cosmics-proof glass. The spot was fixed and steady, as were all the stars looking into the blister; proof positive that the ship's gravity was not being produced by axial spin. The yellow spot itself, shining between Wagoner's elbow and Anne's upper arm, was—

Jupiter.

On either side of the planet were two smaller bright dots; the four Galilean satellites, as widely separated to Paige's naked eye as they would have looked on Earth through a telescope the size of Galileo's.

While Paige hesitated in the doorway to the blister, the little spots that were Jupiter's largest moons visibly drew apart from each other a little, until one of them went into occulation behind Anne's right shoulder. The *Per Aspera* was still accelerating; it was driving toward Jupiter at a speed nothing in

Paige's experience could have prepared him for. Stunned, he made a very rough estimate in his head of the increase in parallax and tried to calculate the ship's rate of approach from that.

The little lunar ferry, humming scarcely louder than a transformer for carrying five people—let alone ten—as far as SV-1, was now hurtling toward Jupiter at about a quarter of the speed of light.

At least forty thousand miles per second.

And the deepening color of Jupiter showed that the *Per Aspera* was still picking up speed.

"Come in, Colonel Russell," Wagoner's voice said, echoing slightly in the blister. "Come watch the show. We've been waiting for you."

CHAPTER TEN: Jupiter V

That is precisely what common sense is for, to be jarred into uncommon sense. One of the chief services which mathematics has rendered the human race in the past century is to put 'common sense' where it belongs, on the topmost shelf next to the dusty canister labeled 'discarded nonsense.'
— ERIC TEMPLE BELL

The ship that landed as Helmuth was going on duty did nothing to lighten the load on his heart. In shape it was not distinguishable from any of the short-range ferries which covered the Jovian satellary circuit, carrying supplies from the regular SV-1-Mars-Belt-Jupiter X cruiser to the inner moons—and, sometimes, some years-old mail; but it was considerably bigger than the usual Jovian ferry, and it grounded its outsize mass on Jupiter V with only the briefest cough of rockets.

That landing told Helmuth that his dream was well on its way to coming true. If the high brass had a real antigravity, there would have been no reason why the ionstreams should have been necessary at all. Obviously, what had been discovered was some sort of partial gravity screen, which allowed a ship to operate with far less rocket thrust than was usual, but which still left it subject to a sizable fraction of the universal G, the inherent stress of space.

Nothing less than a complete, and completely controllable gravity screen would do, on Jupiter.

And theory said that a complete gravity screen was impossible. Once you set one up—even supposing that you could—you would be unable to enter it or leave it. Crossing a boundary-line between a one G field and a no-G field would be precisely as difficult as surmounting a high-jump with the bar set at infinity, and for the same reasons. If you crossed it from the other direction, you would hit the ground on the other side of the line as hard as though you had fallen there from the Moon; a little harder, in fact.

Helmuth worked mechanically at the gang board, thinking. Charity was not in evidence, but there was no special reason why the foreman's board had to be manned on this trick. The work could be as easily supervised from here, and obviously Charity had expected Helmuth to do it that way, or he would have left notice. Probably Charity was already conferring with the senators, receiving what would be for him the glad news.

Helmuth realized suddenly that there was nothing left for him to do now, once this trick was over, but to cut and run.

There could be no real reason why he should be required to re-enact the entire nightmare, helplessly, event for event, like an actor committed to a role. He was awake now, in full control of his own senses, and still at least partially sane. The man in the dream had volunteered—but that man would not be Robert Helmuth. Not any longer.

While the senators were here on Jupiter V, he

would turn in his resignation. Direct—over Charity's head.

The wave of relief came washing over him just as he finished resetting the circuits which would enable him to supervise from the gang board, and left him so startlingly weak that he had to put the helmet down on the ledge before he had raised it half-way to his head. So *that* had been what he had been waiting for: to quit, nothing more.

He owed it to Charity to finish the Grand Tour of the Bridge. After that, he'd be free. He would never have to see the Bridge again, not even inside a viewing helmet. A farewell tour, and then back to Chicago, if there was still such a place.

He waited until his breathing had quieted a little, scooped the helmet up on to his shoulders, and the Bridge . . .

. . . came falling into existence all around him, a Pandemonium beyond broaching and beyond hope, sealed on all sides. The drumfire of rain against his beetle's hull was so loud that it hurt his ears, even with the gain knob of his helmet backed all the way down to the thumb-stop. It was impossible to cut the audio circuit out altogether; much of his assessment of how the Bridge was responding to stress depended on sound; human eyesight on the Bridge was almost as useless as a snail's.

And the Bridge was responding now, as always, with its medley of dissonance and cacophony: *crang . . . crang . . . spungg . . . skreek . . . crang . . . ungg . . . oingg . . . skreek . . . skreek . . .* These structural noises were the only ones that counted; they were the polyphony of the Bridge, everything else was decorative and to be ignored by the Bridge operator— the fioritura shrieking of the winds, the battery of the rain, the pedal diapason of thunder, the distant grumbling roll of the stage-hand volcanoes pushing continents back and forth on castors down below.

This time, however, at long last, it was impossible to ignore any part of this great orchestra. Its composite uproar was enormous, implacable, incredible even for Jupiter, overwhelming even in this season. The moment he heard it, Helmuth knew that he had waited too long.

The Bridge was not going to last much longer. Not unless every man and woman on Jupiter V fought without sleep to keep it up, throughout this passage of the Red Spot and the South Tropical Disturbance—

—if even that would serve. The great groans that were rising through the tornado-riven mists from the caissons were becoming steadily, spasmodically deeper; their hinges were already overloaded. And the deck of the Bridge was beginning to rise and fall a little, as though slow, frozen waves were passing along it from one unfinished end to the other. The queasy, lazy tidal swell made the beetle tip first its nose into the winds, then its tail, then back again, so that it took almost all of the current Helmuth could feed into the magnet windings to keep the craft stuck to the rails on the deck at all. Cruising the deck seemed to be out of the question; there was not enough power left over for the engines—almost every available erg had to be devoted to staying put.

But there was still the rest of the Grand Tour to be made. And still one direction which Helmuth had yet to explore:

Straight down.

Down to the ice; down to the Ninth Circle, where everything stops, and never starts again.

There was a set of tracks leading down one of the Bridge's great buttresses, on to which Helmuth could switch the beetle in nearby sector 94. It took him only a few moments to set the small craft to creeping, head downward, toward the surface.

The meters on the ghost board had already told him that the wind velocity fell off abruptly at twenty-one miles—that is, eleven miles down from the deck—in this sector, which was in the lee of The Glacier, a long rib of mountain-range which terminated nearby. He was unprepared, however, for the near-calm itself. There was some wind, of course, as there was everywhere on Jupiter, especially at this season; but the worst gusts were little more than a few hundred miles per hour, and occasionally the meter fell as low as seventy-five.

The lull was dream-like. The beetle crawled downward through it, like a skin-diver who has already passed the safety-knot on his line, but is too drugged by the ecstasy of the depths to care. At fifteen miles, something white flashed in the fan-lights, and was gone. Then another; three more. And then, suddenly, a whole stream of them.

Belatedly, Helmuth stopped the beetle and peered ahead, but the white things were gone now. No, there were more of them, drifting quite slowly through the lights. As the wind died momentarily, they almost seemed to hover, pulsating slowly—

Helmuth heard himself grunt with astonishment. Once, in a moment of fancy, he had thought of Jovian jellyfish. That was what these looked like—jellyfish, not of the sea, but of the air. They were ten-ribbed, translucent, ranging in size from that of a closed fist to one as big as a football. They were beautiful—and looked incredibly delicate for this furious planet.

Helmuth reached forward to turn up the lights, but the wind rose just as his hand closed on the knob, and the creatures were gone. In the increased glare, Helmuth saw instead that there was a large platform jutting out from the buttress not far below him, just to one side of the rails. It was enclosed and roofed, but the material was transparent. And there was motion inside it.

He had no idea what the structure could be; evidently it was recent. Although he had never been below the deck in this sector before, he knew the plans well enough to recall that they had specified no such excrescence.

For a wild instant he had thought that there was a man on Jupiter already; but as he pulled up just above the platform's roof, he realized that the moving thing inside was—of course—a robot: a misshapen, many-tentacled thing about twice the size of a man. It was working busily with bottles and flasks, of which it seemed to have thousands on benches and shelves all around it. The whole enclosure was a litter of what Helmuth took to be chemical apparatus, and off to one side was an object which might have been a microscope.

The robot looked up at him and gesticulated with two or three tentacles. At first Helmuth failed to understand; then he saw that the machine was pointing to the fanlights, and obediently turned them almost all the way down. In the resulting Jovian gloom he could see that the laboratory—for that was obviously what it was—had plenty of artificial light of its own.

There was, of course, no way that he could talk to the robot, nor it to him. If he wanted to, he could talk to the person operating it; but he knew the assignment of every man and woman on Jupiter V, and running this thing was no part of any of their duties. There was not even any provision for it on the boards—

A white light began to wink on the ghost board. That would be the incoming line for Europa. Was somebody on that snowball in charge of this many-tentacled experimenter, using Jupiter V's booster station to amplify the signals that guided it? Curiously, he plugged the jack in.

"Hello, the Bridge! Who's on duty there?"

"Hello, Europa. This is Bob Helmuth. Is this your robot I'm looking at, in sector ninety-four?"

"That's me," the voice said. It was impossible to avoid thinking of it as coming from the robot itself. "This is Doc Barth. How do you like my laboratory?"

"Very cosy," Helmuth said. "I didn't even know it existed. What do you do in it?"

"We just got it installed this year. It's to study the Jovian life-forms. You've seen them?"

"You mean the jellyfish? Are they really alive?"

"Yes," the robot said. "We are keeping it under our hats until we had more data, but we knew that sooner or later one of you beetle-goosers would see them. They're alive, all right. They've got a colloidal continuum-discontinuum exactly like protoplasm— except that it uses liquid ammonia as a sol substrate, instead of water."

"But what do they live on?" Helmuth said.

"Ah, that's the question. Some form of aerial plankton, that's certain; we've found the digested remnants inside them, but haven't captured any live specimens of it yet. The digested fragments don't offer us much to go on. And what does the plankton live on? I only wish I knew."

Helmuth thought about it. Life on Jupiter. It did not matter that it was simple in structure, and virtually helpless in the winds. It was life all the same, even down here in the frozen pits of a hell no living man would ever visit. And who could know, if jellyfish rode the Jovian air, what Leviathans might not swim the Jovian seas?

"You don't seem to be much impressed," the robot said. "Jellyfish and plankton probably aren't very exciting to a layman. But the implications are tremendous. It's going to cause quite a stir among biologists, let me tell you."

"I can believe that," Helmuth said. "I was just taken aback, that's all. We've always thought of Jupiter as lifeless—"

"That's right. But now we know better. Well, back to work; I'll be talking to you." The robot flourished its tentacles and bent over a workbench.

Abstractedly, Helmuth backed the beetle off and turned it upward again. Barth, he remembered, was the man who had found a fossil on Europa. Earlier, there had been an officer doing a tour of duty in the Jovian system who had spent some of his spare time cutting soil samples, in search of bacteria. Probably he had found some; scientists of the age before spaceflight had even found them in meteors. The Earth and Mars were not the only places in the universe that would harbor life, after all; perhaps it was— everywhere. If it could exist in a place like Jupiter, there was no logical reason to rule it out even on the Sun—some animated flame no one would recognize as life. . . .

He regained the deck and sent the beetle rumbling for the switchyard; he would need to transfer to another track before he could return the car to its garage. It had occurred to him during the ghostly proxy-conversation that he had never met Doc Barth, or many of the other men with whom he had talked so often by ham radio. Except for the Bridge operators themselves, the Jovian system was a community of disembodied voices to him. And now, he would never meet them. . . .

"Wake up, Helmuth," a voice from the gang deck snapped abruptly. "If it hadn't been for me, you'd have run yourself off the end of the Bridge. You had all the automatic stops on that beetle cut out."

Helmuth reached guiltily and more than a little

too late for the controls. Eva had already run his beetle back beyond the danger line.

"Sorry," he mumbled, taking the helmet off. "Thanks, Eva."

"Don't thank me. If you'd actually been in it, I'd have let it go. Less reading and more sleep is what I recommend for you, Helmuth."

"Keep your recommendations to yourself," he growled.

The incident started a new and even more disturbing chain of thought. If he were to resign now, it would be nearly a year before he could get back to Chicago. Antigravity or no antigravity, the senators' ship would have no room for unexpected extra passengers. Shipping a man back home had to be arranged far in advance. Living space had to be provided, and a cargo equivalent of the weight and space requirements he would take up on the return trip had to be dead-headed out to Jupiter V.

A year of living in the station on Jupiter V without any function—as a man whose drain on the station's supplies no longer could be justified in terms of what he did. A year of living under the eyes of Eva Chavez and Charity Dillon and the other men and women who still remained Bridge operators, men and women who would not hesitate to let him know what they thought of his quitting.

A year of living as a bystander in the feverish excitement of direct, personal exploration of Jupiter. A year of watching and hearing the inevitable deaths—while he alone stood aloof, privileged and useless. A year during which Robert Helmuth would become the most hated living entity in the Jovian system.

And, when he got back to Chicago and went looking for a job—for his resignation from the Bridge gang would automatically take him out of government service—he would be asked why he had left the Bridge at the moment when work on the Bridge was just reaching its culmination.

He began to understand why the man in the dream had volunteered.

When the trick-change bell rang, he was still determined to resign, but he had already concluded bitterly that there were, after all, other kinds of hells besides the one on Jupiter.

He was returning the board to neutral as Charity came up the cleats. Charity's eyes were snapping like a skyful of comets. Helmuth had known that they would be.

"Senator Wagoner wants to speak to you if you're not too tired, Bob," he said. "Go ahead; I'll finish up there."

"He does?" Helmuth frowned. The dream surged back upon him. *No.* They would not rush him any faster than he wanted to go. "What about, Charity? Am I suspected of unwestern activities? I suppose you've told them how I feel."

"I have," Dillon said, unruffled. "But we've agreed that you may not feel the same way after you've talked to Wagoner. He's in the ship, of course. I've put out a suit for you at the lock."

Charity put the helmet over his head, effectively cutting himself off from further conversation or from any further consciousness of Helmuth at all.

Helmuth stood looking at the blind, featureless bubble on Charity's shoulders for a moment. Then, with a convulsive shrug, he went down the cleats.

Three minutes later, he was plodding in a spacesuit across the surface of Jupiter V with the vivid bulk of the mother planet splashing his shoulders with color.

A courteous marine let him through the ship's airlock and deftly peeled him out of the suit. Despite a grim determination to be uninterested in the new antigravity and any possible consequence of it, he looked curiously about as he was conducted up toward the bow.

But the ship on the inside was like the ones that had brought him from Chicago to Jupiter V—it was like any spaceship: there was nothing in it to see but corridor walls and cleatwalls, until you arrived at the cabin where you were needed.

Senator Wagoner was a surprise. He was a young man, no more than sixty at most, not at all portly, and he had the keenest pair of blue eyes that Helmuth had ever seen. The cabin in which he received Helmuth was obviously his own, a comfortable cabin as spaceship accommodations go, but neither roomy nor luxurious. The senator was hard to match up with the stories Helmuth had been hearing about the current Senate, which had been involved in scandal after scandal of more than Roman proportions.

There were only two people with him: a rather plain girl who was possibly his secretary, and a tall man wearing the uniform of the Army Space Corps and the eagles of a colonel. Helmuth realized, with a second shock of surprise, that he knew the officer: he was Paige Russell, a ballistics expert who had been stationed in the Jovian system not too long ago. The dirt-collector. He smiled rather wryly as Helmuth's eyebrows went up.

Helmuth looked back at the senator. "I thought there was a whole sub-committee here," he said.

"There is, but we left them where we found them, on Ganymede. I didn't want to give you the idea that you were facing a grand jury," Wagoner said, smiling. "I've been forced to sit in on most of these endless loyalty investigations back home, but I can't see any point in exporting such religious ceremonies to deep space. Do sit down, Mr. Helmuth. There are drinks coming. We have a lot to talk about."

Stiffly, Helmuth sat down.

"You know Colonel Russell, of course," Wagoner

said, leaning back comfortably in his own chair. "This young lady is Anne Abbott, about whom you'll hear more shortly. Now then: Dillon tells me that your usefulness to the Bridge is about at an end. In a way, I'm sorry to hear that, for you've been one of the best men we've had on any of our planetary projects. But, in another way, I'm glad. It makes you available for something much bigger, where we need you much more."

"What do you mean by that?"

"You'll have to let me explain it in my own way. First, I'd like to talk a little about the Bridge. Please don't feel that I'm quizzing you, by the way. You're at perfect liberty to say that any given question is none of my business, and I'll take no offense and hold no grudge. Also, 'I hereby disavow the authenticity of any tape or other tapping of which this statement may be a part.' In short, our conversation is unofficial, highly so."

"Thank you."

"It's to my interest; I'm hoping that you'll talk freely to me. Of course, my disavowal means nothing, since such formal statements can always be excised from a tape; but later on I'm going to tell you some things you're not supposed to know, and you'll be able to judge by what I say that anything you say to me is privileged. Paige and Anne are your witnesses. Okay?"

A steward came in silently with the drinks and left again. Helmuth tasted his. As far as he could tell, it was exactly like many he had mixed for himself back in the control shack from standard space rations. The only difference was that it was cold, which Helmuth found startling but not unpleasant after the first sip. He tried to relax. "I'll do my best," he said.

"Good enough. Now: Dillon says that you regard the Bridge as a monster. I've examined your dossier pretty closely—as a matter of fact I've been studying both you and Paige far more intensively than you can imagine—and I think perhaps Dillon hasn't quite the gist of your meaning. I'd like to hear it straight from you."

"I don't think the Bridge is a monster," Helmuth said slowly. "You see, Charity is on the defensive. He takes the Bridge to be conclusive evidence that no possible set of adverse conditions will ever stop man for long, and there I'm in agreement with him. But he also thinks of it as Progress, personified. He can't admit—you asked me to speak my mind, Senator—he can't admit that the West is a decadent and dying culture. All the other evidence that's available shows that it is. Charity likes to think of the Bridge as giving the lie to that evidence."

"The West hasn't many more years," Wagoner agreed, astonishingly.

Paige Russell mopped his forehead. "I still can't hear you say that," the spaceman said, "without wanting to duck under the rug. After all, MacHinery's with that pack on Ganymede—"

"MacHinery," Wagoner said calmly, "is probably going to die of apoplexy when we spring this thing on him, and I for one won't miss him. Anyhow, it's perfectly true; the dominoes have been falling for some time now, and the explosion Anne's outfit has cooked up is going to be the final blow. Still and all, Mr. Helmuth, the West has been responsible for some really towering achievements in time. Perhaps the Bridge could be considered as the last and mightiest of them all."

"Not by me," Helmuth said. "The building of gigantic projects for ritual purposes—doing a thing for the sake of doing it—is the last act of an already dead culture. Look at the pyramids in Egypt for an example. Or at an even more enormous and more idiotic example, bigger than anything human beings have accomplished yet—the laying out of the 'Diagram of

Power' over the whole face of Mars. If the Martians had put all that energy into survival instead, they'd probably be alive yet."

"Agreed," Wagoner said, "with reservations. You're right about Mars, but the pyramids were built during the springtime of the Egyptian culture. And 'doing a thing for the sake of doing it' is not a definition of ritual; it's a definition of science."

"All right. That doesn't greatly alter my argument. Maybe you'll also agree that the essence of a vital culture is its ability to defend itself. The West has beaten the Soviets for half a century now—but as far as I can see, the Bridge is the West's 'Diagram of Power,' its pyramids, or what have you. It shows that we're mighty, but mighty in a non-survival sort of way. All the money and the resources that went into the Bridge are going to be badly needed, *and won't be there*, when the next Soviet attack comes."

"Correction: it has already come," Wagoner said. "And it has already won. The USSR played the greatest of all von Neumann games far better than we did, because they didn't assume as we did that each side would always choose the best strategy; they played also to wear down the players. In fifty years of unrelenting pressure, they succeeded in converting the West into a system so like the Soviets' as to make direct military action unnecessary; we Sovietized ourselves, and our moves are now exactly predictable.

"So in part I agree with you. What we needed was to sink the energy and the money into the game— into social research, since the menace was social. Instead, typically, we put it into a physical research project of unprecedented size. Which was, of course, just what the theory of games said we would do. For a man who's been cut off from Earth for years, Helmuth, you seem to know more about what's going on down there than most of the general populace does."

"Nothing promotes an interest in Earth like being off it," Helmuth said. "And there's plenty of time to read out here." Either the drink was stronger than he had expected—which was reasonable, considering that he had been off the stuff for some time now—or the senator's calm concurrence in the collapse of Helmuth's entire world had given him another shove toward the abyss; his head was spinning.

Wagoner saw it. He leaned forward suddenly, catching Helmuth flat-footed. "*However*," he said, "it's difficult for me to agree that the Bridge serves, or ever did serve, a ritual purpose. The Bridge served several huge practical purposes which are now fulfilled. As a matter of fact, the Bridge, as such, is now a defunct project."

"Defunct?" Helmuth said faintly.

"Quite. Of course, we'll continue to operate it for a while. You can't stop a process of that size on a dime. Besides, one of the reasons why we built the Bridge was because the USSR expected us to; the game said that we should launch another Manhattan District or Project Lincoln at this point, and we hated to disappoint them. One thing we are *not* going to do this time, however, is to tell them the problem that the project was supposed to solve—let alone that it *can* be solved, and has been.

"So we'll keep the Bridge going, physically and publicly. That'll be just as well, too, for people like Dillon who are emotionally tied up in it, above and beyond their conditioning to it. You're the only person in authority in the whole station who's already lost enough interest in the Bridge to make it safe for me to tell you that it's being abandoned."

"But why?"

"Because," Wagoner went on quietly, "the Bridge has now given us confirmation of a theory of stupendous importance—so important, in my opinion, that the imminent fall of the West seems like a puny event in comparison. A confirmation, incidentally, which contains in it the seeds of ultimate destruction for the Soviets, whatever they may win for themselves in the next hundred years or so."

"I suppose," Helmuth said, puzzled, "that you mean antigravity?"

For the first time, it was Wagoner's turn to be taken aback. "Man," he said at last, "do you know *everything* I want to tell you? I hope not, or my conclusions will be mighty unwelcome to both of us. Do you also know what an anti-agathic is?"

"No," Helmuth said. "I don't even recognize the root of the word."

"Well, that's a relief. But surely Charity didn't tell you we had antigravity. I strictly enjoined him not to mention it."

"No. The subject's been on my mind," Helmuth said. "But I certainly don't see why it should be so world-shaking, any more than I see how the Bridge helped to bring it about. I thought it would be developed independently, for the further exploitation of the Bridge. In other words, to put men down there, and short-circuit this remote control operation we have on Jupiter V. And I thought it would step up Bridge operation, not discontinue it."

"Not at all. Nobody in his right mind would want to put men on Jupiter, and besides, gravity isn't the main problem down there. Even eight gravities is perfectly tolerable for short periods of time—and anyhow a man in a pressure suit couldn't get five hundred miles down through that atmosphere before he'd be as buoyed up and weightless as a fish—and even more thoroughly at the mercy of the currents."

"And you can't screen out the pressure?"

"We can," Wagoner said, "but only at ruinous cost. Besides, there'd be no point in trying. The Bridge is finished. It's given us information in thousands of different categories, much of it very valuable indeed. But the one job that *only* the Bridge could do was that of confirming, or throwing out, the Blackett-Dirac equations."

"Which are—?"

"They show a relationship between magnetism and the spinning of a massive body—that much is the Dirac part of it. The Blackett Equation seemed to show that the same formula also applied to gravity; it says G equals $(2CP/BU_2)$, where C is the velocity of light, P is magnetic moment, and U is angular momentum. B is an uncertainty correction, a constant which amounts to 0.25.

"If the figures we collected on the magnetic field strength of Jupiter forced us to retire the equations, then none of the rest of the information we've gotten from the Bridge would have been worth the money we spent to get it. On the other hand, Jupiter was the only body in the solar system available to us which was big enough in all relevant respects to make it possible for us to test those equations at all. They involve quantities of infinitesimal orders of magnitudes.

"And the figures showed that Dirac was right. *They also show that Blackett was right.* Both magnetism *and* gravity are phenomena of rotation.

"I won't bother to trace the succeeding steps, because I think you can work them out for yourself. It's enough to say that there's a drive-generator on board this ship which is the complete and final justification of all the hell you people on the Bridge have been put through. The gadget has a long technical name— The Dillon-Wagoner gravitron polarity generator, a name which I loathe for obvious reasons—but the technies who tend it have already nicknamed it the spindizzy, because of what it does to the magnetic moment of any atom—*any* atom—within its field.

"While it's in operation, it absolutely refuses to notice any atom outside its own influence. Furthermore, it will notice no other strain or influence which holds good beyond the borders of that field. It's so snooty that it has to be stopped down to almost nothing when it's brought close to a planet, or it won't let you land. But in deep space . . . well, it's impervious to meteors and such trash, of course; it's impervious to gravity; and—it hasn't the faintest interest in any legislation about top speed limits. It moves in its own continuum, not in the general frame."

"You're kidding," Helmuth said.

"Am I, now? This ship came to Ganymede directly from Earth. It did it in a little under two hours, counting maneuvring time. That means that most of the way we made about 55,000 miles per second— with the spindizzy drawing less than five watts of power out of three ordinary No. 6 dry cells."

Helmuth took a defiant pull at his drink. "This thing really has no top speed at all?" he said. "How can you be sure of that?"

"Well, we can't," Wagoner admitted. After all, one of the unfortunate things about general mathematical formulae is that they don't contain cut-off points to warn you of areas where they don't apply. Even quantum mechanics is somewhat subject to that criticism. However, we expect to know pretty soon just how fast the spindizzy can drive an object. We expect you to tell us."

"I?"

"Yes, you, and Colonel Russell, and Miss Abbott too, I hope." Helmuth looked at the other two; both of them looked at least as stunned as he felt. He could not imagine why. "The coming débâcle on Earth makes it absolutely imperative for us—the West—to get inter-stellar expeditions started at once. Richardson Observatory, on the Moon, has two likely-looking systems mapped already—one at Wolf 359, the other at 61 Cygni—and there are sure to be others, hundreds of others, where Earth-like planets are highly probable.

"What we're doing, in a nutshell, is evacuating the West—not physically, of course, but in essence, in idea. We want to scatter adventurous people, people with a thoroughly indoctrinated love of being free, all over this part of the galaxy, if it can be done.

"Once they're out there, they'll be free to flourish, with no interference from Earth. The Soviets haven't the spindizzy yet, and even after they get it, they won't dare allow it to be used. It's too good and too final an escape route for disaffected comrades.

"What we want you to do, Helmuth . . . now I'm getting to the point, you see . . . is to direct this exodus, with Colonel Russell's help. You've the intelligence and the cast of mind for it. Your analysis of the situation on Earth confirms that, if any more confirmation were needed. And—there's no future for you on Earth now."

"You'll have to excuse me for a while," Helmuth said firmly. "I'm in no condition to be reasonable now: it's been more than I could digest in a few moments. And the decision doesn't entirely rest with me, either. If I could give you an answer in . . . let me see . . . about three hours. Will that be soon enough?"

"That'll be fine," the senator said.

For a moment after the door closed behind Helmuth there was silence in the senator's cabin. At last Paige said:

"So it was long life for spacemen you were after, all the time. Long life, by God, for *me*, and for the likes of me."

Wagoner nodded. "This was the one part of this affair that I couldn't explain to you back in Hal Gunn's office," he said. "Until you had ridden in this ship, and understood as a spaceman just what kind of a thing we have in it, you wouldn't have believed me; Helmuth does, you see, because he already has the background. In the same way, I didn't go into the question of the anti-agathic with Helmuth, because that's something he's going to have to experience; you two have the background to understand that part of it through explanation alone.

"Now you see why I didn't give a whistle about your spy, Paige. The Soviets can have the Earth. As a matter of fact they will take it before very long, whether we give into them or not. But we are going to scatter the West throughout the stars, scatter it with immortal people carrying immortal ideas. People like you, and Miss Abbott."

Paige looked back to Anne. She was aloofly regarding the empty space just above Wagoner's head, as though still looking at the bewhiskered picture of the Pfitzner founder which hung in Gunn's office. There was something in her face, however, that Paige could read. He smothered a grin and said: "Why me?"

"Because you're just what we need for the job. I don't mind telling you that your blundering into the Pfitzner project in the first place was an act of Providence from my point of view. When Anne first called your qualifications to my attention, I was almost prepared to believe that they'd been faked. You're going to be liason-man between the Pfitzner side of the project and the Bridge side. We've got the total output to date of both ascomycin and the new anti-agathic salted away in the cargo-hold, and Anne's already shown you how to take the stuff and how to administer it to others. After that—just as soon as you and Helmuth can work out the details—the stars are yours."

"Anne," Paige said. She turned her head slowly toward him. "Are you with this thing?"

"I'm here," she said. "And I'd had a few inklings of what was up before. You were the one who had to be brought in, not I."

Paige thought about it a moment more. Then something both very new and very old occurred to him.

"Senator," he said, "you've gone to an immense amount of trouble to make this whole thing possible—but I don't think you plan to go with us."

"No, Paige, I don't. For one thing, MacHinery and his crew will regard the whole project as treasonous. If it's to be carried out nevertheless, someone has to stay behind and be the goat—and after all, the idea *was* mine, so I'm the logical candidate." He fell silent for a moment. Then he added ruminatively: "The government boys have nobody but themselves to thank for this. The whole project would never have been possible so long as the West had a government of laws and not of men, and stuck to it. It was a long while ago that some people—MacHinery's grandfather among them—set themselves up to be their own judges of whether or not a law ought to be obeyed. They had precedents. And now here we are, on the brink of the most enormous breach of our social contract the West has ever had to suffer—and the West can't stop it." He smiled suddenly. "I'll have good use for that argument in the court."

Anne was on her feet, her eyes suddenly wet, her lower lip just barely trembling. Evidently, over whatever time she had known Wagoner and had known what he had planned, it had never occurred to her that the young-old senator might stay behind.

"That's no good!" she said in a low voice. "They won't listen, and you know it. They might easily hang you for it. If they find you guilty of treason, they'll seal you up in the pile-waste dump—that's the current penalty, isn't it? You can't go back!"

"It's a phony terror. Pile wastes are quick chemical poisons; you don't last long enough to notice that they're also hot," Wagoner said. "And what difference does it make, anyhow? Nothing and nobody can harm me now. The job is done."

Anne put her hands to her face.

"Besides, Anne," Wagoner said, with gentle insistence, "the stars are for young people—eternally young people. An eternal oldster would be an anachronism."

"Why—did you do it, then?" Paige said. His own voice was none too steady.

"Why?" Wagoner said. "You know the answer to that, Paige. You've known it all your life. I could see it in your face, as soon as I told Helmuth that we were going out to the stars. Supposing you tell *me* what it is."

Anne swung her blurred eyes on Paige. He thought he knew what she expected to hear him say; they had talked about it often enough, and it was what he once would have said himself. But now another force seemed to him to be the stronger: a special thing, bearing the name of no established dogma, but nevertheless and unmistakably the force to which he had borne allegiance all his life. He in turn could see it in Wagoner's face now, and he knew he had seen it before in Anne's.

"It's the thing that lures monkeys into cages," he said slowly. "And lures cats into open drawers and up telephone poles. It's driven men to conquer death, and put the stars into our hands. I suppose that I'd call it Curiosity."

Wagoner looked startled. "Is that really what you want to call it?" he said. "Somehow it seems insufficient; I should have given it another name. Perhaps you'll amend it later, somewhere, some day out by Aldebaran."

He stood up and looked at the two for a moment in silence. Then he smiled.

"And now," he said gently, "*nunc dimittis . . .* suffer thy servant to depart in peace."

CHAPTER ELEVEN: Jupiter V

. . . the social and economic rewards for such scientific activities do not primarily accrue to the scientist or to the intellectual. Still, that has perhaps been his own moral speciation, a choice of one properly humane activity: to have knowledge of things, not to have things. If he loves and has knowledge, all is well.

—WESTON LA BARRE

"And so, that's the story," Helmuth said.

Eva remained silent in her chair for a long time.

"One thing I don't understand," she said at last. "Why did you come to me? I'd have thought that you'd find the whole thing terrifying."

"Oh, it's terrifying, all right," Helmuth said, with quiet exultation. "But terror and fright are two different things as I've just discovered. We were both wrong, Evita. I was wrong in thinking that the Bridge was a dead end. You were wrong in thinking of it as an end in itself."

"I don't understand you."

"I didn't understand myself. My fears of working in person on the Bridge were irrational; they came from dreams. That should have tipped me off right away. There was really never any chance of anyone's working in person on Jupiter; but I *wanted to*. It was a death wish, and it came directly out of the goddamned conditioning. I knew, we all knew, that the Bridge couldn't stand forever, but we were conditioned to believe that it had to. Nothing else could justify the awful ordeal of keeping it going even one day. The result: the classical dilemma that leads to madness. It affected you, too, and your response was just as insane as mine: you wanted to have a child here.

"Now all that's changed. The work the Bridge was doing was worth while after all. I was wrong in calling it a bridge to nowhere. And Eva, you no more saw where it was going than I did, or you'd never have made it the be-all and end-all of your existence.

"Now, there's a place to go to. In fact, there are places—hundreds of places. They'll be Earthlike places. Since the Soviets are about to win the Earth, those places will be more Earthlike than Earth itself, at least for the next century or so!"

She said: "Why are you telling me this? Just to make peace between us?"

"I'm going to take on this job, Evita . . . if you'll go along."

She turned swiftly, rising out of the chair with a marvelous fluidity of motion. At the same instant, all the alarm bells in the station went off at once, filling every metal cranny with a jangle of pure horror.

"*Posts!*" the loudspeaker above Eva's bed roared, in a distorted, gigantic caricature of Charity Dillon's voice. "*Peak storm overload! The STD is now passing the Spot. Wind velocity has already topped all*

*previous records, and part of the land mass has begun
to settle. This is an A-1 overload emergency."*

Behind Charity's bellow, they could hear what he
was hearing, the winds of Jupiter, a spectrum of
continuous, insane shrieking. The Bridge was responding with monstrous groans of agony. There was
another sound, too, an almost musical cacophony of
sharp, percussive tones, such as a dinosaur might
make pushing its way through a forest of huge steel
tuning-forks. Helmuth had never heard the sound
before, but he knew what it was.

The deck of the Bridge was splitting up the middle.

After a moment more, the uproar dimmed, and
the speaker said, in Charity's normal voice: "Eva,
you too, please. Acknowledge, please. This is it—
unless everybody comes on duty at once, the Bridge
may go down within the next hour."

"Let it," Eva responded quietly.

There was a brief, startled silence, and then a
ghost of a human sound. The voice was Senator
Wagoner's, and the sound just might have been a
chuckle.

Charity's circuit clicked out.

The mighty death of the Bridge continued to re-
sound in the little room.

After a while, the man and the woman went to the
window, and looked past the discarded bulk of Jupiter
at the near horizon, where there had always been
visible a few stars.

CODA: Brookhaven National Laboratories
(the pile-dump)

*But I say unto you, Love your enemies, bless them
that curse you, do good to them that hate you, and
pray for them which despitefully use you, and perse-
cute you; That ye may be the children of your Father
which is in heaven: for he maketh his sun to rise on*

the evil and on the good, and sendeth rain on the just and on the unjust. For if ye love them which love you, what reward have ye? do not even the publicans the same? And if ye salute your brethren only, what do ye more? do not even the publicans so?

"Every end," Wagoner wrote on the wall of his cell on the last day, "is a new beginning. Perhaps in a thousand years my Earthmen will come home again. Or in two thousand, or four, if they still remember home then. They'll come back, yes; but I hope they won't stay. I pray they will not stay."

He looked at what he had written and thought of signing his name. While he debated that, he made the mark for the last day on his calendar, and the point on his stub of pencil struck stone under the calcimine and snapped, leaving nothing behind it but a little coronet of frayed, dirty blond wood. He could wear that away against the window-ledge, at least enough to expose a little graphite, but instead he dropped the stub in the waste can.

There was writing enough in the stars that he could see, because he had written it there. There was a constellation called Wagoner, and every star in the sky belonged to it. That was surely enough.

Later that day, a man named MacHinery said: "Bliss Wagoner is dead."

As usual, MacHinery was wrong.

A LIFE FOR
THE STARS

To L. Sprague DeCamp

CHAPTER ONE: Press Gang

From the embankment of the long-abandoned Erie-Lackawanna-Pennsylvania Railroad, Chris sat silently watching the city of Scranton, Pennsylvania, preparing to take off, and sucked meditatively upon the red and white clover around him.

It was a first time for each of them. Chris had known since he had been a boy—he was sixteen now—that the cities were deserting the Earth, but he had never seen one in flight. Few people had, for the nomad cities, once gone, were gone for good.

Nor was it a very happy occasion, interesting though it was. Scranton was the only city Chris had ever seen, let alone visited, and the only one he was ever likely to see. It represented what small livelihood his father and his older brother had been able to scratch out of this valley; it was where the money was made, and where it was spent, somehow always managing to go out faster than it came in.

Scranton had become steadily greedier as the money to be made dwindled, but somehow never greedy enough. Now, as it had for so many other towns, the hour of the city's desperation had struck. It was going into space, to become a migrant worker among the stars.

The valley sweltered in the mercilessly hot July sunlight, and the smoke from the plant chimneys rose straight up. There were only a few smokestacks going, though, and those would be shut down shortly, until the city should find another planet on which to work. Nothing would be allowed to smoke in the confined air of a star-cruising vessel, even as big a one as a city—not so much as a cigarette.

Down at the bottom of the railroad embankment, where the tar-paper shacks huddled, a red-necked man in an undershirt and levis scratched at a kitchen garden with a hoe. Chris wondered if he knew what was about to happen. Certainly he was paying no attention; maybe he just didn't care. Chris's own father had reached the gloomy state of mind long ago. But all the same, it was odd that there were no sight-seers other than Chris himself.

A circular belt of cleared land, nothing but raw, red, dry earth, ran around the city, separating it from the shacks, from the battered and flaking sub-urbs, and from all the rest of the world. Inside it, the city looked the same as always, even to the yellow and orange glare of the slag heaps. Scranton was going to leave half its homes behind, but it was taking the slag heaps along; they were part of its stock in trade. Somewhere, out among the stars, there would be a frontier planet with iron ore to process; somewhere else, a planet with a use for slag, or something that might be extracted from slag—a use still beyond speculation, but not to be foreclosed by shortsightedness. People, on the other hand, were largely useless; weight for weight, the slag would be worth more.

At least, that was the hope. What was certain was that there was no more iron ore on Earth worth processing. The voracious Second Millennium—the books called it the "Age of Waste"—had used it all up, except for such artificial mines as used-car dumps and other deposits of scrap and rust. There was still native iron on Mars, of course, but none of that was available for Scranton. Pittsburgh was already on Mars, as well equipped with guns as with blast furnaces. Besides Mars was too small a planet to support more than one steel town, not because the red world was short of iron, but because it was short of oxygen, which was also essential for the making of steel.

Any work Scranton might find to do now would have to lie beyond the reaches of the solar system. There was no iron on Venus or Mercury that a steel town could afford to process—and no iron at all on the other six planets, the five gas giants and the remote ice ball that was Pluto.

The man in the kitchen garden straightened, leaned his hoe against the back of his shack, and went inside. Now the valley outside the raw-earth circle looked deserted indeed, and it suddenly occurred to Chris that this might be more than an appearance. Was there something dangerous about being too close to a city under a spindizzy field? Were he and the lone gardener being foolhardy?

At the moment, the whole world was silent except for the distant grumbling of Scranton itself. He knew he had nothing to fear from the rail bed behind him, for the tracks had been torn up long ago to feed the furnaces. There was a legend in the valley that on quiet nights one could still hear the Phoebe Snow going by, but Chris scoffed at such fairy tales. (Besides, his father had told him, that had been a daytime train.) Even the ties were gone, burned as firewood by the shack dwellers through generations of harsh Pennsylvania winters.

He racked his memory for what little he knew about the behavior of spindizzies, but could come up with nothing but that they were machines and that they lifted things. Though his schooling had been poor and spasmodic, he was a compulsive reader, devouring even the labels on cans if there was nothing else available; but the physics of interstellar flight is an impossible discipline to grasp even for an advanced student without a first-rate teacher to help, and the closest Chris had even come to a good teacher was Scranton's public librarian. She had tried hard; but she did not know the subject.

As a result, Chris stayed where he was. He would probably have done so even had he known positively that there was some danger; for in the valley, anything new was a change—even the fact, disastrous though it was, that Scranton was about to go as permanently out of his life and world as Betelgeuse. His own life thus far had held little but squirrel trapping; stealing eggs from neighbors as badly off as his own family; hunting scrap to sell to the mills; helping Bob nurse their father through repeated bouts of an illness which, but for the fact that there was no one in thirty-second-century America to diagnose it, would have been recognized as the ancient African scourge of *kwashiorkor* or malignant malnutrition; keeping the little girls out of the berry patch; fishing for fingerlings; and watching the rockets of the rich howl remotely through the highest reaches of the indifferent sky.

He had often thought of leaving, though he had no trade to practice and knew of no place in the world where his considerable but utterly untrained brute strength could be sold at any price. But there was loyalty and love in the motherless family, and it had often before sustained them when there had been nothing to eat but fried dough and green tomatoes, and no warmth against the Christmas snows but huddling with the little kids under a heap of the old rags that were their clothes; and in the end, Chris stuck by it as stubbornly and devotedly as Bob always had. In all the depopulated Earth there was no place to which he owed more loyalty, and no place which could offer him more in return—the worst possible substratum for dreams of escape, even for a temperament as naturally sunny and sanguine as Chris's. In a world where a Ph.D. in economics could find no one to teach, nor use his knowledge of how the economy wagged to find any other niche in it—a world in which a thousand penny-ante jobs left him no time even to tend his wife's grave, yet all the same paid him less and less every year—what hope could his boys reasonably cherish for any better future? The answer, alas, was all too obvious; and for the little girls, the foreseeable future was even more grim.

The nomad cities offered no better way of escape. More often than not, Chris had read, star roving was simply another form of starvation, without even the company of a blue sky, a scrub forest or a patch of ground to grow turnips in. Otherwise, why did almost every city which had ever left the Earth fail to come back home? Pittsburgh had made its fortune on Mars, to be sure—but it was a poor sort of fortune that kept you sitting in a city all your life, with nothing to see beyond the city limits but an ochre desert, a desert with no air you could breathe, a desert that would freeze you solid only a few minutes after the tiny sun went down. Sooner or later, too, his father said, Pittsburgh would have to leave the solar system as all the other cities had—not, this time, because it had exhausted the iron and the oxygen, but because there would be too few people left on the Earth to buy steel. There were already too few to justify Pittsburgh's coming back to the once-golden triangle of rivers it had abandoned thirty years ago; Pittsburgh had wealth, but was finding it increasingly hard to spend on the Earth, even for necessities. The nomad cities seemed, like everything else, to be a dead end.

Nevertheless Chris sat on the embankment and watched, for only a single, simple reason: Something was going on. If he envied the city its decision to leave the valley, he was unaware of it. He was there simply to see something happen, for a change.

A brief rustle of shrubbery behind him made him turn. A dog's head peered across the roadbed at him from the foot of the mountainside, surrounded incongruously by the trumpets of tiger lilies; it looked a little as if it were being served up on a platter. Chris grinned.

"Hello, Kelly. Look out for bees."

The dog whuffed and came trotting to him, looking foolishly proud of itself—as it probably was, for Kelly was usually not very good at finding anything, even his own way home. Bob, whose dog Kelly officially was, said that Kelly was a combination of Kerry blue and collie—hence the name—but Chris had never seen a pure sample of either breed, and Kelly did not look anything like the pictures of either. He looked, in point of fact, like a shaggy mutt, which was fortunate for him, since that was what he was.

"What do you make of it, handsome? Think they'll ever get that thing off the ground?"

Kelly gave an imitation of a dog trying to think, registered pain, wagged his tail twice, woofed at a butterfly and sat down, panting. It had obviously always been his impression that he belonged to Chris, an impression Bob had wisely never tried to discourage. Explaining something that abstract to Kelly was

(a) a long and complicated task, and (b) utterly hopeless anyhow. Kelly earned his own keep—he caught rabbits—which made up for the nuisance he was when he caught a porcupine; so nobody in the family but Chris much cared whom he thought he belonged to.

There was at last some activity around the parching city. Small groups of men, made so tiny by distance that they were almost invisible except for their bright yellow steel workers' helmets, were patrolling the bare perimeter. There was probably a law about that, Chris reflected. Equally probably it would be the last Earth law Scranton would ever be *obliged* to observe—no matter how many of them the city fathers took into space of their own free will. No doubt the patrol was looking for rubbernecks who might be standing too close for safety.

He imagined it so vividly that for a moment he had the illusion of hearing their voices. Then he realized with a start that it was not an illusion. A flash of yellow hard hat revealed another group of patrollers working their way through the shacks at the foot of the embankment and coming in his direction.

With the ingrained prudence of the lifelong poacher, he took at once to the bushes on the other side of the roadbed. Not only would he be invisible from there, but, of course, he could no longer see the patrol; however, he could still hear it.

". . . anybody in these shacks. Ask me, it's a waste of time."

"The boss says look, so we look, that's all. Myself, I think we'd make out better in Nixonville."

"Them tramps? They can smell work ten miles away. People on this side of town, they used to *look* for work. Not that there ever was any."

Chris cautiously parted the shrubbery and peered

out. The gang was still out of sight, but there was another group coming toward him from the other direction, walking along the old roadbed. He let the bushes swing closed hastily, wishing that he had retreated farther up the mountainside. It was too late for that now, though. The new patrol was close enough to hear the brush rustle, and would probably see him too if he was in motion.

Down in the valley there was a sudden, slight hum, like bee-buzz, but infinitely gentler, and deeper in tone. Chris had never heard anything exactly like it before, but there could be no doubt in his mind about what it was: Scranton's spindizzies were being tuned. Was he going to have to hide right through the take-off, and miss seeing it? But surely the city wouldn't leave until its patrols were back on board!

The voices came closer, and beside him Kelly growled softly. The boy grasped the dog firmly by the scruff and shook him gently, not daring to speak. Kelly shut up, but all his muscles were tensed.

"Hey! Look what we got here!"

Chris froze as completely as a rabbit smelling fox; but another voice struck in at once.

"You guys get outa here. This here's my place. You got no business with me."

"Yeah? You didn't hear anything about getting out of the valley by noon today? There's a poster on your own front door that says so. Can't read, huh, Jack?"

"I don't do everything any piece of paper says. I live here, see? It's a lousy dump, but it's mine, and I'm staying, that's all. Now blow, will you?"

"Well, now, I don't know if that's all, Jack. It's the law that you're supposed to be vacated. *We* don't want your shack, but it's the law, see?"

"It's the law that I got a right to my own property, too."

A new voice chimed in from the embankment, not fifteen feet from where Chris and Kelly crouched. "Trouble down there, Barney?"

"Squatter. Won't move. Says he owns the place."

"That's a laugh. Get him to show you his deed."

"Ah, why bother with that? We ain't got the time. Let's impress him and get moving."

"No you don't—"

There was the meaty sound of a blow landing, and a grunt of surprise. "Hey, he wants to play rough! All right, mister—"

More impacts, and then the sound of something smashing—glass or crockery, Chris guessed, but it might have been furniture. Before Chris could do more than grab at him convulsively, Kelly burst into a volley of high, howling yelps, broke free, crashed out of the bushes and went charging across the embankment toward the fracas.

"Look out! Hey—Where'd that mutt come from?"

"Out of the bushes there. Somebody's in there still. Red hair, I can see it. All right, Red, out in the open—on the double!"

Chris rose slowly, ready to run or fight at the drop of a hard hat. Kelly, on the far side of the embankment, gave up his idiot barking for a moment, his attention divided between the struggle in the shack and the group now surrounding Chris.

"Well, Red, you're a husky customer. I suppose you didn't hear about any vacate order, either."

"No, I didn't," Chris said defiantly. "I live in Lakebranch. I only came over to watch."

"Lakebranch?" the leader said, looking at another of his leathery-faced patrolmates.

"Hick town, way out back some place. Used to be a resort. Nothing out there now but poachers and scratchers."

"That's nice," the other man said, tipping back his

yellow helmet and grinning. "Nobody'll miss you, I guess, Red. Come along."

"What do you mean, come along?" Chris said, his fists clenching. "I have to be home by five."

"Watch it—the kid's got some beef on him."

The other man, now clearly in charge, laughed scornfully. "You scared? He's a kid, isn't he? Come on, Red, I got no time to argue. You're here past noon, we got a legal right to impress you."

"I told you, I'm due home."

"You should have thought of that before you came here. Move along. You give us a hard time, we give you one, get it?"

Below, three men came out of the shack, holding hard to the gardener Chris had seen earlier. All looked considerably battered, but the sullen redneck was secured all the same.

"We got this one—no thanks to you guys. Thought you was going to be right down. Big help you was!"

"Got another one, Barney. Let's go, Red."

The press-gang leader took Chris by the elbow. He was not unnecessarily violent about it, but the movement was sudden enough to settle matters in Kelly's slow brain. Kelly was unusually stupid, even for a dog, but he now knew which fight interested him most. With a snarl which made even Chris's hackles rise—he had never in his life before heard a dog make such a noise, let alone Kelly—the animal streaked back across the embankment and leaped for the big man's legs.

In the next thirty seconds of confusion Chris might easily have gotten away—there were a hundred paths through the undergrowth that he might have taken that these steel puddlers would have found it impossible to follow—but he couldn't abandon Kelly. And with an instinct a hundred thousand years old, the patrol fell on the animal enemy first, turning their backs on the boy without even stopping to think.

Chris was anything but a trained in-fighter, but he had instincts of his own. The man with Kelly's teeth in him was obviously busy enough. Chris lobbed a knob-kerrie fist at the man next to him. When the target looked stunned but failed to fall, Chris threw the other fist. It didn't land where Chris had meant it to land, exactly, but the man staggered away anyhow, which was good enough. Then Chris was in the middle of the melee and no longer had any chance even to try to call his shots.

After a while, he was on the broken granite of the old roadbed, and no longer cared about Scranton, Kelly or even himself. His head was ringing. Over him, considerable swearing was going on.

"—more trouble than he's worth. Give him a shoe in the head and let's get back!"

"No. No killing. We can impress 'em, but we can't bump 'em off. One of you guys see if you can slap Huggins awake."

"What are you—chicken all of a sudden?"

The press-gang leader was breathing hard, and as Chris's sight cleared, he saw that the big man was sitting on the ground wrapping a bloody leg in a length of torn shirt. Nevertheless he said evenly: "You want to kill a kid because he gave you a fight? That's the lousiest excuse for killing a man I ever heard, let alone a kid. You give me any more of that, I'll take a poke at you myself."

"Ah, shaddup, will you?" the other voice said surlily. "Anyhow we got the dog—"

"You loud-mouthed—*look out!*"

Two men grabbed Chris, one from each side, as he surged to his feet. He struggled fiercely, but all the fight left in him was in his soul, not any in his muscles.

"What a bunch of flap-jaws. No wonder you can't hold your own with a kid. Huggins, put your hat on. Red, don't you listen to that slob, he's been all mouth all his life. Your dog ran away, that's all."

The lie was kindly meant, no matter how clumsy it was, but it was useless. Chris could see Kelly, not far away. Kelly had done the best he could; he would never have another chance.

The youngster the press-gang dragged stumbling toward Scranton had a heart made of stone.

CHAPTER TWO: A Line of Boiling Dust

The city inside the perimeter of raw earth was wavery and unreal. It did not hum any more, but it gave a puzzling impression of being slightly in shadow, though the July sun was still blazing over it. Even in his grief and anger, Chris was curious enough to wonder at the effect, and finally he thought he saw what caused it: The heat waves climbing the air around the town seemed to be detouring it, as though the city itself were inside a dome. No, not a dome, but a bubble, only a part of which was underground; it met the earth precisely at the cleared perimeter.

The spindizzy field was up. It was invisible in itself, but it was no longer admitting the air of the Earth.

Scranton was ready.

Thanks to the scrapping, the patrol was far behind schedule; the leader drove them all through the scabrous, deserted suburbs without any mercy for his own torn leg. Chris grimly enjoyed watching him wince at every other step, but the man did not allow the wound to hold him up, nor did he let any of the lesser bruises and black eyes in the party serve as excuses for foot dragging.

There was no way to tell, by the normal human senses, when the party passed through the spindizzy screen. Midway across the perimeter, which was a good five hundred feet wide, the leader unshipped from his belt a device about as big as an avocado, turned it in his hands until it whined urgently, and then directed the group on ahead of him in single file, along a line which he traced in the dry red ground with the toe of his boot.

As his two guards left his side, Chris crouched instinctively. He was not afraid of them, and the leader apparently was going to stay behind. But the big man saw the slight motion.

"Red, I wouldn't if I were you," he said quietly. "If you try to run back this way after I turn off this gadget—or if you try to go around me—you'll go straight up in the air. Look back and see the dust rising. You're a lot heavier than a dust speck, and you'll go up a lot farther. Better relax. Take it from me."

Chris looked again at the dubious boundary line he had just crossed. Sure enough, there was a hair-thin ruling there, curving away to both sides as far as he could see, where the inert friable earth seemed to be turning over restlessly. It was as though he were standing inside a huge circle of boiling dust.

"That's right, that's what I meant. Now look here." The press-gang leader bent and picked up a stone just about as big as his fist—which was extraordinarily big—and shied it back the way they had come. As the rock started to cross the line above the seething dust, it leaped skyward with an audible screech, like a bullet ricocheting. In less than a second, Chris had lost sight of it.

"Fast, huh? And it'd throw you much farther, Red. In a few minutes, it'll be lifting a whole city. So don't go by how things look. Right where you stand, you're not even on the Earth any more."

Chris looked at the mountains for a moment, and then back at the line of boiling dust. Then he turned away and resumed marching toward Scranton.

And yet they were now on a street Chris had traveled a score of times before, carrying fifty cents for the Sunday paper's Help Wanted ads, or rolling a wheel-barrow not quite full of rusty scrap, or bringing back a flat package of low-grade ground horsemeat. The difference lay only in the fact that just beyond the familiar corner the city stopped, giving place to the new desert of the perimeter—and all in the overarching shadow which was not a shadow at all.

The patrol leader stopped and looked back. "We'll never make it from here," he said finally. "Take cover. Barney, watch that red-neck. I'll take the kid with me; he looks sensible."

Barney started to answer, but his reply was drowned out by a prolonged fifty-decibel honking which made the very walls howl back. The noise was horrifying; Chris had never before heard anything even a fraction so loud, and it seemed to go on forever. The press-gang boss herded him into a doorway.

"There's the alert. Duck, you guys. Stand still, Red. There's probably no danger—we just don't know. But something might just shake down and fall—so keep your head in."

The honking stopped; but in its place Chris could again hear the humming, now so pervasive that it made his teeth itch in their sockets. The shadow deepened, and out in the bare belt of earth the seething dust began to leap into the air in feathery plumes almost as tall as ferns.

Then the doorway lurched and went askew. Chris grabbed for the frame; and just in time, for a second later, the door jerked the other way; and then, back again. Gradually, the quakes became periodic, spacing themselves farther apart in time, and slowly weakening in violence.

After the first quake, however, Chris's alarm began to dwindle into amazement, for the movements of the ground were puny compared to what was going on before his eyes. The whole city seemed to be rocking heavily, like a ship in a storm. At one instant, the street ended in nothing but sky; at the next, Chris was staring at a wall of sheared earth, its rim looming clifflike, fifty feet or more above the new margin of the city; and then the blank sky was back again—

These huge pitching movements should have brought the whole city down in a roaring avalanche of steel and stone. Instead, only these vague twitchings and shudderings of the ground came through, and even those seemed to be fading away. Now the city was level again, amidst an immense cloud of dust, through which Chris could see the landscape begin to move solemnly past him. The city had stopped rocking, and was now turning slowly. There was no longer even the slightest sensation of movement; the illusion that it was the valley that was revolving around the city was irresistible and more than a little dizzying.

I can see where the spindizzy got its name, Chris thought. *Wonder if we go around like a top all the time we're in space? How'll we see where we're going, then?*

But now the high rim of the valley was sinking. In a breath, the distant roadbed of the railroad embankment was level with the end of the street; then the lip of the street was at the brow of the mountain; then with the treetops . . . and then there was nothing but blue sky, becoming rapidly darker.

The big press-gang leader released an explosive sigh. "By thunder," he said, "we got her up." He seemed a little dazed. "I guess I never really believed it till now."

"Not so sure I believe it yet," the man called Barney said. "But I don't see any cornices falling—we don't have to hang around here any longer. The boss'll have our necks for being even this late."

"Yeah, let's move. Red, use your head and don't give us any more trouble, huh? You can see for yourself, there's no place to run to now."

There was no doubt about that. The sky at the end of the street, and overhead too, was now totally black; and even as Chris looked up, the stars became visible—at first only a few of the brightest, but the others came out steadily in their glorious hundreds. From their familiar fixity Chris could also deduce that the city was no longer rotating on its axis, which was vaguely reassuring, somehow. Even the humming had faded away again; if it was still present, it was now inaudible in the general noise of the city.

Oddly, the sunlight was still as intense as ever. From now on, "day" and "night" would be wholly arbitrary terms aboard the city; Scranton had emerged into the realm of Eternal Daylight-Saving Time.

The party walked two blocks and then stopped while the big man located a cab post and pulled the phone from it. Barney objected at once.

"It'll take a fleet of cabs to get us all to the Hall," he complained. "And we can't get enough guys into a hack to handle a prisoner, if he gets rough."

"The kid won't get rough. Go ahead and march your man over. I'm not going to walk another foot on this leg."

Barney hesitated, but obviously the big man's marked limp was an unanswerable argument. Finally he shrugged and herded the rest of his party around the corner. His boss grinned at Chris; but the boy looked away.

The cab came floating down out of the sky at the

intersection and maneuvered itself to rest at the curb next to them with a finicky precision. There was, of course, nobody in it; like everything else in the world requiring an I.Q. of less than 150, it was computer-controlled. The world-wide dominance of such machines, Chris's father had often said, had been one of the chief contributors to the present and apparently permanent depression: the coming of semi-intelligent machines into business and technology had created a second Industrial Revolution, in which only the most highly creative human beings, and those most gifted at administration, found themselves with any skills to sell which were worth the world's money to buy.

Chris studied the cab with the liveliest interest, for though he had often seen them before from a distance, he had of course never ridden in one. But there was very little to see. The cab was an egg-shaped bubble of light metals and plastics, painted with large red-and-white checkers, with a row of windows running all around it. Inside, there were two seats for four people, a speaker grille, and that was all; no controls, and no instruments. There was not even any visible place for the passenger to deposit his fare.

The big press-gang leader gestured Chris into the front seat, and himself climbed into the back. The doors slid shut simultaneously from the ceiling and floor, rather like a mouth closing, and the cab lifted gently until it hovered about six feet above street level.

"Destination?" the Tin Cabby said cheerily, making Chris jump.

"City Hall."

"Social Security number?"

"One five six one one dash zero nine seven five dash zero six nine eight two one seven."

"Thank you."

"Shaddup."

"You're welcome, sir."

The cab lifted vertically, and the gang captain settled back into his seat. He seemed content for the moment to allow Chris to sight-see out the windows at the passing stubby towers of the flying city; he looked relaxed and a little indulgent, but a little wary, too. Finally he said: "I need to dutch-uncle you a little, Red. I didn't call a cab because of the leg—I've walked farther on worse. Feel up to listening?"

Chris felt himself freezing. Distracted though he was by all this enormous budget of new experience and the vast reaches of the unknown which stretched before him, the press-gang leader's remark reminded him instantly of Kelly, and as instantly made him ashamed that he had forgotten. In the same rush of anger he remembered that he had been kidnapped, and that now there was no one left to take care of his father and the little kids but Bob. That had been hard enough to do when there had been two of them. It was bad enough that he would never see Annie and Kate and Bob and his father again, but far worse that they should be deprived of his hands and his back and his love; and worst of all, they would never know what had happened.

The little girls would only think that he and Kelly had run away, and wonder why, and mourn a little until they forgot about it. But Bob and his father might well think that he'd deserted them . . . most likely of all, that he had gone off with Scranton on his own hook, leaving them all to scrounge for themselves.

There was a well-known ugly term for that among the peasantry of the Earth, expressing all the contempt it felt for any man who abandoned his land, no matter how unrewarding it was, to tread the alien streets and star lanes of a nomad city: it was called, "going Okie."

Chris had gone Okie. He had not done it of his own free will, but his father and Bob and the little girls would never know that. For that matter, it would never have happened had it not been for his own useless curiosity; and neither would the death of poor Kelly, who, Chris now remembered too, had been Bob's dog.

The big man in the hard hat saw his expression close down, and made an impatient gesture. "Listen, Red, I know what you're thinking. What good would it do now if I said I was sorry? What's done is done; you're on board, and you're going to stay on board. We didn't put the snatch on you either. If you didn't know about the impressment laws, you've got your own ignorance to blame."

"You killed my brother's dog."

"No, I didn't. I've got a bad rip or two under that rag to prove I had reasons to kill him; but I wasn't the guy who did it, and I couldn't have done it, either. But that's done too, and can't be undone. Right now I'm trying to help you, and I've got about three minutes left to do it in, so if you don't shut up and listen it'll be too late. You *need* help, Red; can't you understand that?"

"Why do you bother?" Chris said bitterly.

"Because you're a bright kid and a fighter, and I like that. But that's not going to be enough aboard an Okie city, believe me. You're in a situation now that's totally new to you, and if you've got any skills you can make a career on here, I'll be darned surprised, I can tell you that. And Scranton isn't going to start educating you this far along in your life. Are you smart enough to take some advice, or aren't you? If you aren't, there's no sense in my bothering. You've got about a minute left to think it over."

What the big man said made a bitter dose to have to swallow, but it did seem to make sense. And it did seem likely, too, that the man's intentions were good—

otherwise, why would he be taking the trouble? Nevertheless Chris's emotions were in too much of a turmoil for him to trust himself to speak; instead, he merely nodded mutely.

"Good for you. First of all, I'm taking you to see the boss—not the mayor, he doesn't count for much, but Frank Lutz, the city manager. One of the things he'll ask you is what you do, or what you know about. Between now and when we get there, you ought to be thinking up an answer. I don't care what you tell him, but tell him *something*. And it had better be the thing you know the most about, because he'll ask you questions."

"I don't know anything—except gardening, and hunting," Chris said grimly.

"No, no, that's not what I mean! Don't you have any book subjects? Something that might be useful in space? If you don't, he'll put you to work pitching slag—and you won't have much of a lifetime as an Okie."

The cab slowed, and then began to settle.

"And if he doesn't seem interested in what you tell him, *don't* try to satisfy him by switching to something else. No true specialist really knows more than one subject, especially at your age. Stick to the one you picked and try to make it sound useful. Understand?"

"Yes, but—"

"No time left for 'buts.' One other thing: If you ever get into a jam on board this burg, you'll need to know somebody to turn to, and it'd better not be Frank Lutz. My name is Frad Haskins—not Fred but Frad, F-R-A-D."

The cab hovered for a moment, and then its hull grated against the cobblestones and the doors slid open. Chris was thinking so hard and in so many directions that for a long moment he did not understand what the press-gang chief was trying to convey by introducing himself. Then the realization hit home, and Chris was struggling unsuccessfully to blurt out his thanks and give his own name at the same time.

"Destination, gentlemen," the Tin Cabby said primly.

"Shaddup. Come along, Red."

Frank Lutz, the city manager of Scranton-in-flight, reminded Chris instantly of a skunk—but by this Chris meant not at all what a city boy would have meant by a skunk. Lutz was small, sleek, handsome, and plump, and even sitting behind his desk, he gave an appearance of slight clumsiness. As he listened to Haskins' account of the two impressments, even his expression had something of the nearsighted amiability of the woods pussy; but as Haskins finished, the city manager looked up suddenly—and Chris knew, if he had ever been in any doubt about it before, that this animal was also dangerous . . . and never more so than when it seemed to be turning its back.

"That impressment law was a nuisance. But I suppose we'll have to make a show of maintaining our pickups until we get to some part of space where the police aren't so thick."

"We've got no drug for them, that's for sure," Haskins agreed obscurely.

"That's not a public subject," Lutz said, with such deadly coldness that Chris was instantly convinced that the slip, whatever its meaning, had been intended by Haskins for his own ears. The big man was a lot more devious than his size or his bluffness suggested. That much was becoming clearer every minute. "As for these samples, I don't suppose they can do anything. They never can."

The deceptively mild hazel eyes, watery and inoffensive, swung suddenly to bear on the red-neck. "What's your name?"

"Who wants to know? That's what I want to know. You got no right—"

"Don't buck me, bum, I haven't got the time. So you've got no name. Have you a trade?"

"I'm no bum, 'm a puddler," the red-neck said indignantly. "A *steel* puddler."

"Same thing. Anything else?"

"I been a puddler twenty years. 'M a Master Puddler, fair an' square. I got seniority, see? I don' need to be anything else, see? I got a trade. Nobody knows it like I do."

"Been working lately?" the city manager said quietly.

"No. But I got seniority. And a card. 'M no bum, 'm a craftsman, see?"

"If you were a Genius Puddler I couldn't use you, buddy . . . not even if, as and when we ever see any steel again. This is a Bessemer-process town, and it was one even back when you were an apprentice. You didn't notice? Tough. Barney, Huggins, this one's for the slag heaps."

This order was not executed without a good deal of renewed shouting and struggling, during which Lutz looked back down at his papers, as obviously harmless a critter as a skunk which had just happened upon a bird's egg and was wondering if it might bite, his small hands moving tentatively. When the noise was over, he said: "I hope your luck was better, Frad. How about it, sonny? Have you got a trade?"

"Yes," Chris said instantly. "Astronomy."

"What? At your age?" The city manager stared at Haskins. "What's this, Frad—another one of your mercy projects? Your judgment gets worse every day."

"It's all news to me, boss," Haskins said with complete and obvious honesty. "I thought he was just a scratcher. He never said anything else to me."

The city manager drummed delicately on the top

of his desk. Chris held his breath. His claim was ridiculous and he knew it, but he had been able to think of nothing else to answer which would have had a prayer of interesting the boss of a nomad city. Insofar as he had been able to stay awake past dusk, Chris had read a little of everything, and of his reading he had retained best the facts and theories of history; but Haskins had cautioned him to espouse something which might be useful aboard an Okie city, and plainly it didn't qualify. The fragments of economics he had picked up from his father might possibly have been more useful had there been more of them, and those better integrated into *recent* history, but his father had never been well enough to do that job since Chris had reached the age of curiosity. He was left with nothing but his smattering of astronomy, derived from books, most of which had been published before he was born, and from many nights spent lying on his back in the fields, breathing clover and counting meteors.

But he had no hope that it would work. A nomad city would need astronomy for navigation, primarily, a subject about which he knew nothing—indeed he lacked even the rudimentary trigonometry necessary to approach it. His knowledge of the parent subject, astronomy, was purely descriptive, and would become obsolete the minute Scranton was far enough away from the Sun to make the constellations hard to recognize—which in fact had probably happened already.

Nevertheless, Frank Lutz seemed to be a little bit baffled, for the first time. He said slowly:

"A Lakebranch kid who claims he's an astronomer! Well, at least it's new. Frad, you've let the kid sell you a hobby. If he ever got through grammar school I'll eat your tin hat, paint and all."

"Boss, I swear I never heard a word of all this until now."

"Hmm. All right, sonny. Name the planets, going outward from the Sun."

That was easy, but the next ones would surely be harder. "Mercury, Venus, Earth, Mars, Jupiter, Saturn, Uranus, Neptune, Pluto, Proserpina."

"You left out a few didn't you?"

"I left out about five thousand," Chris said, as steadily as he could manage. "You said planets—not asteroids or satellites."

"All right, what's the biggest satellite? And the biggest asteroid?"

"Titan, and Ceres."

"What's the nearest fixed star?"

"The Sun."

The city manager grinned, but he did not seem to be much amused. "Oho. Well, it won't be, not much longer. How many months in a light-year?"

"Twelve, just like any other year. A light-year isn't a measure of time, it's a measure of distance—the distance light travels in a year. Months don't have anything to do with it. You might as well ask how many weeks there are in an inch."

"There are fifty-two weeks to the inch—or it'll seem like that, once you're as old as I am." Lutz drummed on the desk again. "Where'd you get all this stuff? You won't pretend you had any schooling in Lakebranch, I hope?"

"My father taught almost all his life at the University, till it was shut down," Chris said. "He was the best there was. I got most of it from him. The rest I read about, or got from observation, and paper and pencil."

Here Chris was on firm ground, provided only that he be allowed one lie: the substitution of astronomy for economics. The next question did not bother him in the least, for it was thoroughly expectable:

"What's your name?"

"Crispin deFord," he said reluctantly.

There was a surprised guffaw from the remainder
of the audience, but Chris did his best to ignore it.
His ridiculous name had been a burden to him through
so many childhood fights with the neighbors that he
was now able to carry it with patience, though still
not very gladly. He was surprised, however, to see
Haskins raising his bushy bleached eyebrows at him
with every evidence of renewed interest. What that
meant, Chris had no idea; the part of his brain that
did his guessing was almost worn out already.

"Check that, somebody," the city manager said.
"We've got a couple of people left over from the
S.U. faculty, at least. By Hoffa, Boyle Warner was a
Scranton prof, wasn't he? Get him up here, and let's
close this thing out."

"What's the matter, boss?" Haskins said, with a
broad grin. "Running out of trick questions?"

The city manager smiled back, but again the smile
was more than a little frosty. "You could call it that,"
he said, with surprising frankness. "But we'll see if
the kid can fool Warner."

"The ole bassar must be good for something,"
somebody behind Chris mumbled. The voice was
quiet, but the city manager heard it; his chin jerked
up, and his fist struck a sudden, terrible blow on the
top of his desk.

"He's good for getting us where we're going, and
don't you forget it! Steel is one thing, but stars are
another—we may never see another lie or another
ingot without Boyle. Next to him we're *all* puddlers,
just like that red-neck. And that may go for the kid
here, too."

"Ah, boss, don't lay it on. What can *he* know?"

"That's what I'm trying to find out," Lutz said, in a
white fury. "What do you know about it? Anybody
here know what a geodesic is?"

Nobody answered.

"Red, do you know?"

Chris swallowed. He knew the answer, but he found it impossible to understand why the city manager considered it worth all this noise.

"Yes, sir. It's the shortest distance between two points."

"Is that all?" somebody said incredulously.

"It's all there is between us and starvation," Lutz said. "Frad, take the kid below and see what Boyle says about him; on second thought, I don't want to pull Boyle out of the observatory, he must be up to his eyebrows in course-corrections. Get to Boyle as soon as he's got some free time. Find out if there ever was any Professor deFord at S.U.; and then get Boyle to ask the kid some hard questions. *Real* hard. If he makes it, he can be an apprentice. If he doesn't, there are always the slag heaps; this has taken too long already."

CHAPTER THREE: "Like a Barrel of Scrap"

Even a city which has sloughed off its slums to go space flying has hidey holes, and Chris had lost no time in finding one of his own. He had located it with the simple instinct of a hunted animal going to ground.

Not that anybody was hunting for him—not yet. But something told him that it would be only a matter of time. Dr. Boyle Warner, the city's astronomer, had been more than kind to him, but he had asked hard questions all the same; and these had revealed quickly enough that Chris's knowledge of astronomy, while extraordinary in a youngster with no formal education worth mentioning, was too meager to be of any help to Dr. Warner or of any use to the city.

Dr. Warner signed him on as an apprentice anyhow, and so reported to the city manager's office, but not without carefully veiled misgivings, and an open warning:

"I can think of very little for you to do around the observatory that would be useful, Crispin, I'm sorry to say. If I so much as set you to work sweeping the place, one of Frank Lutz's henchmen would find out about it sooner or later; and Frank would point out quite legitimately that I don't need so big a fellow as you for so light a task as that. While you're with me, you'll have to appear to be studying all the time."

"I will be studying," Chris said. "That's just what I'd like."

"I appreciate that," Dr. Warner said sadly. "And I sympathize. But Crispin, it can't last forever. Neither I nor anyone else in Scranton can give you in two years the ten years of study that you've missed, let alone any part of what it took me thirty more years to absorb. I'll do my best, but that best can only be a pretense—and sooner or later they'll catch us at it."

After that, Chris already knew, would come the slag heaps—hence the hidey hole. He wondered if they would send Dr. Warner to the slag heaps too. It didn't seem very likely, for the frail, pot-bellied little astrophysicist could hardly last long at the wrong end of a shovel, and besides he was the only navigator the city had. Chris mentioned this guardedly to Frad Haskins.

"Don't you believe it," Frad said grimly. "The fact is that we've got no navigator at all. Expecting an astronomer to navigate is about like asking a chicken to fry an egg. Doc Warner ought to be a navigator's assistant himself, not a navigator-in-chief, and Frank Lutz knows it. If we ever run across another city with a spare *real* navigator to trade, Frank could send Boyle Warner to the slag heaps without blinking an eye. I don't say that he would, but he might."

It could hardly be argued that Haskins knew his boss, and after only one look of his own at Lutz, Chris was more than ready to agree. Officially, Chris continued to occupy the single tiny room at the university dormitory to which he had been assigned as Dr. Warner's apprentice, but he kept nothing there but the books that Dr. Warner lent him, the mathematical instruments from the same source, and the papers and charts that he was supposed to be working on; plus about a quarter of the rough clothing and the even rougher food which the city had issued him as soon as he had been given an official status. The other three-quarters of both went into the hole, for Chris had no intention of letting himself be caught at an official address when the henchmen of Frank Lutz finally came looking for him.

He studied as hard in the hole as he did in the dormitory and at the observatory, all the same. He was firmly determined that Dr. Warner should not suffer for his dangerous kindness if there was anything that Chris could possibly do to avoid it. Frad Haskins, though his visits were rare—he had no real business at the university—detected this almost at once; but he said only:

"I knew you were a fighter."

For almost a year Chris was quite certain that he was making progress. Thanks to his father, for example, he found it relatively easy to understand the economy of the city—probably better than most of its citizens did, and almost certainly better than either Frad Haskins or Dr. Warner. Once aloft, Scranton had adopted the standard economy of all tribes of highly isolated nomad herdsmen, to whom the only real form of wealth is grass: a commune, within which everyone helped himself to what he needed, subject only to the rules which established the status of his job in the community. If Frad Haskins needed to ride in a cab, for instance, he boarded it, and gave the Tin Cabby his social security number—but if, at the end of the fiscal year, his account showed more cab charges than was reasonable for his job, he would hear about it. And if he or anyone else took to hoarding physical goods—no matter whether they were loaves of bread or lock washers, they could not by definition be in anything but short supply on board an Okie city—he would do more than hear about it: The penalties for hoarding of any kind were immediate and drastic.

There was money aboard the city, but no ordinary citizen ever saw it or needed it. It was there to be used exclusively for foreign trade—that is, to bargain for grazing rights, or other privileges and supplies which the city did not and could not carry within the little universe bounded by its spindizzy field. The ancient herdsmen had accumulated gold and jewels for the same reason. Aboard Scranton, the equivalent metal was germanium, but there was actually very little of it in the city's vaults; since germanium had been the universal metal base for money throughout this part of the galaxy ever since space flight had become practical most of the city's currency was paper—the same "Oc dollar" everyone used in trading with the colonies.

All this was new to Chris in the specific situation in which he now found himself, but it was far from new to him in principle. As yet, however, he was too lowly an object in Scranton to be able to make use of his understanding; and remembering the penury into which his father had been driven, back on Earth, he was far from sure that he would ever have a use for it.

As the year passed, so also did the stars. The city manager, according to Haskins, had decided not to cruise anywhere inside "the local group"—an arbitrary sphere fifty light-years in diameter, with Sol at its center. The planetary systems of the local group had been heavily settled during the great colonial Exodus of 2375-2400, mostly by people from Earth's fallen Western culture who were fleeing the then world-wide Bureaucratic State. It was Lutz's guess—quickly confirmed by challenges received by Scranton's radio station—that the density of older Okie cities would be too high to let a newcomer into competition.

During this passage, Chris busied himself with trying to identify the stars involved by their spectra. This was the only possible way to do it under the circumstances, for of course their positions among the constellations changed rapidly as the city overtook them. So did the constellations themselves, although far more slowly.

It was hard work, and Chris was often far from sure his identifications were correct. All the same, it was impressive to know that those moving points of light all around him were the almost legendary stars of colonial times, and even more impressive to find that he had one of those storied suns in the small telescope. Their very names echoed with past adventure: Alpha Centauri, Wolf 359, RD-4°4048', Altair, 61 Cygni, Sirius, Kruger 60, Procyon, 40 Eridani. Only a very few of these, of course, lay anywhere near the city's direct line of flight—indeed, many of them were scattered "astern" (that is, under the keel of the city), in the imaginary hemisphere on the other side of his home Sun. But most of them were at least visible from here, and the rest could be photographed. The city, whatever Chris thought of it as a home, had to be given credit for being a first-class observatory platform.

How he saw the stars was another matter, and one that was a complete mystery to him. He knew that Scranton was now traveling at a velocity many times that of light, and it seemed to him that under these circumstances there should have been no stars at all still visible in the city's wake, and those to the side and even straight ahead should be suffering considerable distortion. Yet in fact he could see no essential change in the aspect of the skies. To understand how this could be so would require at least some notion of how the spindizzies worked, and on this theory Dr.

Warner's explanations were even more unclear than usual . . . so much so that Chris suspected him of not understanding it any too well himself.

Lacking the theory, Chris's only clue was that the stars from Scranton-in-flight looked to him much as they always had from a field in the Pennsylvania backwoods, where the surrounding Appalachians had screened him from the sky glare of Scranton-on-the-ground. From this he deducted that the spindizzy screen, though itself invisible, cut down the apparent brightness of the stars by about three magnitudes, as had the atmosphere of the Earth in the region where Chris had lived. Again he didn't know the reason why, but he could see that the effect had some advantages. For instance, it blanked out many of the fainter stars completely to the naked eye, thus greatly reducing the confusing multitudes of stars which would otherwise have been visible in space. Was that really an unavoidable effect of the spindizzy field—or was it instead something imposed deliberately, as an aid to navigation?

"I'm going to ask Lutz that question myself," Dr. Warner said, when Chris proposed it. "It's no help to me; in fact, it takes all the fun out of being an astronomer in free space. And there's no time like the present. Come along, Crispin—I can't very well leave you in charge, and the only other logical place for Lutz to see an apprentice of mine is with me."

It seemed to Chris that nobody aboard Scranton ever said anything officially to him but "Come along," but he went. He did not relish the prospect of seeing the city manager again, but it was probably true that he would be safer under the astronomer's wing than he would be anyplace else; in fact, he was both surprised by, and a little admiring of, Dr. Warner's boldness.

But if Boyle Warner ever asked the question, Chris never heard the answer.

Frank Lutz did not believe in making people who came to see him on official business wait in ante-chambers. It wasted his time as well as theirs, and he at least had none to waste—and they had better not have. Nor were there many details of his admin-istration that he thought he needed to keep secret, not now that those who might oppose him no longer had any place to run to. To remind his people who was boss, he occasionally kept the mayor waiting out of earshot, but everyone else came and went quite freely when he held court.

Dr. Warner and Chris sat in the rearmost benches—for Lutz's "court" was actually held in what once had been a courtroom—and waited patiently to work their way forward to the foot of the city manager's desk. In the process, the astronomer fell into a light doze; Frank Lutz's other business was nothing to him, and in addition his hearing was no better than usual for a man his age. Both Chris's curiosity and his senses, on the other hand, shared the acuity of his youth, and the latter had been sharpened by almost a life-time of listening and watching for the rustle of small animals in the brush; and the feeling of personal danger with which Frank Lutz had filled him on their first encounter was back again, putting a razor edge upon hearing and curiosity alike.

"We're in no position to temporize," the city man-ager was saying. "This outfit is big—the biggest there is—and it's offering us a fair deal. The next time we meet it, it may not be so polite, especially if we give it any sass this time around. I'm going to talk turkey with them."

"But what do they want?" someone said. Chris craned his neck, but he did not know the man who had spoken. Most of Lutz's advisers were nonenti-ties, in any event—except for those like Huggins, who were outright thugs.

"They want us to veer off. They've analyzed our

course and say we're headed for a region of space that they'd had staked out long before we showed up. Now this, let me point out, is actually all to the good. They have a preliminary survey of the area, and we don't—everything ahead of *us* is all alike, until we've had some experience of it. Furthermore, one of the things they offer in payment is a new course which they say will take us into an iron-bearing star cluster, very recently settled, where there's likely to be plenty of work for us."

"So *they* say."

"And I believe them," Lutz said sharply. "Everything they've said to me, they've also said on the open air, by Dirac transmitter. The cops have heard every word, not only locally, but wherever in the whole universe that there's a Dirac transceiver. Big as they are, they're not going to attempt to phony an open contract. The only question in my mind is, what ought to be the price?"

He looked down at the top of his desk. Nobody seemed to have any suggestions. Finally he looked up again and smiled coldly.

"I've thought of several, but the one I like best is this: They can help us run up our supplies. We haven't got the food to reach the cluster that they've designated—I'd hoped we'd make a planetfall long before we had to go that far—but that's something that they can't know, and that I'm not going to tell them."

"They'll know when you ask for the food, Frank—"

"I'm not such an idiot. Do you think any Okie city would ever sell food at *any* price? You might as well try to buy oxygen, or money. *I'm* going to ask them to throw in some minor piece of machinery or other, it doesn't matter what, and two or three technicians to man and service it; and as an evidence of good faith, I'll offer back for these oh-so-valuable technicians a big batch of our people—people that are of

no use to us. There won't be so many of them that a
town *that* size would have any difficulty in absorbing
them—but to us, they'll represent just the number
of extra mouths to feed that would prevent us from
reaching the iron-bearing cluster that Amalfi's offered to guide us to. Food will never be mentioned.
It'll be just a standard swap of personnel, under the
usual Okie 'rule of discretion.' "

There was a long minute of respectful silence.
Even Chris was forced to admire the ingenuity of the
scheme, insofar as he understood it. Frank Lutz
smiled again and added:

"And this way we get rid of every single one of
those useless bums and red-necks we had to take
aboard under the impressment laws. The cops will
never know it; and neither will Amalfi; he has to
carry enough food and, ah, medicines to maintain a
crew of well over a million. He'll swallow another
three hundred yokels without as much effort as you'd
swallow an aspirin, and probably think it a fair trade
for two technies and a machine that are useless to
him. The most beautiful part of it all is, it might even
be a fair trade—which brings me to my next point—"

But Chris did not stay to hear the next point. After
a last, quick, regretful glance at the drowsing astronomer who had befriended him, he stole out of the
court as silently as any poacher, and went to ground.

The hole was structurally an accident. Located in a
warehouse at the edge of the city nearest the university, it was in the midst of an immense stack of heavy
crates which evidently had shifted during the first
few moments of take-off, thus forming a huge and
unpredictable three-dimensional maze which no map
of the city would ever show. By worrying a hole in
the side of one crate with a pocketknife, Chris had
found that it contained mining machinery (and, evidently, so did all the others, since they all bore the

same stenciled code number). The chances were good, he thought, that the crates would not be unstacked until Scranton made its first planetfall; the city in flight would have nothing to dig into.

Nor did Chris have any reason to leave the hole, at least for now. The warehouse itself had a toilet he could visit, and seemed to be unfrequented; and of course it didn't need a watchman—Who would bother to steal heavy machinery, and where would they run with it? If he was careful not to set any fires with his candles—for the hole, although fairly well ventilated through the labyrinth, was always pitch dark—he would probably be safe until his food ran out. After that, he would have to take his chances . . . but he had been a poacher before.

But nothing in his plans had allowed for a visitor.

He heard the sounds of the approach from some distance and blew out his candle at once. Maybe it was only a casual prowler; maybe even only a strayed child—maybe, at the worst, another refugee from Lutz's flesh-trading deal, looking for a hole. There were plenty of holes amid the piled-up crates, and the way to this one was so complex that two of them could live in the heap for weeks without encountering each other.

But his heart sank as he realized how quietly the footsteps were approaching. The newcomer was negotiating the maze with scarcely a false turn, let alone a noisy blunder.

Someone knew where he was—or at least knew where his hole was.

The footsteps became louder, slowed, and stopped. Now he could distinctly hear someone breathing.

Then the beam of a hand torch caught him full in the face.

"Hell, Chris. Make a light, huh?"

The voice was that of Frad Haskins. Anger and relief flooded through Chris at the same time. The big man had been his first friend, and almost his name-brother—for after all, Fradley O. Haskins is not much more ridiculous a name than Crispin deFord—but that blow of light in the face had been like a betrayal.

"I've only got candles. If you'd set the flashlight on end, it'd be just as good—maybe better."

"Okay." Haskins sat down on the floor, placing the torch on the small crate Chris used for a table, so that it made a round spot of light on the boards overhead. "Now tell me something. Just what do you think you're doing?"

"Hiding," Chris said, a little sullenly.

"I can see that. I knew what this place was from the day I saw you toting books into it. I have to keep in practice on this press-gang dodge; I'll need it some day on some other planet. But in your case, what's the sense? Don't you *want* to be transferred to a bigger city?"

"No, I don't. Oh, I can't say that Scranton's been like home to me. I hate it. I wish I could really go home. But Frad, at least I'm getting to know the place. I already knew part of it, back while it was on the ground. I don't want to be kidnapped twice, and go through it all again—aboard some city where I don't know even as much about the streets as I knew about Scranton—and maybe find out that I hate it even worse. And I don't like being swapped, like— like a barrel of scrap."

"Well, maybe I can't blame you for that—though it's standard Okie procedure, not anything that Lutz thought up in his own head. Do you know where the 'rule of discretion' came from?"

"No."

"From the trading of players between baseball teams. It's that old—more than a thousand years. The contract law that sanctions it is supposed to be a whale of a lot older, even."

"All right," Chris said. "It could even be Roman, I suppose. But Frad, I'm not a barrel of scrap and I still don't want to be swapped."

"Now that part of it," the big man said patiently, "is just plain silly. You've got no future in Scranton, and you ought to know it by now. On a really big town you could probably find something to do—and the least you'll get is some schooling. All our schools are closed, for good and forever. And another thing: We've only been aloft a year, and it's a cinch we've got some hard times ahead of us. An older town would be a darn sight safer—not absolutely safe, no Okie ever is; but safer."

"Are you going, too?"

Haskins laughed. "Not a chance. Amalfi must have ten thousand of the likes of me. Besides, Lutz needs me. He doesn't know it, but he does."

"Well . . . then . . . I'd rather stay with you."

Haskins smote one fist into the other palm in exasperation. "Look, Red . . . Cripes, what do you say to this kid? Thanks, Chris; I—I'll remember that. But if I'm lucky, I'll have a boy of my own some day. This isn't the day. If you don't face facts right now, you aren't going to get a second chance. Listen, I'm the only guy who knows where you are, yet, but how long can that last? Do you know what Frank will do when he roots you out of a hole full of cached food? *Think,* please, will you?"

Chris's stomach felt as though he had just been thrown out of a window.

"I guess I never thought of that."

"You need practice. I don't blame you for that. But I'll tell you what Frank will do: *He'll have you shot.* And nobody else in town'll even raise an eyebrow. In the Okie lawbook, hoarding food comes under the head of endangering the survival of the city. Any such crime is a capital crime—and not only in Scranton, either."

There was a long silence. At last, Chris said quietly: "All right. Maybe it is better this way. I'll go."

"That's using your head," Haskins said gruffly. "Come on, then. We'll tell Frank you were sick. You *look* sick, right enough. But we'll have to hustle— the gigs leave in two hours."

"Can I take my books?"

"They're not yours, they're Boyle Warner's," Fred said impatiently. "I'll get 'em back to him later. Pick up the torch and let's go—you'll find plenty of books where you're going." He stopped suddenly and glared at Chris through the dim light. "Not that you care where you're going! You haven't even asked the name of the town."

This was true; he had not asked, and now that he came to think about it, he didn't care. But his curiosity came forward even through the gloom of the maze, and even through his despair. He said, "So I haven't. What is it?"

"New York."

CHAPTER FOUR: Schoolroom in the Sky

The sight from the gig was marvelous beyond all imagination: an island of towers, as tall as mountains, floating in a surfaceless, bottomless sea of stars. The gig was rocket-powered, so that Chris was also seeing the stars from space in all their jeweled majesty for the first time in his life; but the silent pride of the great human city, aloof in its spindizzy bubble—which was faintly visible from the outside—completely took precedence. Behind the gig, Scranton looked in comparison like a scuttleful of old stove bolts.

The immigrants were met at the perimeter by a broad-shouldered, crew-cut man of about forty, in a uniform which made all of Chris's hackles rise; cops were natural enemies, here as everywhere. But the perimeter sergeant, who gave his name as Anderson, did no more than herd them all into separate cubicles for interviews.

There was nobody in Chris's cubicle but Chris himself. He was seated before a small ledge or banquette, facing a speaker grille which was set into the wall. From this there issued the questions, and into this he spoke his answers. Most of the questions were simple matters of vital statistics—his name, his age, point of origin, date of boarding Scranton and so on—but he rather enjoyed answering them; the fact was that never before in his life had anyone been interested enough in him to ask them. In fact he himself did not know the answers to some of them.

It was also interesting to speculate on the identity of the questioner. It was a machine, Chris was almost sure, and one speaking not from any vocabulary of prerecorded words sounded by a human voice, but instead from some store of basic speech sounds which it combined and recombined as it went along. The result was perfectly understandable and nonmechanical, carrying many of the stigmata of real human speech—for example, the sentences emerged in natural speech rhythms, and with enough inflection so that key words and even punctuation could be distinguished—yet all the same he would never have mistaken it for a human voice. Whatever the difference was, he thought of it as though the device were speaking all in capital letters.

Even in an age long dominated by computers, to the exclusion, in many cases, of human beings, Chris had never heard of a machine with intelligence enough to be able to construct its speech in this fashion, let alone one intelligent enough to be given the wide discretionary latitude implied by the conduct of this interview. He had never before heard of a machine which referred to itself as "we," either.

"HOW MUCH SCHOOLING HAD YOU HAD BEFORE YOU WERE IMPRESSED, MR. DEFORD?"

"Almost none."

"DID YOU RECEIVE ANY SCHOOLING ABOARD SCRANTON?"

"A little. Actually it was only just tutoring—the kind of thing I used to get from my father, when he felt up to it."

"IT IS RATHER LATE TO START, BUT WE CAN ARRANGE SCHOOLING FOR YOU IF YOU WISH—"

"Boy, do I!"

"THAT IS THE QUESTION. AN ACCELERATED SECONDARY EDUCATION IS PHYSICALLY VERY TRYING. IT IS POSSIBLE THAT YOU WOULD HAVE NO NEED OF IT HERE, DEPENDING UPON YOUR GOALS. DO YOU WISH TO BE A PASSENGER, OR A CITIZEN?"

On the surface, this was a perfectly easy question. What Chris most wanted to do was to go home and back to being a citizen of nothing more complicated than the Commonwealth of Pennsylvania, Western Common Market, Terran Confederation. He had had many bad nights spent wondering how his family was doing without him, and what they had thought of his disappearance, and he was sure that he would have many more. Yet by the same token, by now they had doubtless made whatever adjustment was possible for them to the fact of his being gone; and an even more brutal fact was that he was now sitting on a metropolis of well over a million people which was floating in empty space a good twenty light-years away from Sol, bound for some destination he could not even guess. This monstrous and wonderful construct was not going to turn itself into his personal Tin Cabby simply because he said he wanted to go home, or for any other reason.

So if Chris was stuck with the city, he reasoned, he might as well be a citizen. There was no point in being a passenger when he had no idea where he was going, or whether it would be worth the fare when he got there. Being a citizen, on the other hand, sounded as though it conferred some privileges; it would be worth while knowing what they were. It would also be worth knowing whether or not the two terms the machine had used carried some special technical meaning of which he ought to be wary.

"Who'm I talking to?"

"THE CITY FATHERS."

This reply nearly threw him completely off course; he tabled the baker's dozen of questions it raised only by a firm exercise of will. What was important about it right now was that it told him that he was talking to a responsible person—whatever the meaning of "Person" might be when one is dealing with a machine with a collective personality.

"Am I entitled to ask questions too?"

"YES, WITHIN LIMITS IT WOULD TAKE TOO LONG TO DEFINE FOR THE PURPOSE OF THIS INTERVIEW. IF YOU ASK US QUESTIONS, WE WILL AT PRESENT EITHER ANSWER OR NOT ANSWER."

Chris thought hard. The City Fathers, despite their mention of time limitations, waited him out without any evidence of impatience. Finally he said:

"What's the most important single difference between a passenger and a citizen."

"A CITIZEN LIVES AN INDEFINITELY PROLONGED LIFE."

Nothing they could have said could have been farther from any answer that Chris might have expected. It was so remote from anything he had ever thought or read about that it was almost meaningless to him. Finally he managed to ask cautiously: "How long is indefinitely?"

"INDEFINITELY LONG. OUR PRESENT MAYOR WAS BORN IN 2998. THE AGE OF THE OLDEST CITY MAN OF WHOM WE HAVE ANY RECORD IS FIVE HUNDRED AND THIRTEEN YEARS, BUT IT IS STATISTICALLY DEFENSIBLE TO ASSUME THAT THERE ARE SEVERAL OLDER SPECIMENS, SINCE THE FIRST OF THE ANTIDEATH DRUGS WAS DISCOVERED IN THE YEAR 2018."

Antideath drugs! The dose was now entirely too big to swallow. It was all Chris could do to cling to the one microgram of it that seemed to have some meaning for him right now: that were he to live a long time—a very long time—he might some day find his way back home, no matter how far he had wandered in the meantime. All the rest would have to be thought through later. He said:

"I want to be a citizen."

"IT IS REQUIRED THAT WE INFORM YOU THAT YOU ARE PERMITTED TO CHANGE YOUR MIND UNTIL YOUR EIGHTEENTH BIRTHDAY, BUT THAT A DECISION TO BECOME A PASSENGER MAY NOT THEREAFTER BE RESCINDED, EXCEPT BY SPECIAL ORDER OF THE MAYOR." A thin slot which Chris had not noticed until now suddenly spat out upon the banquette a long white card. "THIS IS YOUR CITY REGISTRATION, WHICH IS USED TO OBTAIN FOOD, CLOTHING, HOUSING AND OTHER NECESSIITES. WHEN IT IS REJECTED ON PRESENTATION, YOU WILL KNOW THAT THE GOODS OR SERVICES YOU HAVE CLAIMED HAVE BEEN DISALLOWED. THE CARD IS INDESTRUCTIBLE EXCEPT BY CERTAIN SPECIAL TECHNIQUES, BUT WE ADVISE YOU NOT TO LOSE IT, SINCE FOUR TO SIX HOURS WILL ELAPSE BEFORE IT CAN BE RETURNED TO YOU. IT IS PRESENTLY VALIDATED FOR ACCELERATED SCHOOLING. IF YOU HAVE NO FURTHER QUESTIONS, YOU MAY LEAVE."

The accelerated schooling to which the City Fathers had remanded Chris did not at first seem physically strenuous at all. In fact it seemed initially to be no more demanding than sleeping all day might be. (This to Chris was a Utopian notion; he had never had the opportunity to try sleeping as a career, and so had no idea how intolerably exhausting it is.)

The "schoolroom" was a large gray, featureless chamber devoid of blackboard or desk; its only furniture consisted of a number of couches scattered about the floor. Nor were there any teachers; the only adults present were called monitors, and their duties appeared to be partly those of an usher, and partly those of a nurse, but none pertinent to teaching in any sense of the term Chris had ever encountered. They conducted you to your couch and helped you to fit over your head a bright metal helmet which had inside it what seemed to be hundreds of tiny, extremely sharp points which bit into your scalp just enough to make you nervous, but without enough pressure to break the skin. Once this gadget, which was called a toposcope, was adjusted to their satisfaction, the monitors left, and the room began to fill with the gray gas.

The gas was like a fog, except that it was dry and faintly aromatic, smelling rather like the dried leaves of mountain laurel that Bob had liked to add sparingly to rabbit stews. But like a thick fog, it made it impossible to see the rest of the room until the session was over, when it was sucked out with a subdued roar of blowers.

Thus Chris could never decide whether or not he actually slept while class was in session. The teaching technique, to be sure, was called hypnopaedia, an ancient word from still more ancient Greek roots which when translated literally meant "sleep-teaching." And, to be sure, it filled your head with strange voices and strange visions which were remarkably like dreams. Chris also suspected that the gray gas not only cut off his vision, but also his other senses; otherwise he should surely have heard such random sounds as the coughing of other students, the movements of the monitors, the whir of the ventilators, the occasional deep sounds of the city's drivers, and even the beating of his own heart; but none of these came through, or if they did, he did not afterwards have any memory of them. Yet the end result of all this was almost surely not true sleep, but simply a divorcing of his mind from every possible bodily distraction which might have come between him and his fullest attention to the visions and voices which were poured directly into his mind through the shiring helmet of the toposcope.

It was easy to understand why no such distraction could be tolerated, for the torrent of facts that came from the memory cells of the City Fathers into the prickly helmet was overwhelming and merciless. More than once, Chris saw ex-Scrantonites, all of them older than he was, being supported by monitors out of the classroom at the end of a session in a state closely resembling the kind of epileptic fit called "petit mal" . . . nor were they ever allowed back on their couches again. He himself left the sessions in a curious state of wobbly, washed-out detachment which became more and more marked every day, despite the tumbler of restorative drink which was the standard antidote for the gray gas: a feeling of weakness which no amount of sleep seemed to make up for.

The drink tasted funny, furthermore, and besides, it made him sneeze. But on the day after he had refused it for the first time, the memory banks decanted a double dose of projective Riemannian geometry, and he awoke to find four monitors holding him down on the couch during the last throes of a classical Jacksonian seizure.

His education nearly stopped right there. Luckily, he had the sense to admit that he had skipped drinking the anticonvulsant drug the day before; and the records of the patterns of electrical activity of his brain which the toposcope had been taking continued to adjudge him a good risk. He was allowed back into the hall—and after that he was no longer in any doubt that learning can be harder physical labor than heaving a shovel.

The voices and the visions resumed swarming gleefully inside his aching head.

In retrospect, Chris found Okie history the least difficult subject to absorb, because the part of it dealing with the early years of the cities, and in particular with what had happened on Earth before the first of the cities had left the ground, was already familiar to him. Nevertheless he was now hearing it for the first time from the Okie point of view, which omitted great swatches which an Earthman would have considered important, and instead brought to the fore for study many events of which Chris had never heard but which obviously were essential for the understanding of how the cities had gone into space and prospered in it. It was, perhaps predictably, like seeing the past life of the Earth through the wrong end of a telescope.

As the memory banks told the story (without the pictures and sounds and other sensations, which, though they were so vivid as to become at once a part of Chris's immediate experience, could not possibly be reproduced in print), it went like this:

"The exploration of the solar system was at first primarily the province of the military, who alone could demand the enormous sums of money necessary for space travel under rocket power, which is essentially a brute-force method of propulsion directly dependent upon how much power is thrown away. The highest achievement of this phase was the construction of a research and observation station upon Proserpina II, the second satellite of the most remote of all the planets from Sol. Proserpina Station was begun in 2016; it was, however, still not completed when it was abandoned temporarily twenty-eight years later.

"The reasons for the abandonment of Proserpina

Station and all other solar system colonies at this time may be found in the course of contemporary Terrestrial politics. Under the relentless pressure of competition from the USSR and its associated states, the Earth's Western culture had undertaken to support a permanent war economy, under the burden of which its traditional libertarian political institutions were steadily eroded away. By the beginning of the twenty-first century it was no longer realistically possible to see any difference between the rival cultures, although their outward forms of government continued to be called by different names. Both were police states in which the individual citizen had lost all right to juridical defense, and both operated under a totally controlled economy. In the West, the official term for this form of public policy was 'anti-Communism'; in the East it was called 'anti-Fascism,' and both terms were heavily laden with mob emotion. The facts of the matter, however, were that neither state was economically either fascist or communist, and that as economic systems neither fascism nor communism has ever been tried in recorded Terrestrial history.

"It was during this period that two Western research projects under the direction of the Alaskan senator Bliss Wagoner discovered the basic inventions upon which the second phase of space flight was to be based. The first of these was the Dillon-Wagoner gravitronpolarity generator, now known as the spindizzy, which was almost immediately developed into an interstellar drive. The second was ascomycin, the first of the anti-agathics, or death-postponing drugs. The first interstellar expedition was launched from the Jovian satellary system in 2021 under Wagoner's personal direction, although Wagoner himself was arrested and executed for his complicity in this 'treasonable' event. Though no record exists of the fate of this expedition, it is certain that it survived, since the second expedition, more than three hundred and fifty years later, found the planets of the stars of the local group well scattered with human beings speaking recognizable Terrestrial languages.

"At this time an attempt was made to settle the rivalry between the two power blocs by still another personal pact between their respective leaders, President MacHinery of the Western Common Market and Premier Erdsenov of the USSR. This took place in 2022, and the subsequent Cold Peace provided little incentive for space flight. In 2027 MacHinery was assassinated, and Erdsenov proclaimed himself premier and president of a United Earth; however, Erdsenov was himself assassinated in 2032. During this same year, an underground Western group calling itself the Hamiltonians succeeded in escaping from the solar system in a large number of small spindizzy-powered craft which they had built from funds collected secretly to finance a supposed new American revolution, thus leaving behind the vast majority of their followers. No survivors of the Hamiltonian exodus have thus far been found; they succeeded, however, in escaping the Terror, the worldwide program by which a United Earth government was actually established for the first time.

"One of the first acts of this government, now called the Bureaucratic State, was the banning in 2039 of spaceflight and all associated sciences. The existing colonies on the planets and satellites of the solar system were not evacuated home, but were simply cut off and abandoned. The consolidation of the State proceeded rapidly, and historians generally agree that the fall of the West must be dated no later than the year 2105. Thus began a period of systematic oppression and exploitation unmatched on Earth even by the worst decades of the Roman Empire.

"In the meantime the interstellar exiles continued to consolidate new planets and to jump from star to star. In 2289, one such expedition made its first contact with what proved to be a planet of the Vegan Tyranny, an interstellar culture which, we now know, had ruled most of this quadrant of the galaxy for eight to ten thousand years, and was still in the process of expanding. The Vegans were quick to see potential rivals even in these unorganized and badly supplied colonists, and made a concerted attempt to stamp out all the colonies. However, the distances involved were so vast that the first real engagement of the Vegan War, the battle of Altair, did not occur until 2310. The colonial forces were defeated and scattered, but not before inflicting sufficient damage to set back the Vegans' timetable for razing the colonial planets—permanently, as it turned out.

"In 2375, the spindizzy was independently rediscovered on Earth and the Thorium Trust's Plant Number Eight used it to wrench its entire installation from off the ground and leave the Earth, using the plant as a self-contained spaceship. Other plants followed, and shortly thereafter, whole cities. Many of these were driven to leave as much by the permanent depression which had settled over the Earth as by the long-established political repressions of the Bureaucratic State. These escaping cities quickly found the earlier Earth colonies among the nearby stars, to which they provided badly needed industrial strength, and with whom they joined forces against Vega. The outcome was both triumphant and shameful. In 2394 one of the escaping cities, Gravitogorsk-Mars, now calling itself the Interstellar Master Traders, was responsible for the sacking of the new Earth colony on Thor V; this act of ferocity earned for them the nickname of 'the Mad Dogs,' but it gradually became a model for dealing with Vegan planets. The capital world of the Tyranny, Vega II, was invested in 2413 by a number of armed cities, including IMT, whose task it was to destroy the many orbital forts surrounding the planet, and by the Third Colonial Navy under Admiral Alois Hrunta, who was charged with occupying Vega II in the event of its surrender. Instead, Admiral Hrunta scorched the planet completely, and led the Third Navy off into an uncharted quadrant with the intention of founding his own interstellar empire. In 2451 the colonial court found him guilty *in absentia* of atrocities and attempted genocide, and an attempt to bring him to justice culminated in 2464 in the battle of BD 40° 4048′, which was destructive but completely indecisive for both sides. The same year Alois Hrunta declared himself Emperor of Space.

"The Exodus of Earth's industrial power had by now become so marked that the Bureaucratic State no longer had a productive base upon which to rest, and it is generally agreed that it collapsed in 2522. In the same year there began the police interregnum, a limited government deriving its powers from a loose confederation based roughly upon the ancient United Nations, but without sufficient popular base or industrial support to control the economy. Realizing, however, that the only hope for the restoration of economic health to Earth lay in the colonists and the free cities, the confederation proclaimed an amnesty for everyone in space, and at the same time instituted a limited but systematic program for the policing of those nomad cities which had begun to prey upon colony planets or upon each other.

"The confederation is still the only operative government in this arm of the galaxy. The poisoning of Alois Hrunta in 3089 was followed by the rapid Balkanization of the Hruntan Empire, which was never even at its best highly cohesive, and although there is a present self-styled Emperor of Space, Arpad Hrunta, his realm does not appear to be of any importance. Effectively, today, law and order in Arm II are provided by the Earth police, and its economy is supported by the migrant cities. Both systems are haphazard and inefficient, and often operate at cross purposes.

"It is impossible to predict when better methods will emerge, or what they will be."

CHAPTER FIVE: "Boy, You Are Dumb!"

While the memory cells chattered and called up dreams, the immense city soared outward among the stars, at what seemed like a breakneck pace after the tentative first explorations of Scranton within the local group. The streets were thronged 24 hours a day with myriads of people hurrying on unimaginable errands; and in addition to the constant flitting of Tin Cabs, there was often the distant but edgy roar of subway trains coursing through tunnels bored through the very granite keel of the city. All of this activity seemed purposeful and even cheerful, but it was also extremely bewildering.

Chris's schooling left him very little time to explore it. Not all of his education was machine education, either, for, as he slowly realized, no one really *learns* anything through hypnopaedia; machine teaching at its best enables the student to accumulate nothing better than facts; it does not show how to tie them together, let alone how to do something with them. To train the intelligence—not just the memory— a real human tutor is required.

The one assigned to Chris, a stocky, fierce, white-haired woman named Dr. Helena Braziller, was far and away the best teacher Chris had ever encountered in his life—and far and away the worst taskmaster. The City Fathers wore him out only by taxing his memory; whereas Dr. Braziller made him *work*.

"The fundamental equation of the Blackett-Dirac scholium reads as follows:

$$P = \frac{BG^{1/2}U}{2C}$$

Where P is magnetic moment, U is angular momentum, C and G have their usual values, and B is a constant with the value 0.25 approximately. A first transform of this identity gives:

$$G = \left(\frac{2PC}{BU}\right)^2$$

Which is the usual shorthand form of the primary spindizzy equation, called the Locke Derivation. Blackett, Dirac and Locke all assumed that it would hold true for large bodies, such as gas-giant planets and suns. Show on the blackboard by dimensional analysis why this assumption is invalid."

As far as Chris was concerned, the answer could have been much more simply arrived at; Dr. Braziller could just have told him that this relationship between gravitation and the spin of a body applied only to electrons and other submicroscopic objects, and disappeared, for all practical purposes, in the world of the macrocosm; but that was not her way. Had she only told him that, it would have come into his mind as a fact like any other fact—for instance, like the facts that the memory cells of the City Fathers were constantly pouring into his ears and eyes—but by her lights he would not have understood it. She wanted him to repeat not only the original reasoning of Blackett, Dirac and Locke, but to see for himself, not just because she told him so, where they had gone astray, and hence why a natural law which had first been proposed in the gas-lit, almost prehistoric year of 1891, and was precisely formulated as the Lande Factor in 1940, nevertheless failed to lift so much as a grain of sand off the Earth until the year 2019.

"But Dr. Braziller, why isn't it enough to see that they made a mistake? We know that now. Why repeat it?"

"Because that's what all these great men have labored toward: so that you could do it right, yourself. Up until about the thirteenth century, nobody in the world except a few dedicated scholars could do long division; then Fibonacci introduced the Arabic numbers to the West. Now, any idiot can do what it took a great mind to do in those days. Are you going to complain that because Fibonacci found a better way to do long division, you shouldn't be required to learn why it's better? Or that because a great inventor like Locke didn't understand dimensional analysis, you should be allowed to be just as ignorant, after all these years? They spent their lives making things simple for you that were enormously difficult for them, and until you understand the difficulties, you can't possibly understand the simplifications. Go back to the blackboard and try again."

Being in a "live" class had its compensations, though; and one of these was Piggy Kingston-Throop. Piggy— his real name was George, but nobody ever called him that, not even Dr. Braziller—was not much of a prize as a friend and companion, but he was the only member of the small class who was exactly Chris's age; all the others were much younger. From this Chris deduced that Piggy was not a student, which turned out to be true.

Piggy seemed glad enough to encounter someone who was as retarded as he was, whatever the reasons, and who knew less than he ʲʲd about a great many subjects which were commonplaces to him. And in many ways he was quite a pleasant sort of fellow; blond, plump and affable, with a ready wit and a tendency to be unimpressed by almost everything that other people considered important. In this last, he made a particularly good foil for Chris, who in his ignorance and in the strangeness of his situation often could not help but be earnest to the point of grimness over what later turned out to be trivia.

Not that Chris allowed these differences over value judgments always to be resolved in Piggy's favor; they quarreled over them almost from the beginning. The first of these tangles, which soon proved to be a model for the others, involved the subject of the antiagathic drugs.

"You're going to be a citizen, aren't you, Piggy?"

"Oh, sure. I'm all set."

"I wish I were. My trouble is, I don't even know what I want to do—let alone what I'm good at."

Piggy turned and stared at him. They had paused on the way from school on the Tudor Tower Place bridge leading over 42nd Street. Long ago, the view from here across First Avenue to the East River had been blocked by the UN Building, but that had been demolished during the Terror, and there was nothing to mark where it had stood but a plaza; and on the far side of that, starry space itself.

"What do you mean, *do?*" Piggy said. "Oh, maybe you'll have a little trouble, what with not having been born here. But there's ways around that. Don't believe everything they tell you."

Like many of the things Piggy said, fully 80 per cent of this speech meant nothing to Chris. In self-defense, he could do nothing but answer the question. "You know all this better than I do. But the laws do say pretty clearly that a man has to be good for something before he's allowed to become a citizen and be started on the drug treatments. Let's see; there are supposed to be three ways to go about it; and I ought to have them straight, because I just had them put into my head a few days ago."

He concentrated a moment. He had discovered a useful trick for dredging up the information which had been implanted in his mind from the memory cells: If he half closed his eyes and imagined the gray gas, in a moment he would begin to feel, at least in retrospect, the same somnolence under which the original facts had been imparted, and they would come back in very much the same words. It worked equally well this time; almost at once, he heard his own voice saying, in a curious monotone imitation of the City Fathers:

" 'There are three general qualifications for citizenship. They are: (1) Display of some obviously useful talent, such as computer programming, administration, or another gift worth retaining, as opposed to depending upon the accidents of birth to provide new such men for each succeeding generation; (2) a demonstrable bent toward any intellectual field, including scientific research, the arts and philosophy, since in these fields one lifetime is seldom enough to attain masterhood, let alone put it to the best use; and (3) passage of the Citizenship Tests, which are designed to reveal reserves and potentials in the latematuring eighteen-year-old whose achievement record is unimpressive.' No matter how you slice it, it doesn't sound easy!"

"That's only what the City Fathers say," Piggy said scornfully. "What do they know about it? They're only a bunch of machines. They don't know anything about people. Those rules don't even make sense."

"They make sense to me," Chris objected. "It's a cinch the antiagathics can't be given to everybody—from what I hear, they're scarcer than germanium. On Scranton, the big boss wouldn't even allow them to be mentioned in public. So there's got to be *some* way of picking who gets them and who doesn't."

"Why?"

"Why? Well, to begin with, because a city is like an island—an island in the middle of the biggest ocean you can think of, and then some. Nobody can get on, and nobody can get off, except for a couple of guys now and then. If everybody gets this drug and lives forever, pretty soon the place is going to be so crowded that we'll all be standing on each other's feet."

"Ah, cut it out. Look around you. Are *we* all standing on each other's feet?"

"No, but that's because the drugs are restricted, and because not everybody's allowed to have children, either. For that matter, look at you, Piggy—your father and your mother are both big wheels on this town, but you're an only child, and furthermore, the first one they've been allowed to have in a hundred and fifty years."

"Leave them out of this," Piggy growled. "They didn't play their cards right, I'll tell you that. But that's none of your business."

"All right. Take me, then. Unless I turn out to be good for something before I'm eighteen—and I can't think what it would be—I won't be a citizen and I won't get the drugs. Or even if I do get to be a citizen, say by passing the Tests, I'll still have to prove myself useful stock before I'm allowed to have even one kid of my own. That's just the way it has to be when the population has to be kept stable; it's simple economics, Piggy, and there's a subject I think I know something about."

Piggy spat reflectively over the railing, though it was hard to tell whether or not he was expressing an opinion, and if so, whether it referred to economics alone or to the entire argument. "All right, then," he said. "Suppose you get the drugs, and they let you have a kid. Why shouldn't they give the kid the drugs too?"

"Why should they, unless he qualifies?"

"Boy, you *are* dumb! That's what the Citizenship Tests are for, can't you see that? They're an out—an escape hatch, a dodge—and that's all they are. If you don't get in any other way, you get in that way. At least you do if you've got any sort of connections. If you're a nobody, maybe the City Fathers rig the Tests against you—that's likely enough. But if you're a somebody, they're not going to be too tough. If they are, my father can fix their wagon—he programs 'em. But either way, there's no way to study for the Tests, so they're obviously a sell."

Chris was shaken, but he said doggedly: "But they're not supposed to be that kind of test at all. I mean, they're not supposed to show whether or not you're good at dimensional analysis, or history, or some other subject. They're supposed to show up gifts that you were born with, not anything that you got through schooling or training."

"Spindizzy whistle. A test you can't study for is a test you can't pass unless it's rigged—otherwise it doesn't make any sense at all. Listen, Red, if you're so sold on this idea that everybody who gets to take the drugs has to be a big brain, what about the guardian they handed you over to? He's got no kids of his own, and he's nothing but a cop . . . but he's almost as old as the Mayor!"

Up to now, Chris had felt vaguely that he had been holding his own; but this was like a blow in the face.

Chris had originally been alarmed to find that his ID card assigned him lodgings with a family, and horrified when the assignment number turned out to belong to Sgt. Anderson. His first few weeks in the Andersons' apartment—it was in the part of the city once called Chelsea—were prickly with suspicion, disguised poorly by as much formality as his social inexperience would allow.

It soon became impossible, however, to continue believing that the perimeter sergeant was an ogre; and his wife, Carla, was as warm and gracious a woman as Chris had ever met. They were childless, and could not have welcomed Chris more wholeheartedly had he been one of their own. Furthermore, as the City Fathers had of course calculated, Anderson was the ideal guardian for a brandnew young passenger, for few people, even the Mayor, knew the city better.

He was, in fact, considerably more than a cop, for the city's police force was also its defense force—and its Marines, should the need for a raid or a boarding party ever arise. Technically, there were many men on the force who were superior to the perimeter sergeant, but Anderson and one counterpart, a dark taciturn man named Dulany, headed picked squads and were nearly independent of the rest of the police, reporting directly to Mayor Amalfi.

It was this fact which opened the first line of friendly communication between Chris and his guardian. He had not yet even seen Amalfi with his own eyes. Although everyone in the city spoke of him as if they knew him personally, here at last was one man who really did, and saw him several times a week. Chris was unable to restrain his curiosity.

"Well, that's just the way people talk, Chris. Actually hardly anyone sees much of Amalfi, he's got too much to do. But he's been in charge here a long time and he's good at his job; people feel that he's their friend because they trust him."

"But what is he *like?*"

"He's complicated—but then most people are complicated. I guess the word I'm groping for is 'devious.' He sees connections between events that nobody else sees. He sizes up a situation like a man looking at a coat for the one thread that'll make the whole thing unravel. He has to—he's too burdened to deal with things on a stitch-by-stitch basis. In my opinion he's killing himself with overwork as it is."

It was to this point that Chris returned after his upsetting argument with Piggy. "Sergeant, the other day you said that the Mayor was killing himself with overwork. But the City Fathers told me he's several centuries old. On the drugs, he ought to live forever, isn't that so?"

"Absolutely not," Anderson said emphatically: "*Nobody* can live forever. Sooner or later, there'd be an accident, for one thing. And strictly speaking, the drugs aren't a 'cure' for death anyhow. Do you know how they work?"

"No," Chris admitted. "School hasn't covered them yet."

"Well, the memory banks can give you the details— I've probably forgotten most of them. But generally, there are several antiagathics, and each one does a different job. The main one, ascomycin, stirs up a kind of tissue in the body called the reticulo-endothelial system—the white blood corpuscles are a part of it—to give you what's called 'nonspecific immunity.' What that means is that for about the next seventy years, you can't catch any infectious disease. At the end of that time you get another shot, and so on. The stuff isn't an antibiotic, as the name suggests, but an endotoxin fraction—a complex organic sugar called a mannose; it got its name from the fact that it's produced by fermentation, as antibiotics are.

"Another is TATP—triacetylthiparanol. What this does is inhibit the synthesis in the body of a fatty stuff called cholesterol; otherwise it collects in the arteries and causes strokes, apoplexy, high blood pressure and so on. This drug has to be taken every day, because the body goes right on trying to make cholesterol every day."

"Doesn't that mean that it's good for something?" Chris objected tentatively.

"Cholesterol? Sure it is. It's absolutely essential in the development of a fetus, so women have to lay off TATP while they're carrying a child. But it's of no use to men—and men are far more susceptible to circulatory diseases than women.

"There are still two more antiagathics in use now, but they're minor; one, for instance, blocks the synthesis of the hormone of sleep, which again is essential in pregnancy but a thundering nuisance otherwise; that one was originally found in the blood of ruminant animals like cows, whose plumbing is so defective that they'd die if they lay down."

"You mean you *never sleep?*"

"Haven't got the time for it," Anderson said gravely. "Or the need any longer, thank goodness. But ascomycin and TATP between them prevent the two underlying major causes of death: heart diseases and infections. If you prevent those alone, you extend the average lifetime by at least two centuries.

"But death is still inevitable, Chris. If there isn't

an accident, there may be cancer, which we can't
prevent yet—oh, ascomycin attacks tumors so strongly
that cancer doesn't kill people any longer, in fact the
drug even offers quite a lot of protection against hard
radiation; but cancer can still make life so agonizing
that death is the only humane treatment. Or a man
can die of starvation, of being unable to get the
antiagathics. Or he can die of a bullet—or of overwork. We live long lives in the cities, sure; *but there
is no such thing as immortality.* It's as mythical as
the unicorn. Not even the universe itself is going to
last forever."

This, at last, was the opportunity Chris had been
hoping for, though he still hardly knew how to grasp
it.

"Are—are the drugs ever stopped, once a man's
been made a citizen?"

"Deliberately? I've never heard of such a case,"
Anderson said, frowning. "Not on our town. If the
City Fathers want a man dead, they shoot him. Why
let him linger for the rest of his seventy-year stanza?
That would be outrageously cruel. What would be
the reason for such a procedure?"

"Well, no tests are foolproof. I mean, supposing
they make a man a citizen, and then discover that he
really isn't—uh—as big a genius as they thought he
was?"

The perimeter sergeant looked at Chris narrowly,
and there was quite a long silence, during which
Chris could clearly hear the pulsing of his own blood
in his temples. At last Anderson said slowly:

"I see. It sounds to me like somebody's been
feeding you spindizzy whistle. Chris, if only geniuses
could become citizens, how long do you think a city
could last? The place'd be depopulated in one crossing. That isn't how it works at all. The whole reason
for the drugs is to save skills—and it doesn't matter

one bit what the skills are. All that matters is whether or not it would be logical to keep a man on, rather than training a new one every four or five decades.

"Take me for an example, Chris. I'm nobody's genius; I'm only a boss cop. But I'm good at my job, good enough so that the City Fathers didn't see any reason to bother raising and training another one from the next generation; they kept this one, which is me; but a cop is, all the same, all I am. Why not? It suits me, I like the work, and when Amalfi needs a boss cop he calls me or Dulany—not any officer on the force, because none of them have the scores of years of experience at this particular job that we do under their belts. When the Mayor wants a perimeter sergeant he calls me; when he wants a boarding squad he calls Dulany; and when he wants a specific genius, he calls a genius. There's one of everything on board this town—partly because it's so big—and so long as the system works, no need for more than one. Or more than X, X being whatever number you need."

Chris grinned. "You seemed to remember the details all right."

"I remembered them all," Anderson admitted. "Or all that they gave me. Once the City Fathers put a thing into your head, it's hard to get rid of."

As he spoke, there was a pure fluting sound, like a brief tune, somewhere in the apartment. The perimeter sergeant's heavy head tipped up; then he, too, grinned.

"We're about to have a demonstration," he said. He was obviously pleased. He touched a button on the arm of his chair.

"Anderson?" a heavy voice said. Chris thought instantly that the father bear in the ancient myth of Goldilocks must have sounded much like that.

"Yes—Here, Sir."

"We're coming up on a contract. It looks fairly good to me and the City Fathers, and I'm about to sign it. Better come up here and familiarize yourself with the terms, just in case: This'll be a rough one, Joel."

"Right away." Anderson touched the button, and his grin became broader and more boyish than ever.

"The Mayor!" Chris burst out.

"Yep."

"But what did he mean?"

"That he's found some work for us to do. Unless there's a hitch, we should be landing in just a few days."

CHAPTER SIX: A Planet Called Heaven

Nothing could be seen of Heaven from the air. As the city descended cautiously, the spindizzy field became completely outlined as a bubble of boiling black clouds, glaring with blue-green sheets and slashes of lightning, and awash with streams of sleet and rain. At lower altitude the sleet disappeared, but the rain increased.

After so many months of starlit skies and passing suns, the grumbling, closed-in darkness was oppressive, even alarming. Sitting with Piggy on an old pier at the foot of Gansevoort Street, from which Herman Melville had sailed into the distant South Sea marvels of *Typee, Omoo* and *Mardi,* Chris stared at the globe of thunder around the city as nervously as though he had never seen weather before. Piggy, for once, was in no better shape, for he never *had* seen weather before; this was New York's first planetfall since he had been born.

How Amalfi could see where he was going was hard to imagine; but the city continued to go down anyhow; it had a contract with Heaven, and work was work. Besides, there would have been no point in waiting for the storms to clear away. It was always and everywhere like this on Heaven, except when it was worse. The settlers said so.

"Wow!" Chris said, for the twelfth or thirteenth time. "What a blitzkrieg of a storm! Look at *that!* How far up are we still, Piggy?"

"How should I know?"

"D'you think Amalfi knows? I mean really knows?"

"Sure, he knows," Piggy said miserably. "He always does the tough landings. He never misses."

WHAM!

For a second the whole sphere of the spindizzy field seemed to be crawling with electric fire. The noise was enormous and bounded back again and again from the concrete sides of the towers behind them. It had never occurred to Chris that a field which could protect a whole city from the hard radiation, the hard stones and the hard vacuum of space might pass noise when there was air outside it as well as inside—but it surely did. The descent already seemed to have been going on forever.

After a while, Chris found that he was beginning to enjoy it. Between thunder rolls, he shouted maliciously:

"He must be flying sidewise this time. Bet he's lost."

"What do you know about it? Shut up."

"*I've* seen thunderstorms. You know what? We're going to be up here forever. Sailing under a curse, like IMT." The sky lit. *WHAM!* "Hey, what a beauty!"

"If you don't shut up," Piggy said with desperate grimness, "I'm going to poke you right in the snoot."

This was hardly a very grave threat, for although Piggy outweighed Chris by some twenty pounds, most of it was blubber. Amid the excitement of the storm Chris almost made the mistake of laughing at him; but at the same instant, he felt the boards of the ancient pier begin to shudder beneath them to the tramp of steel boots. Startled, he looked back over his shoulder, and then jumped up.

Twenty men in full space armor were behind them, faceless and bristling, like a phalanx of giant robots. One of them came forward, making the planks of the pier groan and squeal under the weight, and suddenly spoke to him.

The voice was blarey and metallic, as though the gain had been turned up in order to shout across acres of ground and through cannonades of thunder, but Chris had no difficulty in recognizing it. The man in the armor was his guardian.

"CHRIS!" The volume of sound suddenly went down a little. "Chris, what are you doing here? And Kingston-Throop's kid! Piggy, you ought to know better than this. We're landing in twenty minutes—and this is a sally port. Beat it—both of you."

"We were only looking," Piggy said defiantly. "We can look if we want."

"I've got no time to argue. Are you going or not?"

Chris pulled at Piggy's elbow. "Come on Piggy. What's the sense of being in the way?"

"Let go. I'm not in the way. They can walk right by me. I don't have to go just because he says so. He's not *my* guardian—he's only a cop."

A steel arm reached out, and steel pincers opened at the end of it. "Give me your card," Anderson's voice said harshly. "I'll let you know later what you're charged with. If you won't move now, I'll assign two men to move you—though I can't spare the men, and when that winds up on your card you may spend the rest of one lifetime wishing it hadn't."

"Oh, all right. Don't throw your weight around. I'm going."

The bulbous steel arm remained stiffly extended, the pincers menacingly open. "I want the card."

"I said I was going!"

"Then go."

Piggy broke and ran. After a puzzled look at the armored figure of his guardian, Chris followed, dodging around and through the massive blue-steel statues standing impassively along almost the whole length of the pier.

Piggy had already vanished. As Chris ran for home, his mind full of bewilderment, the city grounded in a fanfare of lightning bolts.

Unfortunately, so far as Chris was concerned the City Fathers took no notice of the landing: his schooling went on regardless, so that he got only the most confused picture of what was going on. Though the municipal pipeline, WNYC, had five-minute news bulletins on tap every hour for anyone who wanted to dial into them, decades of the uneventfulness of interstellar travel had reduced the WNYC news bureau to a state of vestigial ineptitude— the pipeline's only remaining real function was the broadcasting of the city's inexhaustible library of music and drama; Chris suspected that most of the citizens found the newscasts almost as dim-witted and uninformative as he did. What little meaningful information he was able to garner, he got from Sgt. Anderson, and that was not very much, for the perimeter sergeant was hardly ever home now; he was too busy consolidating the beachhead on Heaven. Nevertheless, Chris picked up a few fragments, mostly from conversations between the sergeant and Carla:

"What they want us to do is to help them industrialize the planet. It sounds easy, but the kicker is that their social setup is feudal—the sixty-six thousand people they call the Elect are actually only free landholders or franklins, and below *them* there's a huge number of serfs—nobody's ever bothered to count them. The Archangels want it to stay that way even after they've got their heavy industries established."

"It sounds impossible," Carla said.

"It is impossible, as they'll find out when we've finished the job. But that's exactly the trouble. We're not allowed to change planets' social systems, but we can't complete this contract without starting a revolution—a long, slow one, sure, but a revolution all the same. And when the cops come here afterward and find that out, we'll have a Violation to answer for."

Carla laughed musically. "The cops! My dear, is that still a three-letter word for you? What else are you? How many more centuries is it going to take you to get used to it?"

"You know what I mean," Anderson said, frowning. "So all right, I'm a cop. But I'm not an Earth cop, I'm a *city* cop, and that makes all the difference. Well, we'll see. What's for lunch? I've got to go in half an hour."

The storm, as predicted, went on all the time. When he had the chance, Chris watched the machinery being uncrated and readied, and followed it to the docks at the working perimeter of the city, beyond which always bobbed and crawled a swarm of the glowing swamp vehicles of the colonists of Heaven. Though these came in all sizes, they were all essentially of the same design: a fat cylinder of some transparent cladding, ribbed with metal, provided on both sides with caterpillar treads bearing cleats so large that they could also serve as paddles where the going underfoot became especially sloppy. The shell was airtight, for buoyancy, but Chris was sure that the vessel could make little or no headway afloat, even if it were equipped somewhere with a screw propeller; under those circumstances it probably could do no more than try to maintain its position as best it could while it radioed for help. It was certainly well studded with antennae. Mainly, it seemed to be designed to shed water, rather than to swim in it.

How could any sort of industry be possible under these soggy conditions? He could not imagine how even an agricultural society could survive amidst these perpetual torrents, especially since there was very little land area above water on the planet. But then he recalled a little of the history of the colonization of Venus, which had presented somewhat similar problems. There, farming eventually had been taken beneath the sea; but even that needed an abundance of energy, and besides, the people of Heaven hadn't even gotten that far—they seemed to be living mostly on fish and mudweed.

He listened as closely as possible to the conversations of the colonists on the docks—not the conversations in English with the Okies, which were technical and unrevealing, but what the colonists said to each other in their own language. This was a gluey variant of Russian, the now dead Universal language of deep space, which the memory cells had been cramming into Chris's head at a cruel rate almost since the beginning of his city education. It was a brute of a language to master, especially on board a town where it was very seldom used, and perhaps for this reason the colonists, though mostly they were circumspect even in their private conversations, did not really seem to believe that the Okies spoke it; their very possession of it assured them that their history was safely pre-Okie. Quite certainly it never occurred to them that it might be understood, however imperfectly, by a teen-age boy standing about the quaysides gawping at their powerboats.

Between these eavesdroppings and the increasingly rare visits home of his guardian, Chris gradually built up a fuzzy picture of what the colonists seemed to want. As a citizen he could have asked the City Fathers directly for the text of the contract, but access to this was denied to passengers. In general, however, he gathered that the Archangels proposed to establish an economy like that of Venus, complete with undersea farming and herding, with the aid of broadcast power of the kind that kept the city's Tin Cabs in the air. The Okies were to do the excavating in the shifting, soaking terrain, and were to build the generator-transmitter station involved. They were also to use city facilities to refine the necessary power metals, chiefly thorium, of which Heaven had an abundance beyond its ability to process. After the economy was revamped, the Archangels hoped to have their own refineries, and to sell the pure stuffs to other planets. Curiously, they also had enough germanium to be willing to pay for the job in this metal, although it too was notoriously difficult to refine; this was fortunate for them, since without any present interstellar trade, they were woefully short of Oc Dollars.

Once the whole operation had rumbled and sloshed out into the field and was swallowed up in the enveloping, eternal storm, Sgt. Anderson's absences became prolonged, and the number of colonists to be found on the docks also diminished sharply. Now there were only a few of the swamp vehicles— inexplicably called swan boats—to be seen at the end of each day, when Chris was released from school, and these were mostly small craft whose owners were engaged in dickering with individual Okies for off-planet curios to give to their ladies. This commerce also was bogging down rather rapidly, for the single citizen had no use for money, and the lords and franklins of Heaven had few goods to barter. Soon the flow of information available to Chris had almost stopped, frustrating him intensely.

In this extremity he had an inspiration. He still carried with him a small, cheap clasp knife with a tiny compass embedded in its handle, the last of the exceedingly few gifts his father had ever been able to give him; perhaps it would have status here as an off-planet curio. When the notion first occurred to him, he rejected it with distress at even having thought of it—but when first Sgt. Dulany, and then his own guardian, were officially posted on the "Missing" list, he hesitated no longer. His only remaining doubt was whether or not the compass would work here, amid so much electrical activity (but then it had never worked very well on Earth, either).

He waited until he saw the lord of a six-man swan boat stalking disappointedly away from a deal he had been unable to close, and then approached him with the knife outstretched on his palm.

"*Gospodin*—"

The man, a huge burly fellow with a face like one of the eternal thunderclouds of his planet, stopped in his tracks and looked down. "Boy? Did you speak?"

"Yes sir. With your permission, I have here useful tool, earthly in origin. Would my lord care to examine?"

"But you speak our language," the man said, still frowning. He took the knife abstractedly; it was plain that he was interested, but Chris's stumbling Russian seemed to interest him more. "How is that?"

"By listening, lord. It is very hard, but I am trying. Please see object, it is from Earth, from *kolkhoz* of Pennsylvania. Genuine antique, touched once by human hands in factory."

"Well, well. How does it work?"

Chris showed him how to pry out the two blades, but his attempts to explain the compass were dismissed with a brusque gesture. Either his command of the language was insufficient to make the matter clear, or the lord already had recognized that such a thing would be useless in the lightning-stitched ether of Heaven.

"Hmm. Sleazy, to be sure, but perhaps my lady would like it for her charm-necklace. What do you ask for it?"

"Lord, I would like to drive your swan boat one time, one distance. I ask no more."

The colonist stared at him for a long moment, and then burst into deep guffaws of laughter. "Come along, come along," he said when he had recovered a little. "Sharp traders, you tramps, but this is the best story yet—I'll be telling it for years! Come along—you have a bargain."

Still chortling, he led the way to the dock, where they were both stopped by a perimeter cop who recognized Chris. Between them, the boy and the lord explained the bargain, and the Okie guard dubiously allowed Chris to board the swan boat.

In the forward cabin of the bobbing cylinder, two other colonists confronted them at once, wearing expressions at once nervous and angry, but the owner shushed them with a swift slash of one hand. He still seemed to be highly amused.

"It's only an infant. It traded me a bangle to learn how to mush the boat about. There's nothing to that. Go on aft; I'll join you in a minute."

To judge by their expressions, the other two still disapproved, but they took orders. The big man sat Chris down in a bucket seat before the broad front window and showed him how to grasp the two handles, one on each side of the half-circle of the control wheel, which were the throttles of the vehicle.

"It's not enough simply to turn the wheel, because you must also deliver power to one tread or the other. To do that, you push the handle forward or back, to speed the treads or slow them down. Past the red mark here, the tread will reverse. If you're not getting any traction, tilt the whole wheel forward on its column; that blows the tanks and allows the boat to settle in the mud. When the ground gets harder, the boat will of course climb up by itself and that will start the pumps; as the pressure in the tanks rises, the steering column tilts back to its original position automatically. Understand me so far?"

"But can I try?"

"Well, I suppose so. Yes. I have some talking to do abaft. Let me back the craft away from the pier, and then you can try crawling in a circle just outside the perimeter. Make sure you can always see your city beacon there."

"Let me back it up, lord?" Chris said urgently.

"All right," the big man said with amused indulgence. "But don't be rough with it. Gently back of the red line on both throttles. That's it. Not so fast. Gently! Now into neutral on the left. That's it; see how it turns around?"

There was a shout from somewhere in the rear of the vessel, to which the big man responded with a tremendously rapid burst of speech, only a few words of which were intelligible to Chris. "I have to leave for a few minutes," he added. "Remember, don't try anything tricky, and don't lose sight of the beacon."

"No, lord."

As the boat's owner left the cabin, Chris caught a few more words, amusedly beginning to relate the story of the dock boy who had picked up a few stammering words of the language and immediately had decided that he was a pilot; then the voices dwindled to a blurred murmur. Chris spent the next few minutes testing the controls of the boat in small jerks and spurts, being as inexpert about it as he could manage, although the machine was really not difficult to master. Then, as directed, he set it to crawling in a fixed circle, counter-clockwise, left the bucket seat, and edged his way back to the door leading to the next chamber.

He had no idea what it was that he expected to overhear—he was simply avid for more information, to relieve the recent famine. He was certainly unprepared for what he got.

The men were talking in a rapid patois which differed sharply from the form of the Universal Language which the memory cells had been teaching him, but many phrases were clear and distinct:

". . . can't be done without keeping the city, that's all there is to it."

". . . Disable it? . . . Don't even have a blueprint of the machinery, let alone a map."

"That can come later, after we've occupied . . . We've got thousands of commoners to throw away, but the defenses—It's essential first to immobilize their Huacu, or whatever they call it here. We can't afford to fight on their terms."

"Then what's the problem? We've got their two chief generals for hostages. We can hold them forever if necessary . . . Don't even know the name of Castle Wolfwhip, let alone where it—"

There the conversation ended abruptly. With a grinding thump, the swan boat hit something and began clumsily to try to climb it. Chris was thrown to the deck, and on the other side of the doorway there was the sound of scrambling and of angry shouting. Then that too was cut off as the bulkhead swung to, of its own inertia.

Fighting to regain his balance against the blind lurching of the boat, Chris scrambled up, and dogged the bulkhead tightly closed all the way around. Was there any way to lock it, too? Yes, there was a big bolt that could be thrown which would hold the whole series of dogs in place, provided that it could not be unbolted from the other side. Well, he'd have to take his chances on that, though a fat padlock to complete the job would have made him feel more comfortable. Then, he clambered up the tilted, pitching deck to the control seat.

The boat had been doing its best to travel in a circle, but Chris had failed to realize that mud is a shifting, inexact sort of medium in which to turn a machine loose. The circle had been precessing, and the boat had run head-on into a dock. Okie cops were running toward it.

Chris reversed both engines, backing away from the city as rapidly as the boat would go, but that was not half as fast as he would have liked. Then he switched the vehicle around, end for end, and set it to whining and sliding squarely into the teeth of the storm, aiming it for the pip on the cross hairs which showed on the control board as its homing signal.

Where that might wind him up, he had no idea. He could only hope that it might be Castle Wolfwhip, and that he would find Anderson and Dulany there—and that the six furious colonists in back of the locked bulkhead would not be able to burn their way out before he got there.

CHAPTER SEVEN: Why Not to Keep Demons

Before tbe swan boat had been on its slobbering way outward for more than five minutes, the sodium-yellow glare of the city's dockside beacon dimmed and vanished as swiftly as if it had been snuffed out. Except for his prisoners, whom he was trying to ignore, Chris was alone in the shell of the boat, like a chick in an egg, with nothing for company but the unfamiliar instruments, the grunting of the engines, and the flash and crash of the eternal storm.

He studied the control board intently, but it told him very little that he did not already know. All the lettering on and around the instruments were in the Cyrillic alphabet—and although the City Fathers expected citizens to be able to speak the Universal Language, up to now they had given Chris not even a first lesson in how to read it. Even so obvious a device as the swan boat's radio set was incomprehensible to him in detail; after a brief study, he gave up all hope of finding the city's master frequency and calling for pursuit and aid. He could not even decide whether it was an AFM or a PM tuner, let alone read the calibrations on the dial.

Nevertheless he urgently needed to signal. Above all, he needed to let the city know the details, fragmentary though they were, of the plotting that he had overheard. Running away with the plotters in their own swan boat had been an impulse of desperation, which he was already beginning more and more to regret. If only he had managed somehow to get back on shore, and told somebody in Amalfi's office what he had learned, pronto!

But the question was, would they have listened, or believed him if they had? Nobody who was anybody aboard the city seemed to want to bother with youngsters until they had become citizens; the adults were all too old, somehow, to be even approachable—and for that matter citizens paid very little attention to passengers of any age.

Of course, Chris could have told the City Fathers what he knew, easily enough—but everything that was told the City Fathers went into the memory cells, which was the equivalent of putting it in dead storage. The City Fathers never took action on what they knew, or even volunteered information, unless directed; otherwise they only held it until it was asked for, which might take centuries.

In any event the die was cast. Now he also needed someone in the city to know where he was going, and to follow him. But among the glittering, enigmatic instruments before him he could find no way to bring that about, nor did he in fact know even vaguely how the city might chase after him if it did know what his situation was. The Tin Cabs operated upon broadcast power which faded out at the city's perimeter, and to the best of Chris's knowledge, the city had no ground vehicles capable of coping with shifting, ambiguous, invisible terrain of this kind. Somewhere in storage, true, it did have a limited number of larger military aircraft, but how could you fly one of them in this region of perpetual storm? And even if you could, what would you look for, in a world where even the largest villages and castles produced and consumed so little power that detecting instruments would be unable to differentiate a city from a random splatter of lightning bolts?

The swan boat churned onward single-mindedly. After a while, Chris noticed that it had been at least several minutes since he had had to apply corrections in order to keep the green pip on the cross hairs. Experimentally, he let go of the controls entirely. The pip stayed centered. Some signal—perhaps simply his keeping the pip centered for a given length of time—had cut in an automatic pilot.

That was a help, in a way, but it deprived him of anything to do but worry, and added a new worry to the list: How could he cut the autopilot *out* of the circuit if he needed to? The pertinent switch was doubtless in plain sight and clearly marked, but again, he couldn't read the markings. As for his prisoners, they were being disturbingly quiet. In the back of his mind he had been anticipating some attempt to burn through the door—surely they had some sort of hand weapon back there which might serve the purpose—but they hadn't so much as pounded on it.

He hoped fervently that they were just being fatalistic about their captivity. If their silence meant that they were satisfied with it, that was bad news. The news was bad enough already, for he had no idea what he was going to do with them, or with the boat, when he got to Castle Wolfwhip—

And no time left to invent any plan, for in the next flash of lightning he saw the castle.

It was still several miles away, but even at this distance its massiveness was awe-inspiring. There were many towers in the city that were smaller; despite the lack of any adjacent structure with which to compare it, Chris guessed that the black, windowless pile could not be less than thirty stories high.

At first, he thought it was surrounded by a moat, but that was only an effect of foreshortening brought on by distance. Actually, it stood in the middle of a huge lake, so storm-lashed that Chris could not imagine how the clumsy swan boat could survive on it, let alone make any headway.

He pulled back on the throttles; but as he had suspected, the boat no longer answered to the manual controls. It plowed doggedly forward into the water. A moment later, the compressed air tanks blew with a bubbling roar, and the lake closed over the boat completely. It was now traveling on the bottom.

Now he no longer had even the lightning flashes to see by—nothing but the lights inside the boat, which did not penetrate the murky water at all. It was as though the transparent shell had abruptly gone opaque.

After what seemed a long while—though it was probably no more than ten minutes—the treads made a grinding noise, as if they had struck stone, and the vehicle came gradually to a halt. On a hunch, Chris tried the manuals again, but there was still no response.

Then the outside lights came on.

The swan boat was sitting snugly in a berth within a sizable cavern. Through the rills of yellow water draining down its sides, Chris saw that it had a reception committee: four men, with rifles. They looked down into the boat at him, grinning unpleasantly. While he stared helplessly back, the engines quit—

—and the outside door swung open.

They put him in the same cell with Anderson and Dulany. His guardian was appalled to see him—"Gods

of all stars, Irish, now they're snatching children!"
—and then, after he had heard the story, thoroughly
disgusted. Dulany, as usual, said very little, but he
did not look exactly pleased.

"There's probably a standard recognition signal you
should have sent, except that you wouldn't have
known what it was," Anderson said. "These petty barons did a lot of fighting among themselves before we
got here—fleecing us is probably the first project
they've been together on since this mudball was
colonized."

"Bluster," Dulany commented.

"Yes, it's part of the feudal *mores*. Chris, those
men in the boat are going to take a lot of ribbing
from their peers, regardless of the fact that they
were never in any danger and they had sense enough
to let you spin your own noose. They'll be likely to
take it out on you when you're taken out for questioning."

"I've already been interviewed," Chris said grimly.
"And they did."

"You have? Murder! There goes that one up the
flue, Irish."

"Complication," Dulany agreed.

Anderson fell silent, leaving Chris to wonder what
they had been talking about. Evidently they had
been planning something which his news had torpe-
doed—though it was hard to imagine even the beginnings of such a plan, for their captors, out of a
respect for the two Okies which Chris knew to be
more than justified, had left them nothing but their
underwear. At last the boy said hesitantly:

"What could I have done if my interview were still
coming up?"

"Located our space suits," Anderson said gloomily.
"Not that they'd have let you search the place, that's
for sure, but you might have gotten a hint, or tricked

them into dropping one. Even wary men sometimes underestimate youngsters. Now we'll just have to think of something else."

"There are dozens of space suits standing around the wall of that big audience chamber," Chris said. "If you could only get there, maybe one of them would fit one of you."

Dulany only smiled slightly. Anderson said: "Those aren't suits, Chris; they're armor—plate armor. Useless here, but they have some kind of heraldic significance; I think the Barons used to collect them from each other, like scalps."

"That may be," Chris said stubbornly, "but there were at least two real suits there. I'm sure of that."

The two sergeants looked at each other. "Is it possible—?" Anderson said. "They've got the bravado for it, all right."

"Could be."

"By Sirius, there's a bluff we've got to call! Get busy on that lock, Irish!"

"In my underwear? Nix."

"What difference does that—oh, I see." Anderson grimaced impatiently. "We'll have to wait for lights out. Happily it won't be long."

"How are you going to bust the lock, Sergeant Dulany?" Chris asked. "It's almost as big as my head!"

"Those are the easy kinds," Dulany said loquaciously.

Chris in fact never did find out what Dulany did with the lock, for the operation was performed in the dark. Standing as instructed all the way to the back of the cell, he did not even hear anything until the huge, heavy door was thrown back with a thunderous crash.

The crash neatly drowned out the only yell the guard outside managed to get off. In this thunder-ridden fortress, nobody would think anything of such a noise. Then there was a jangle of keys, and two loud clicks as the unfortunate man was manacled with his own handcuffs. The Okies rolled him into the cell.

"What'll I do if he comes to?" Chris whispered hoarsely.

"Won't for hours," Dulany's voice said. "Shut the door. We'll be back."

From the boarding-squad sergeant, nine words all in one speech had the reassuring force of an oration. Chris grinned and shut the door.

Nothing seemed to happen thereafter for hours, except that the thunder got louder. That was certainly no novelty on Heaven. But was it possible for even the heaviest thunderclap to shake a pile of stone as squat and massive as Castle Wolfwhip? Surely it couldn't last long if that were the case—and yet it was obviously at least a century old, probably more.

The fourth such blast answered his question. It was an explosion, and it was *inside* the building. In response, all the lights came on; and Chris saw that the door had been jarred open.

When he went over to close it again, he found himself looking down a small precipice. The corridor floor had collapsed. Several stunned figures were sitting amid the rubble it had made on the story below it. Considering the size of the blocks of which it had been made, they were lucky that it hadn't killed them.

Still another explosion, and this time the lights went back out. Quite evidently, the suits Chris had seen in the audience hall had indeed been Anderson's and Dulany's battle dress. Well, this ought to cure the baron of Castle Wolfwhip of the habit of exhibiting his scalps. It ought to cure him of the habit of kidnapping Okies, too. It occurred to Chris that the whole plan of using Anderson and Dulany as hostages, even in their underwear, was about as safe an operation as trying to imprison two demons in a corncrib.

Then they were back. Seeing them hovering in the collapsed corridor, their helmet lamps making a shifting, confusing pattern of shadows, Chris realized, too, what kind of vehicle the city would have sent out after him if he had managed to get word back.

"You all right?" Anderson's PA speaker demanded. "Good. Didn't occur to me that the floor might go."

They came into the cell. The guard, who had just recovered his senses, took one look and crawled into the corner farthest from the two steel figures.

"Now we've got a problem. We've got a safe-conduct out of the castle, but we can't carry you through that storm, and we don't dare risk putting you in one of their suits."

"Boat," Dulany said, pointing at Chris.

"That's right, I forgot, he knows how to drive one. Okay, boy, stick your elbows out and we'll fly you out to where there's a floor you can walk on. Irish, let's go."

"One minute." Dulany unhooked a bunch of keys from his waist and tossed them into the corner where the guard was cowering. "Right."

Only Anderson joined him in the swan boat, still in his armor; Dulany stayed airborne, in radio communication with Anderson, in case the colonials should have the notion of making the boat turn around and return home on autopilot. After he saw the holes the two cops had torn through the great walls of Castle Wolfwhip, Chris doubted that they'd even entertain such a notion, but obviously it was sensible not to take chances where it wasn't necessary.

The moment the boat was crawling across the bottom of the lake, Anderson took his helmet off and turned promptly to studying the control board. Finally he nodded and snapped three switches.

"That should do it."

"Do what?"

"Prevent them from putting this tub under remote control. In fact from this point on they won't even be able to locate her. Now Irish can shoot on ahead of us and get the word to the Mayor." He put the helmet back on and spoke briefly, then doffed it.

"Now, Chris," he said grimly, "comes the riot act."

CHAPTER EIGHT: The Ghosts of Space

The "riot act" was every bit as unpleasant as he had foreseen it would be, but somehow he managed to live through it—mostly by bearing in mind as firmly as possible that he had it coming. He was never likely to become a real Okie by stealing the property of people who had hired the city on to do a job, no matter how good he thought his reasons were.

And in this first disastrous instance he had simply been in the way. The city would have known soon enough in any event of the fact that Anderson and Dulany were being held prisoner, since the colonists of Heaven could not have used them effectively as hostages without notifying Amalfi of the fact; and there was no doubt in Chris's mind that the two cops could have gotten out of Castle Wolfwhip without his intervention, and perhaps a good deal faster, too. Above all, they might have been gotten out by Amalfi *without violence*, and thus saved the contract intact. The appearance of Chris as a third prisoner had been totally unwelcomed to *both* sides, and had turned what had been merely a tense situation into an explosion.

In the end, they gave him full marks for imagination and boldness, as well as for coolness under fire, but by that time Chris had learned enough about the situation to feel that his chances of ever becoming a citizen were not worth an Oc dollar. The new contract was considerably more limited than the old, and called for reparations for the damage the two sergeants had done to Castle Wolfwhip; under it, the city stood to gain considerably less than before.

Chris was astonished that there was any new contract at all, and said so, rather hesitantly. Anderson explained:

"Violence between employer and employee is as old as man, Chris, but the work has to be done all the same. The colonists as a corporate entity disown the kidnapper and claim the right to deal with him according to their own system of justice, which we're bound to respect. Damage to real property, on the other hand, has to be paid for—and the city can't disown Irish and me because we're officers and agents of the city."

"But what about the scheme to ground the city and take it over?"

"We know nothing about that except what you overheard. That would have no status in a colonial court, and probably wouldn't even if you were a citizen—in this case, if you were of legal age."

And there it was again. "Well, there's something else I've been wondering about," Chris said. "Why is the age to start the drugs fixed at eighteen? Wouldn't they work at any age? Suppose we took aboard a man forty years old who also happened to be a red-hot expert at something we needed. Couldn't you start him on the drugs anyhow?"

"We could and we would," Anderson assured him. "Eighteen is only the *optimum* age, the earliest age at which we can be sure the specimen is physically mature. You see the drugs can't set the clock back.

They just arrest aging from the moment when they're first given. Tell me, have you ever heard of the legend of Tithonus?"

"No, I'm afraid not."

"I don't know it very well myself; ask the City Fathers. But briefly, he got himself in the good books of the goddess of dawn, Eos, and asked for the gift of immortality. She gave it to him, but he was pretty old at the time. When he realized that he was just going to stay that way forever, he asked Eos to take the gift back. So she changed him into a grasshopper, and you know how long *they* live."

"Hmm. A man who was going to be a permanent seventy-five wouldn't be much good to himself, I guess. Or to the city either."

"That's the theory," the perimeter sergeant agreed. "But of course we have to take 'em as we find 'em. Amalfi went on the drugs at fifty—which, for him, happened to be his prime."

Thus his education went on, much as before, except that he stayed scrupulously away from the docks. Since the new contract was limited to three months, there probably wouldn't have been much to see down there anyhow—or so he told himself, not without a suspicion that there were a few holes in his logic. In addition, he got some sympathy and support from a wholly unexpected source: Piggy Kingston-Throop.

"It just goes to show you how much truth there is in all this jabber about citizenship," he said fiercely, at their usual after-class meeting. "Here you go and do them a big fat favor, and all they can think of to do is lecture you for getting in their way. They even go right on doing business with these guys who were going to grab the city if they could."

"Well, we do have to eat."

"Yeah, but it's dirty money all the same. Come to think of it, though, if I'd have been in your shoes I'd have handled it differently."

"I know," Chris said, "that's what they all keep telling me. I should never have gotten into the boat in the first place."

"Pooh, that part's all right," Piggy said scornfully. "If you hadn't gotten into the boat they'd never have known about the plot to take the city—that's the favor you did them, and don't you forget it. They're on their guard now. No, I mean what happened after you locked the guys up in the back cabin. You said that the boat had bumped into the dock and was trying to climb it, right?"

"Yes."

"And a lot of cops came running?"

"I don't know about a lot," Chris said cautiously. "There were three or four, I think."

"Okay. Now if it had been me, I would have just stopped the boat right there, and gotten out, and told the cops what I'd heard. Let *them* drag it out of the guys you'd locked up. You know how the City Fathers cram all that junk into our heads in class—well, they can take stuff out the same way. Dad says it's darned unpleasant for the victim, but they get it."

Chris could only shrug helplessly. "You're right. That would have been the sensible thing to do. And it seems obvious the way you tell it. But all I can say is it didn't occur to me." He thought a moment, and then added: "But in a way I'm not too sorry, Piggy. That way, I never would have gotten to Castle Wolfwhip at all—sure, it would have been better if I hadn't—but it sure was exciting while I was there."

"Boy, I'll bet it was! I wish I'd been there!" Piggy began to shadowbox awkwardly. "I wouldn't have hidden in any cell, believe you me. I'd have showed 'em!"

Chris did his best not to laugh. "Going by what I heard, if you'd gone along with the sergeants—if they'd let you—you'd have been killed by your own friends. Those weren't just rotten eggs they were throwing around."

"All the same, I'll bet—Hullo, we're lifting."

The city had not lifted yet, but Chris knew what Piggy meant; he too could hear the deepening hum of the spindizzies. "So we are. That three months sure went by in a hurry."

"Three months isn't much in space. We'll be eighteen before we know it."

"That," Chris said gloomily, "is exactly what I'm afraid of."

"Well, *I* don't give a darn. This whole deal about your running off with the boat proves that they don't mean what they say about earning citizenship. Like I say, the whole thing's just a scheme to keep kids in line, so they won't have to be watched so much. The minute you actually *do* something for the survival of the city, bingo! the roof falls on you. Never mind that, it was a good thing to do and shows you've got guts—you've caused them trouble, and that's what the system's supposed to prevent."

There was, Chris saw, something to be said for the theory, no matter how exaggerated Piggy's way of putting it was. In Chris's present state of discouragement, it would be a dangerously easy point of view to adopt.

"Well, Piggy, what I want to know is, what are you going to do if you're wrong? I mean, supposing the City Fathers decide not to make you a citizen, and it turns out that they can't be fixed? Then you'll be stuck with being a passenger for the rest of your life—and it'd only be a normal lifetime, too."

"Passengers aren't as helpless as they think," Piggy said darkly. "Some one of these days the Lost City is going to come back, and when that happens, all of a sudden the passengers are going to be top dog."

"The Lost City? I never heard of it."

"Of course you haven't. And the City Fathers won't ever tell you about it, either. But word gets around."

"Okay, don't be mysterious," Chris said. "What's it all about?"

Piggy's voice dropped to a hoarse whisper. "Do you swear not to tell anybody else, except another passenger?"

"Sure."

Piggy looked elaborately over both shoulders before going on. As usual, they were the only youngsters on the street, and none of the adults were paying the slightest attention to them.

"Well," he said in the same tone of voice, "it's like this. One of the first cities ever to take off was a big one. Nobody knows its name, but *I* think it was Los Angeles. Anyhow, it got lost, and ran out of drugs, and then out of food, way off in some part of space that was never colonized, so it couldn't find any work either. But then they made a planetfall on a new world, something nobody had ever seen before. It was like Earth—bigger, but the same gravity, and a little more oxygen in the air, and a perfect climate—like spring all year round, even at the poles. If you planted seeds there, you had to jump back in a hurry or the plant would hit you under the chin, they grew so fast.

"But that wasn't the half of it."

"It sounds like plenty," Chris said.

"That was all good, but they found something else even better. There was a kind of grain growing wild there, and when they analyzed it to see whether or not it was good to eat, *they found it contained an antideath drug*—not any of ours, but better than all of ours rolled into one. They didn't even have to extract it—all they had to do was make bread out of the plant."

"Wow. Piggy, is this just a story?"

"Well, I can't give you an affidavit," Piggy said,

offended. "Do you want to hear the rest or don't you?"

"Go ahead," Chris said hastily.

"So then the question was, what were they going to do with their city? They didn't need it. Everything they needed came right up out of the ground while their backs were turned. So they decided to stock it up and send it out into space again, to look for other cities. Whenever they make contact with a new Okie town, they take all the passengers off—nobody else—and take them back to this planet where *everybody* can have the drugs, because there's never any shortage."

"Suppose the other city doesn't want to give up its passengers?"

"Why wouldn't it want to? If it had any use for them, they'd be citizens, wouldn't they?"

"Yes, but just suppose."

"They'd give them up anyhow. Like I said, the Lost City is *big*."

Unfortunately for the half-million other questions Chris wanted to ask, at that point the city moaned softly to the sound of the take-cover siren. The boys parted hurriedly; but Chris, after a moment's thought, did not go home. Instead, he holed up in a public information booth, where he fed his card into the slot and asked for the Librarian.

He had promised not to mention the Lost City to anyone but another passenger, which ruled out questioning his guardian, or the City Fathers directly; but he had thought of a way to ask an indirect question. The Librarian was that one of the 134 machines comprising the City Fathers which had prime charge of the memory banks, and was additionally charged with teaching; it did not collect information, but only catalogued and dispensed it. Interpretation was not one of its functions.

"CARD ACCEPTED. PROCEED."

"Question: Do any antiagathics grow naturally—I mean, do they occur in plants that could be raised as crops?"

A brief pause. "A PRECURSOR OF THE ANTISLEEP DRUG IS A STEROID SUBSTANCE OCCURRING NATURALLY IN A NUMBER OF YAMLIKE PLANTS FOUND ON EARTH, LARGELY IN CENTRAL AND SOUTH AMERICA. THIS SAPOGENIN IS NOT, HOWEVER, IN ITSELF AN ANTIAGATHIC, AND MUST BE CONVERTED; HUNDREDS OF DIFFERENT STEROIDS ARE PRODUCED FROM THE SAME STARTING MATERIAL.

"ASCOMYCIN IS PRODUCED BY DEEP-TANK FERMENTATION OF A MICROORGANISM AND HARVESTED FROM THE BEER. THIS PROCEDURE MIGHT BROADLY BE DEFINED AS CROPRAISING.

"ALL OTHER KNOWN ANTIAGATHICS ARE WHOLLY SYNTHETIC DRUGS."

Chris sat back, scratching his head in exasperation. He had hoped for a clear-cut, yes-or-no answer, but what he had gotten stood squarely in the middle. No antiagathics were harvested from real crops; but if a crop plant could produce something at least enough like an antiagathic to be converted into one, then that part of Piggy's astounding story was at least possible. Unhappily, he could think of no further questions sufficiently indirect to keep his main point of interest hidden.

Then he noticed that the booth had not returned his card to him. This was quite usual; it meant only that the Librarian, which spent its whole mechanical life substituting free association for thinking, had a related subject it would talk about if he liked. Usually it wasn't worth while exploring these, for the Librarian could go on forever if so encouraged; all he needed to do now was to say "Return," and he could take his card and go. But the take-cover alert wasn't over yet; so, instead, he said, "Proceed."

"SUBJECT, ANTIAGATHICS AS BY-PRODUCTS OF AGRICUL-

TURE. SUB-SUBJECT, LEGENDARY IDYLLIC PLANETS." Chris sat bolt upright. "ANTIAGATHICS AS BY-PRODUCTS OF AGRICULTURE, USUALLY IN THE DAILY BREAD, IS ONE OF THE COMMON FEATURES OR DIAGNOSTIC SIGNS OF THE LEGENDARY PLANETS OF NOMAD-CITY MYTHOLOGY. OTHERS INCLUDE: EARTHLIKE GRAVITY BUT GREATER LAND AREA; EARTHLIKE ATMOSPHERE BUT MORE ABUNDANT OXYGEN; EARTHLIKE WEATHER BUT WITH UNIFORM CLIMATE, AND COMPLETE ISOLATION FROM EXISTING TRADE LANES. NO PLANET MATCHING THIS DESCRIPTION IN ANY PARTICULAR HAS YET BEEN FOUND. NAMES OFTEN GIVEN TO SUCH WORLDS INCLUDE: ARCADY, BRADBURY, CELEPHAIS . . ."

Chris was so stunned that the Librarian had worked its way all the way through "ZIMIAMVIA" and had begun another alphabetical catalogue before he thought to ask for his card back. His question had not been very crafty, after all.

By the time he emerged from the booth, the storms of Heaven had vanished and the city was once more soaring amid the stars. Furthermore, he was late for dinner.

So, after all, there had been no secret to keep. Chris told the Andersons the story of his failure to outwit the Librarian; it made the best possible excuse for his lateness, since it was true, and it reduced Carla to tears of helpless laughter. The perimeter sergeant was amused, too, but there was an undercurrent of seriousness beneath his amusement.

"You're learning, Chris. It's easy to think that because the City Fathers are dead, they're also stupid; but you see that that isn't the case. Otherwise they would never have been given the power that they wield—and in some departments their power is absolute."

"Even over the Mayor?"

"Yes and no. They can't forbid the Mayor anything. But if he goes against their judgment more often than they're set to tolerate, they can revoke his office. That's never happened here, but if it does, we'll have to sit still for it. If we don't, they'll stop the machinery."

"Wow. Isn't it dangerous to give machines so much power? Suppose they had a breakdown?"

"If there were only a few of them, that would be a real danger; but there are more than a hundred, and they monitor and repair each other, so in fact it will never happen. Sanity and logic is their stock in trade— which is why they can accept or reject the results of any election we may run. The popular will is some-times an idiot, but no human being can be given the power to overrule it; not safely. But the machines can.

"Of course, there are stories about towns whose City Fathers ran amok with them. They're just sto-ries, like Piggy's 'Lost City'—but they're important even when they're not true. Whenever a new way of living appears in the universe, the people who adopt it see quickly enough that it isn't perfect. They try to make it better, sure; but there are always some things about it that can't be changed. And the hopes and fears that are centered on those points get turned into stories.

"Piggy's myth, for instance. We live long lives in the cities, but not everybody can have the gift. It's impossible that everyone should have it—the whole universe isn't big enough to contain the sheer mass of flesh that would accumulate if we all lived and bred as long as we each wanted to. Piggy's myth says it is possible, which is untrue; but what *is* true about it is that it points to one of the real dissatisfactions with our way of living, real because nothing can be done about it.

"The story of the runaway City Fathers is another. No such thing has ever happened as far as I know, and it doesn't seem to be possible. But no live man *likes* to take orders from a bunch of machines, or to think that he may lose his life if they say so—but he might, because the City Fathers are the jury aboard most cities. So he invents a cautionary tale about City Fathers running amok, though actually he's talking not about the machines at all—he's warning that *he* may run amok if he's pushed too far.

"The universe of the cities is full of these ghosts. Sooner or later somebody is going to tell you that some cities go bindlestiff."

"Somebody has," Chris admitted. "But I didn't know what he meant."

"It's an old Earth term. A hobo was an honest migratory worker, who lived that way because he liked it. A tramp was the same kind of fellow, except that he wouldn't work—he lived by stealing or begging from settled people. In hobo society both kinds were more or less respectable. But the bindlestiff was a migrant who stole from other migrants—he robbed their bindles, the bags they carried their few belongings in. That man was an outcast from both worlds.

"It's common talk that some cities in trouble have gone bindlestiff—taken to preying on other cities. Again, there are no specific instances. IMT is the town that's most often mentioned, but the last we heard of IMT, she wasn't a bindlestiff—she'd been outlawed for a horrible crime on a colony planet, but technically that makes her only a tramp. A mean one, but still only a tramp."

"I see," Chris said slowly. "It's like the story about City Fathers going crazy. Cities do starve, I know that; and the bindlestiff story says, 'How will *we* behave when the pinch comes?'"

Anderson looked gratified. "Look at that," he said to Carla. "Maybe I should have been a teacher!"

"Nothing to do with you," Carla said composedly.

"Chris is doing all the thinking. Besides, I like you better as a cop."

The perimeter sergeant sighed, a little ruefully. "Oh, well, all right. Then I'll give you only one more story. You've heard of the Vegan orbital fort?"

"Oh, sure. That was in the history, way back."

"Good. Well, for once, that's a real thing. There was a Vegan orbital fort, and it did get away, and nobody knows where it is now. The City Fathers say that it probably died when it ran out of supplies, but it was a pretty big job and might well have survived under circumstances no ordinary city could live through. If you ask the City Fathers for the probabilities, they tell you that they can't give you any figures—which is a bad sign in itself.

"Now, that's as far as the facts go. But there's a legend to go with them. The legend says that the fort is foraging through the trade lanes, devouring cities—just the way a dragonfly catches mosquitoes, on the wing. Nobody has actually seen the fort since the scorching of Vega, but the legend persists; every time a city disappears, the word goes around, first, that a bindlestiff got it, and next, that the fort got it.

"What's it all about, Chris? Tell me."

Chris thought for a long time. At last he said:

"I'm kind of confused. It ought to be the same kind of story as the others—something people are afraid of. Like meeting up some day with a planet, like the Vegan system, where the people have more on the ball than we do and will gobble us up the way we did Vega—"

Anderson's big fist crashed down on the dinner table, making all the plates jump. "Precisely!" he crowed. "Look there, Carla—"

Carla's own hands reached out and covered the Sergeant's fist gently. "Dear, Chris isn't through yet. You didn't give him a chance to finish."

"I didn't? But—sorry, Chris. Go ahead."

"I don't know whether I'm through or not," Chris said, embarrassed and floundering. "This one story just confuses me. It's not as simple as the others; I think I'm sure of that."

"Go ahead."

"Well, it's sensible to be afraid of meeting somebody stronger than yourself. It might well happen. And there is a real Vegan orbital fort, or at least there was one. The other stories don't have that much going for them that's real—except the things people are actually afraid of, the things the stories *actually* are about. Does this make sense?"

"Yes. The things the stories symbolize."

"That's the word. To be afraid of the fort is to be afraid of a real thing. But what does the story symbolize? It's got to be the same kind of thing in the end—the fear people have of themselves. The story says, 'I'm tired of working to be a citizen, and obeying the Earth cops, and protecting the city, and living a thousand years with machines bossing me, and taking sass from colonists, and I don't know what all else. If I had a great big city that I could run all by myself, I'd spend the next thousand years smashing things up!'"

There was a long, long silence, during which Chris became more and more convinced that he had again talked out of turn, and far too much. Carla did not seem to be upset, but her husband looked stunned and wrathful.

"There *is* something wrong with the apprenticeship system," he growled at last, though he did not appear to be speaking to either of them. "First the Kingston-Throop kid—and now this. Carla! You're the brains in the family. Did it ever occur to you that that fort legend had anything to do with education?"

"Yes, dear. Long ago."

"Why didn't you say so?"

"I would have said so as soon as we had a child;

until then, it wasn't any of my business. Now Chris has said it for me."

The perimeter sergeant turned a lowering face on Chris. "You," he said, "are a holy terror. I set out to teach you, as I was charged to do, and you wind up teaching me. Not even Amalfi knows this side of the fort story, I'll swear to that—and when he hears it, there's going to be a real upheaval in the schools."

"I'm sorry," Chris said miserably. He did not know what else to say.

"Don't be sorry!" Anderson roared, surging to his feet. "Stick to your guns! Let the other guy be afraid of ghosts—you know the one thing about ghosts that you need to know, no matter what kind of ghosts they are: They have nothing to do with the dead. It's *always* themselves that people are afraid of."

He looked about distractedly. "I've got to go topside. Here's my hurry—where's my hat?" He roared out, banging one hand against the side of the door, leaving Chris frozen with alarm.

Then Carla began to laugh all over again.

CHAPTER NINE: The Tramp

But if the errand on behalf of which Sgt. Anderson had undertaken his rhinoceros-charge exit had really had anything to do with education, Chris had yet to see it reflected in his own. That got steadily harder, as the City Fathers, blindly and impersonally assuming that he had comprehended what they had already stuffed into his head, began to build his store of knowledge toward some threshold where it would start to be useful for the survival of the city. As this process went forward, Chris's old headaches dwindled into the category of passing twinges; these days, he sometimes felt actively, physically sick from sheer inability to make sense of what was being thrust upon him. In a moment of revulsion, he told the City Fathers so.

"IT WILL PASS. THE NORMAL HUMAN BEING FEELS AN AVERAGE OF TWENTY SMALL PAINS PER HOUR. IF ANY PERSIST, REPORT TO MEDICAL."

No, he was not going to do that; he was not going to be invalided out of his citizenship if he could help it. Yet it seemed to him that what he was suffering couldn't fairly be called "small pains." What to do, since he feared that Medical's cure would be worse than the disease? He didn't want to worry the Andersons, either—he had repaid their kindnesses with enough trouble already.

That left nobody to talk to but Dr. Braziller, that fearsome old harpy who seldom spoke in any language but logarithms and symbolic logic. Chris stood off from this next-but-worst choice for weeks; but in the end he had to do it. Though there was nothing physically wrong with him even now, he had the crazy notion that the City Fathers were about to kill him; one more stone of fact on his head and his neck would break.

"And well it might," Dr. Braziller told him, in her office after class. "Chris, the City Fathers are not interested in your welfare; I suppose you know that. They're interested in only one thing: the survival of the city. That's their prime directive. Otherwise they have no interest in people at all; after all, they're only machines."

"All right," Chris said, blotting his brow with a trembling hand. "But Dr. Braziller, what good will it do the city for them to blow all my fuses? I've been trying, really I have. But it isn't good enough for them. They keep right on piling the stuff in, and it makes no *sense* to me!"

"Yes, I've noticed that. But there's reason behind what they're doing, Chris. You're almost eighteen; and they're probing for some entrance point into your talents—some spark that will take fire, some bent of yours that might some day turn into a valuable specialty."

"I don't think I have any," Chris said dully.

"Maybe not. That remains to be seen. If you have one, they'll find it; the City Fathers never miss on this kind of thing. But Chris, my dear, you can't expect it to be easy on you. Real knowledge is always hard to come by—and now that the machines think you might actually be of some use to the city—"

"But they can't think that! They haven't found anything!"

"I can't read their minds, because they haven't any," Dr. Braziller said quietly. "But I've seen them do this before. They wouldn't be driving you in this way if they didn't suspect that you're good for something. They're trying to find out what it is, and unless you want to give up right now, you're going to have to sit still while they look. It doesn't surprise me that it makes you ill. It made me ill, too; I feel a little queasy just remembering it, and that was eighty years ago."

She fell silent suddenly, and in that moment, she looked even older than she had ever seemed before . . . old, and frail, and deeply sad, and—could it be possible?—beautiful.

"Now and then I wonder if they were right," Dr. Braziller told the heaped papers on her desk. "I wanted to be a composer. But the City Fathers had never heard of a successful woman composer, and it's hard to argue with that kind of charge. No, Chris, once the machines have fingered you, you have to be what they want you to be; the only alternative is to be a passenger—which means, to be nothing at all. I don't wonder that it makes you ill. But, Chris—fight back, fight back! Don't let those cabinetheads lick you! Stick them out. They're only probing, and the minute we find out what they want, we can bear down on it. I'll help wherever I can—*I hate those things*. But first, we have to find out what they want. Have you got the guts, Chris?"

"I don't know. I'll try. But I don't know."

"Nobody knows, yet. They don't know themselves— that's your only hope. They want to know what you can do. You have to show them. As soon as they find out, you will be a citizen—but until then, it's going to be rough, and there will be nothing that anybody can do to help you. It will be up to you, and you alone."

It was heartening to have another ally, but Chris would have found Dr. Braziller's whole case more convincing had he been able to see the faintest sign of a talent—any talent at all—emerging under the ungentle ministrations of the machines. True, lately they had been bearing down heavily on his interest in history—but what good was that aboard an Okie city? The City Fathers themselves were the city's historians, just as they were its library, its accounting department, its schools and much of its government. No live person was needed to teach the subject or to write about it, and at best, as far as Chris could see, it could never be more than a hobby for an Okie citizen.

Even in the present instance, Chris was not being called upon to *do* anything with history but pass almost incredibly hard tests in it—tests which consisted largely of showing that he had retained all of the vast mass of facts that the City Fathers were determinedly shoving into him. And this was no longer just history from the Okie point of view. Whole systems of world and interstellar history—Machiavelli, Plutarch, Thucydides, Gibbon, Marx, Pareto, Spengler, Sarton, Toynbee, Durant and a score of others—came marching through the gray gas into his head, without mercy and with apparent indifference to the fact that they all contradicted each other fatally at crucial points.

There was no punishment for failures, since the City Fathers' pedagogy made failure of memory impossible, and it was only his memory that they seemed to be exploiting here. Instead, punishment was continuous: It lay in the certainty that though today's dose had been fiendish, tomorrow's would be worse.

"Now there you're wrong," Dr. Braziller told him. "Dead though they are, the machines aren't ignorant of human psychology—far from it. They know very well that some students respond better to reward than to punishment, and that others have to be driven by fear. The second kind is usually the less intelligent, and they know that too; how could they *not* know it after so many generations of experience? You're lucky that they've put you in the first category."

"You mean they're *rewarding* me?" Chris squeaked indignantly.

"Certainly."

"But how?"

"By letting you go on studying even when they're not satisfied with your progress. That's quite a concession, Chris."

"Maybe so," Chris said glumly. "But I'd get the point faster if they handed out lollipops instead."

Dr. Braziller had never heard of lollipops; she was an Okie. She only responded, a little primly: "You'd get it fast enough if they decided on a punishment system for you instead. They're rigidly just, but know nothing about mercy; and leniency with children is utterly foreign to them—which is one reason why I'm here."

The city hummed onward, and so did the days— and the months. Only Chris seemed to be making no progress in any visible direction.

No, that wasn't quite true. Piggy was going nowhere, either, as far as Chris could see. But there the situation was even more puzzling and full of complications. To begin with, ever since Chris had first met him, Piggy had been denying that he cared about what happened to him when he turned eighteen; so it was odd—though not entirely surprising—to discover that he did care, after all. In fact, though his situation appeared to be now quite hopeless, Piggy was full of loud self-confidence, belied in the next breath by dark hints of mysterious plans to cinch what was supposed to be cinched already, and even darker hints of awful things to come if it didn't turn out to be cinched. It was all more than Chris could manage to sort out, especially considering his inability to see more than half a minute into his own future. Some days he felt as though Piggy's old accusation—"Boy, you *are* dumb!"—were written on his forehead in letters of fire.

Although Piggy said almost nothing about it, Chris gathered that he had already approached his father on the subject of biasing the City Fathers in his favor on the Citizenship Tests, and had been rebuffed with a loud roar, only slightly tempered by the intervention of his mother. There was of course no way to study for the Tests, since they measured nothing but potentials, not achievements; which meant, in turn, that there was no such thing as a pony or a crib for them.

Now, it was obvious, Piggy was thinking back to Chris's adventure on Heaven. Judging by the questions he asked about it, Chris deduced that Piggy was searching for something heroic to do, in order to do it much better than Chris had. Chris was human enough to doubt that Piggy could make a much better showing, but in any event the city was still in space, so no opportunity offered itself.

Occasionally, too, he would disappear after class for several days running. On his return, his story was that he had been prowling around the city eavesdropping on the adult passengers. They were, Piggy said, up to something—just possibly, the building of a secret Dirac transmitter with which to call the Lost

City. Chris did not believe a word of this, nor did he think Piggy did either.

The simple, granite-keel facts were that time was running out for both of them, and that desperation was setting in: for Piggy because he had never tried, and for Chris because nothing he tried seemed to get him anywhere. All around them their younger schoolmates seemed to be opening into talents with the violence and unpredictability of popcorn, turning everything the memory cells fed them into salt and savor no matter how high the heat was turned up. In comparison, Chris felt as retarded as a dinosaur, and just as clumsy and gigantic.

It was in this atmosphere of pervasive, incipient failure that Sgt. Anderson one evening said calmly:

"Chris, the Mayor wants to talk to you."

From anyone else, Chris would have taken such an announcement as a practical joke, too absurd to be even upsetting. From Sgt. Anderson he did not know how to take it; he simply stared.

"Relax—it isn't going to be an ordeal, and besides I didn't say he wanted to *see* you. Sit back down and I'll explain."

Numbly, Chris did so.

"What's happened is this: We're approaching another job of work. From the first contacts we had with these people, it sounded simple and straightforward, but of course nothing ever is. (Amalfi says the biggest lie it's possible to tell in the English language is, 'It was as simple as that.') Supposedly we were going to be hired on to do a straightforward piece of local geology and mining—nothing so tricky as changing the whole setup of a planet; just a standard piece of work. You've seen the motto on City Hall?"

Chris had. It read: MOW YOUR LAWN, LADY? It had never seemed very dignified to him, but he was beginning to understand what it implied. He nodded.

"Well, that's the way it's always supposed to be: We come in, we do a job, we go out again. Local feuds don't count; we take no part in them.

"But as we got closer to signing a contract with this place—it's called Argus Three—we began to get hints that we were second comers. Apparently there'd already been one city on Argus, hired to do the job, but hadn't done it well.

"We tried to find out more about this, naturally, to be sure the Argidae were telling a straight story; we didn't want to be poaching on any other city's contract. But the colonists were very vague about the whole thing. Finally, though, they let it slip that the other city was still sitting on their planet, and still claimed to be working on the job, even though the contract deadline had passed. Tell me—what would you do in a case like that, if you were Amalfi?"

Chris frowned. "I don't know any other answer but the one in the books. If the planet has an over-stayed city, it's supposed to call the cops. All other cities should stay clear, otherwise they might get involved in the shooting, if there is any."

"Right; and this appears to be a classic case. The colonists can't be too explicit because they know that every word they broadcast to us is going to be over-heard; but the City Fathers have analyzed what Argus Three *has* sent us, and the chances are a hundred to one that that other city has settled on Argus Three for good . . . in short, that it means to take over the planet. The Argidae don't want to call the cops, for reasons we don't know. Instead, they seem to be trying to hire us to take on this tramp city and clear him out. If we tackle that, there *will* be shooting, that's for sure—and the cops will probably show up anyhow before it's over.

"Obviously, as you say, the thing to do is get out of the vicinity, fast. Cities ought not to fight with each other, let alone get involved in anything like a Violation. But Argus Three's offering us sixty-three million dollars in metal to slough them of the tramp before the cops arrive, and the Mayor thinks we can do it. Also, he hates tramps—I think he might even have taken on the job for nothing. The fact, anyhow, is that he *has* taken it."

The perimeter sergeant paused and eyed Chris, seemingly waiting for comments. At last Chris said: "What did the City Fathers say?"

"They said NO in a loud voice until the money was mentioned. After that they ran an accounting of the treasury, and gave Amalfi his head. They had a few additional facts to work from that I haven't told you yet, most of which seem to indicate that we can dispossess this tramp without too much damage to our own city, and very possibly before the cops even hear that anything's happening. All the same, bear in mind that they think of nothing but the city as a whole. If some of us get killed in the process they won't care, as long as the city itself gets off cleanly. They're not sentimental."

"I already know that," Chris said, with feeling. "But—how do I come into all this? Why does the Mayor want to talk to me? I don't know anything but what you've told me—and besides, he's already made up his mind."

"He's made up his mind," Anderson agreed, "but you know a lot that he doesn't know. As we get closer to Argus Three, he wants you to listen to the broadcasts from the Argidae, and anything we may pick up from the tramp, and fill him in on any clues you hear."

"But why?"

"Because you're the only person on board who knows the tramp at first hand," the perimeter sergeant said, with slow, deliberate emphasis. "It's your old friend Scranton."

"But—that can't be so! There were hundreds of us put on board from Scranton—all adults but me—"

"Press-gang sweepings," Anderson said with cold disgust. "Oh, there were one or two specialists we found a use for, but none of them ever paid any attention to city politics. The rest were bulgy-muscled misfits, a large proportion of them psychotics. We cured them, but we couldn't raise their IQ's; without something to sell, or the Interplanetary Grand Prix, or heavy labor to keep their minds off their minds, they're just so many vegetables. We—Irish and I—couldn't find even one worth taking into our squads. We've made citizens of the three good specialists, but the rest will be passengers till they die.

"But you're the happy accident of that crew right now, Chris. The City Fathers say that your history aboard Scranton shows that you *know* something about the town. Amalfi wants to mine that knowledge. Want to tackle it?"

"I—I'll try."

"Good." The perimeter Sergeant turned to the miniature tape recorder at his elbow. "Here's a complete transcript of everything we've heard from Argus Three so far. After you've heard it and made any comments that occur to you, Amalfi will begin to feed us the live messages, from the bridge. Ready?"

"No," Chris said, more desperately than he could ever have imagined possible for him. "Not yet. My head is about to bust already. Do I get off from school while this is going on? I couldn't take it, otherwise."

"No," Anderson said, "you don't. If a live message comes through while you're in class, we'll pull you out. But you'll go right back in again. Otherwise your schooling will go right on just as before, and if you can't take the new burden, well, that'll be too bad. You'd better get that straight right away, Chris.

This isn't a vacation, and it isn't a prize. It's a job, *for the survival of the city*. Either you take it or you don't; either way, you get no special treatment. Well?"

For what seemed to him to be a long time, Chris sat and listened to his echoing Okie headache. At last, however, he said resignedly:

"I'll take it."

Anderson snapped the switch, and the tape began to run on the spools.

The earliest messages, as Anderson had noted, were vague and brief. The later ones were longer, but even more cryptic. Chris was able to worry very little more information out of them than Amalfi and the City Fathers already had. As promised, he spoke to Amalfi—but from the Andersons' apartment, through a hookup which fed what he had to say to the mayor and to the machines simultaneously.

The machines asked questions about population, energy resources, degree of automation and other vital matters, not a one of which Chris could answer. The Mayor mostly just listened; on the few occasions when his heavy voice cut in, Chris was unable to figure out what he was getting at.

"Chris, this railroad you mentioned; how long before you were born had it been pulled up?"

"About a century, sir, I think. You know Earth went back to the railroads in the middle two thousands, when all the fossil fuels ran out and they had to give up the highways to farmland."

"No, I didn't know that. All right, go ahead."

Now the City Fathers were asking him about armament. He had no answer for that one, either.

There came a day, however, when this pattern changed suddenly and completely. He was, indeed, pulled out of class for the purpose, and hurried into a small anteroom containing little but a chair and two television screens. One of the screens showed Sgt. Anderson; the other, nothing but a testing pattern.

"Hello, Chris. Sit down and pay attention: this is important. We're getting a transmission from the tramp city. We don't know whether it's just a beacon or whether they want to talk to us. Amalfi thinks it's unlikely that they'd be putting out a beacon in their situation, regardless of the law—they've broken too many others already. He's going to try to raise them, now that you're here; he wants you to listen."

"Right, sir."

Chris could not hear his own city calling, but after only a few minutes—for they were quite close to Argus Three now—the test pattern on the other screen vanished, and Chris saw an odiously familiar face.

"Hullo. This here's Argus Three."

" 'This here' is *not* Argus Three," Amalfi's deep voice said promptly. " 'This here' is the city of Scranton, Pennsylvania, and there's no point in your hiding it. Get me your boss."

"Now wait a minute. Just who do you think—"

"This *here* is New York, New York, calling, and I said, 'Get me your boss.' Go do it."

The face by now was both sullen and confused. After a moment's hesitation, it vanished. The screen flickered, the test pattern came back briefly, and then a second familiar face was looking directly at Chris. It was impossible to believe that the man couldn't see him, and the idea was outright frightening.

"Hello, New York," he said, affably enough. "So you've got us figured out. Well, we've got you figured out, too. This planet is under contract to us; be notified."

"Recorded," Amalfi said. "We also have it a matter

of record that you are in Violation. Argus Three has made a new contract with us. It'd be the wisest course to clear ground and spin."

The man's eyes did not waver. Chris realized suddenly that it was an image of Amalfi he was staring at, not at Chris himself. "Spin yourself," he said evenly. "Our argument is with the colonists, not with you. We don't spin without a Vacate order from the cops. Once you mix into this, you may find it hard to mix out again. Be notified."

"Your self-confidence," Amalfi said, "is misplaced. Recorded."

The image from Scranton contracted to a bright point and vanished. The Mayor said at once:

"Chris, do you know either of those guys?"

"Both of them, sir. The first one's a small-time thug named Barney. I think he was the one who killed my brother's dog when I was impressed, but I didn't see who did it."

"I know the type. Go ahead."

"The other one is Frank Lutz. He was the city manager when I was aboard. It looks as if he still is."

"What's a city manager? Never mind, I'll ask the machines. All right. He looks dangerous; is he?"

"Yes, sir, he is. He's smart and he's tricky—and he has no more feeling than a snake."

"Sociopath," Amalfi said. "Thought so. One more question: Does he know you?"

Chris thought hard before answering. Lutz had seen him only once, and had never had to think about him as an individual again—thanks to the life-saving intervention of Frad Haskins. "Sir, he just might, but I'd say not."

"Okay. Give the details to the City Fathers and let them calculate the probabilities. Meanwhile we'll take no chances. Thanks, Chris. Joel, come topside, will you?"

"Yes, sir." Anderson waited until he heard the Mayor's circuit cut out. Then his image, too, seemed to be staring directly at Chris. In fact, it was.

"Chris, did you understand what Amalfi meant about taking no chances?"

"Uh—no, not exactly."

"He meant that we're to keep you out of this Lutz's sight. In other words, *no deFord expeditions on this job.* Is that clear?"

It was all too clear.

CHAPTER TEN: Argus Asleep

The Argus system was well named: It was not far inside a crowded and beautiful cluster of relatively young stars, so that the nights on its planet had indeed a hundred eyes, like the Argus of the myth. The youth of the cluster went far toward explaining the presence of Scranton, for like all third-generation stars, the sun of Argus was very rich in metals, and so were its planets.

Of these there were only a few—just seven, to be exact, of which only the three habitable ones had been given numbers, and only Argus III actually colonized; II was suitable only for Arabs, and IV for Eskimos. The other four planets were technically of the gas giant class, but they were rather undernourished giants: the largest of them was about the size of Sol's Neptune. The closeness of the stars in the cluster to each other had swept up much of the primordial gas before planet formation had gotten a good start; the Argus system was in fact the largest yet to be encountered in the cluster.

Argus III, as the city droned down over it, looked heart-stoppingly like Pennsylvania. Chris began to

feel a little sorry for the coming dispossession of
Scranton—of which he had no doubts whatsoever—
for surely the planet must have provided an intolerable temptation. It was mountainous over most of its
land area, which was considerable: water was confined to many thousands of lakes, and a few small
and intensely salty seas. It was also heavily wooded—
almost entirely with conifers, or plants much like
them, for evolution here had not yet gotten as far as
a flowering plant. The firlike trees had thick boles
and reared up hundreds of feet, noble monsters with
their many shoulders hunched, as they had to be to
bear their own weight in the two-G gravitation of
this metal-heavy planet. The first sound Chris heard
on Argus III after the city grounded was the explosion of a nearby seed cone, as loud as a crack of
thunder. One of the seeds broke a window on the
thirtieth floor of the McGraw-Hill Greenhouse,
and the startled staff there had had to hack it to
bits with fire axes to stop its germinating on the
rug.

Under these circumstances it hardly mattered where
the city settled; there was iron everywhere: and con-
versely there was no place on the planet which would
be out of eavesdropping or of missile range of Scranton, to the mutual inconvenience of both parties.
Nevertheless, Amalfi chose a site with great care,
one just over the horizon from the great scar in the
ground Scranton had made during its fumbled mining attempt, and with the highest points of an
Allegheny-like range reared up between the two
Okies. Only then did the machinery begin to rumble
out into the forests.

Chris was beginning to practice thinking like
Amalfi—not very confidently to be sure, since he
had never seen the man, but at least it made a good
game. The landing, Chris concluded tentatively, had

been chosen mostly to prevent Scranton from seeing what the city was doing without sending over planes: and secondly to prevent foot traffic between the two cities. Probably it would never come to warfare between the two cities, anyhow, for nothing would be more likely to bring the cops to the scene in a hurry; and besides, it was already quite clear from New York's history that Amalfi actively hated anything that did the city damage, whether it was bombs or only rust.

In the past, his most usual strategy had been to outsit the enemy. If that failed, he tried to outperform them. As a last resort, he tried to bring them into conflict with themselves. There were no pure cases of any of these policies on record—every example was a mixture, and a complicated one—but these three flavorings were the strongest, and usually one was far more powerful than the other two. When Amalfi salted his dish, you could hardly taste the pepper or the mustard.

Not everyone could eat it thereafter, either: there were, Chris suspected, more subtle schools of Okie cookery. But that was how Amalfi did it, and he was the only chef the city had. Thus far, the city had survived him, which was the only test that counted with the citizens and the City Fathers.

On Argus III, it seemed, Amalfi's hope was to starve Scranton out by outperforming it. The city had the contract; Scranton had lost it. The city could do the job; Scranton had made a mess of it, and left behind a huge yellow scar around its planetfall which might not heal for a century. And while New York worked and Scranton starved—here was where a faint pinch of outsittery was added to the broth— Scranton couldn't carry through on its desperate hope of seizing Argus III as a new home planet; though the Argidae could not yell for the cops at the first

sign—or the last—of such a piracy, New York could
and would. Okie solidarity was strong, and included
a firm hatred of the cops . . . but it did not extend to
encouraging another incident like Thor V, or bucking
the cops against another city like IMT. Even the
outlaw must protect himself against the criminally
insane, especially if they seem to be on his side.

Okay; if that was what Amalfi planned, so be it.
There was nothing that Chris could say about it,
anyhow. Amalfi was the mayor, and he had the citizens and the City Fathers behind him. Chris was
only a youngster and a passenger.

But he knew one thing about the plan that neither
Amalfi nor any other New Yorker could know, except
himself:

It was not going to work.

He knew Scranton; the city didn't. If this was how
Amalfi planned to proceed against Frank Lutz, it
would fail.

But was he reading Amalfi's mind aright? That was
probably the first question. After several days of
worrying—which worsened his school record drastically
—he took the question to the only person he knew
who had ever seen Amalfi: his guardian.

"I can't tell you what Amalfi's set us up to do, you
aren't authorized to know," the perimeter sergeant
said gently. "But you've done a lot of good guessing.
As far as you've guessed, Chris, you're pretty close."

Carla banged a coffee cup angrily into a saucer.
"Pretty close? Joel, all this male expertise is a pain in
the neck. Chris is right and you know it. Give him a
break and tell him so."

"I'm not authorized," Anderson said doggedly, but
from him that was tantamount to an admission. "Besides, Chris is wrong on one point. We can't sit there
forever, just to prevent this tramp from taking over
Argus Three. Sooner or later we'll have to be on our

own way, and we can't overstay our contract, either—
we've got Violations of our own on our docket that
we care about, whether Scranton cares about Violations or not. We have a closing date that we mean to
observe—and that makes the problem *much* stiffer."

"I see it does," Chris said diffidently. "But at least
I understood part of it. And it seems to me that there
are two big holes in it—and I just hope I'm wrong
about those."

"Holes?" the perimeter sergeant said. "Where?
What are they?"

"Well, first of all, they're probably pretty desperate over there, or if they aren't now, they soon will
be. The fact that they're in this part of space at all,
instead of wherever it was the Mayor directed them,
back when I came on board here, shows that something went wrong with their first job, too."

Anderson snapped a switch on his chair. "Proba-
bility?" he said to the surrounding air.

"SEVENTY-TWO PER CENT," the air said back, making
Chris start. He still had not gotten used to the idea
that the City Fathers overheard everything one said,
everywhere and all the time; among many other
things, the city was their laboratory in human psychology, which in turn enabled them to answer such
questions as Anderson had just asked.

"Well, score another for you," the sergeant said in
a troubled voice.

"But I hadn't quite gotten to my point yet, sir.
The thing is, now *this* job has gone sour on them too,
so they must be awfully low on supplies. No matter
how good our strategy is, it has to assume that the
other side is going to react logically. But desperate
men almost never behave logically; look at German
strategy in the last year of World War Two, for
instance."

"Never heard of it," Anderson admitted. "But it
seems to make sense. What's the other hole?"

"The other one is really only a guess," Chris said.
"It's based on what I know about Frank Lutz, and I
only saw him twice, and heard one of his aides talk
about him. But I don't think he'd ever allow anybody
to outbluff him; he'd always fight first. He has to
prove he's the toughest guy in any situation, or his
goose is cooked—somebody else'll take over. It's always like that in a thug society—look at the history
of the Kingdom of Naples, or Machiavelli's Florence."

"I'm beginning to suspect you're just inventing
these examples," Anderson said, frowning blackly.
"But again, it does make a certain amount of sense—
and nobody but you knows even a little about this
man Lutz. Supposing you're right; what could we do
about it that we're not doing now?"

"You could use the desperation," Chris said eagerly.
"If Lutz and his gang are desperate, then the ordinary citizen must be on the edge of smashing things
up. And I'm sure they don't have any 'citizens' in our
sense of the word, because the aide I mentioned
before let slip that they were short on the drugs. I
think he meant me to overhear him, but it didn't
mean anything to me at the time. The man on the
street must hate the gang even in good times. We
could use them to turn Lutz out."

"How?" Anderson said, with the air of a man pos-
ing a question he knows to be unanswerable.

"I don't know exactly. It'd have to be done more
or less by feel. But I used to have at least two friends
over there, one of them with constant access to Lutz.
If he's still around and I could sneak over there and
get in touch with him—"

Anderson held up a hand and sighed. "I was kind
of afraid you were going to trot out something like
that. Chris, when are we going to cure you of this
urge to go junketing? You know what Amalfi said
about that."

"Circumstances alter cases," Carla put in.

"Yes, but—oh, all right, all right, I'll go one step farther, at least." Once more he snapped the switch, and said to the air: "Comments?"

"WE ADVISE AGAINST SUCH A VENTURE, SERGEANT ANDERSON. THE CHANCE THAT MISTER DEFORD WOULD BE RECOGNIZED IS PROHIBITIVELY HIGH."

"There, you see?" Anderson said. "Amalfi would ask them the same question. He ignores their advice more often than not, but in this case what they say is just what he's already decided himself."

"Okay," Chris said, not very much surprised. "It's a pretty fuzzy sort of idea, I'll admit. But it was the only one I had."

"There's a lot to it. I'll tell the Mayor your two points, and suggest that we try to do something to stir up the animals over there. Maybe he'll think of another way of tackling that. Cheer up, Chris; it's a darned good thing you told me all this, so you shouldn't feel bad if a small part of what you said gets rejected. You can't win them all, you know."

"I know," Chris said. "But you can try."

If Amalfi thought of any better idea for "stirring up the animals" in Scranton, Chris did not hear of it; and if he tried it, obviously it had no significant effect. While the city worked, Scranton sat sullenly where it was, ominously silent, while New York's contract termination date drew closer and closer. Poor and starving though it must have been, Scranton had no intention of being outsat at the game of playing for so rich a planet as Argus III; if Amalfi wanted Scranton off the planet, he was going to have to throw it off—or call for the cops. Frank Lutz was behaving pretty much as Chris had predicted, at least so far.

Then, in the last week of the contract, the roof fell in.

Chris got the news, as usual, from his guardian. "It's your friend Piggy," he said wrathfully. "He had the notion that he could pretend to turn his coat, worm his way into Scranton's government, and then pull off some sort of coup. Of course Lutz didn't believe him, and now we're all in the soup."

Chris was torn between shock and laughter. "But how'd he get there?"

"That's one of the worst parts of it. Somehow he sold two women on the idea of being deadly female spies, concubine type, as if a thug government ever had any shortage of women, especially in a famine! One of them is a sixteen-year-old girl whose family is spitting flames, for every good reason. The other is a thirty-year-old passenger who's the sister of a citizen, and *he's* one of Irish Dulany's fighter pilots. The sister, the City Fathers tell us now, is a borderline psychotic, which is why she never made citizenship herself; but they authorized the brother to teach her to fly because it seemed to help her clinically. She stole the boarding-squad plane for the purpose, and by the time we got the whole story from the machines, it was all over."

"You mean that the City Fathers heard Piggy and the others planning all this?"

"Sure they did. They hear everything—you know that."

"But why didn't they tell somebody?" Chris demanded.

"They're under orders never to volunteer information. And a good thing too, almost all the time; without such an order they'd be jabbering away on all channels every minute of the day—they have no judgment. Now Lutz is demanding ransom. We'd pay any reasonable sum, but what he wants is the planet—you were right again, Chris, logic has gone out the window over there—and we can't give him what we don't own, and we wouldn't if we could. Piggy has gotten us into a war, and not even the machines can see what the consequences will be."

Chris blew out his breath in a long gust. "What are we going to do?"

"Can't tell you."

"No, I don't want to know about tactics or anything like that. Just a general idea. Piggy *is* a friend of mine—it sounds silly right now, but I really like him."

"If you don't like a man when he's in trouble, you probably never liked him at all," the perimeter sergeant agreed reflectively. "Well, I can't tell you very much more, all the same. In general terms, Amalfi is stalling in a way he hopes will give Lutz the idea that he's going to give in, but won't give the Argidae the same impression; the machines have run him up a set of key words that should convey the one thing to the colonists and the other to Scranton. Contract termination is only a week away, and if we can stall Lutz until the day before that—well, I can't say what we'll do. But generally, again, we'll move in there and deprive him of his marbles. That'll give us a day to get out of this system before the cops come running, and when they do catch us, at least they'll find that we have a fulfilled contract. Incidentally, it also gives us a day to collect our pay—"

"OVERRIDE," the City Fathers said suddenly, without being asked anything at all.

"Woof! Sorry. Either I've already said one word too many, or I was going to. Can't say anything else, Chris."

"But I thought they never volunteered information!"

"They don't," Anderson said. "That wasn't volunteered. They are under orders from Amalfi to monitor talk about this situation and shut it up when it begins to get too loose. That's all I can say—and it's none of it the best news I ever spread."

Only a week to go—and the contract date, Chris realized for the first time, was exactly one day before his birthday. Everything was going to be gained or lost within the same three days: for himself, for Piggy and his two victims, for Scranton, for Argus III, for the city.

And again he knew, as surely as he knew his left hand from his right, that Amalfi's present plan was not going to work.

And again the rock upon which it was sure to founder was Frank Lutz.

Chris did not doubt that Amalfi could outsmart Lutz hands down in any face-to-face situation, but that was not what this was. He did doubt, and doubted most thoroughly, that any list of trigger words the City Fathers could prepare could fool Lutz for long, no matter how well they lulled the hundred eyes of Argus to sleep; the city manager of Scranton was educated, shrewd, experienced in the ways of politics and power—and by now, on top of all that, he would be almost insanely suspicious. Suspicion of everyone had been normal for him even in good times; if he suspected his friends when things were going right, he would hardly be more trustful of his enemies in the very last days of a disaster.

Chris knew very little yet about the politics of Okie cities, but he knew his history. Also, he knew skunks; he had often marveled at the obduracy with which poor Kelly had failed to profit by his tangles with them. Maybe the dog had liked them; they are affectionate pets for a cautious master. But the human variety was not worth the risk. One look at Frank Lutz had taught Chris that.

And even supposing that Lutz did not shoot from

the hip while New York was still trying to stall, bringing down upon the city a rain of missiles or whatever other bombardment Scranton was able to mount; even supposing that Lutz was totally taken in by Amalfi's strategy, so that New York took his city away from him at the very last minute, without firing a shot or losing a man; even supposing all this—and it was an impossible budget of suppositions—Piggy and the two women prisoners would not survive it. In New York only Chris could know with what contempt Lutz treated the useless people aboard his own town; and only Chris could guess what short shrift he would give three putative refugees from a great city that did tolerate passengers.

Piggy's pitiful expedition was probably heaving slag right now. If Lutz allowed them to live, more or less, through the next week, he would certainly have them executed the instant he saw his realm toppling, no matter how fast Amalfi moved upon Scranton when the H-hour arrived—it takes no more than five seconds to order that hostages be sacrificed. That was the whole and only reason why the many wars of medieval Earth had gone on so many years after all the participants had forgotten why they had been started or, if they remembered, no longer cared: there was still ransom money to be made.

His guardian was already impatient of that kind of example, however. As for Amalfi and the City Fathers, they had made their position too clear to be worth appealing to now. Were Chris to go back to them, they would give him more than another No; such an approach would give them all the reasons they could possibly need to put Chris under a 24-hour watch.

Yet this time he *knew* they were wrong; and this time he planned very carefully, fighting off the constant conviction that these ancient men and machines could not possibly have made a mistake . . . and would snap the switch on him at any moment.

If they knew what he was up to, they remained inactive, and kept their own counsel. He trudged out of the city the next night. Nobody tried to stop him. Nobody even seemed to see him go.

That was exactly what he had hoped for; but it made him feel miserably in the wrong, and on his own.

CHAPTER ELEVEN: The Hidey Hole

Ordinarily Chris would not have ventured into a strange wilderness at night; even under present circumstances, he would have left perhaps an hour before sunrise, leaving himself only enough darkness to put distance between himself and any possible pursuit. But on Argus III, he had several advantages going for him.

One of these was a homing compass, a commonplace Okie object the needle of which always pointed toward the strongest nearby spindizzy field. On most planets, cities tended to keep a fractional field going to prevent the local air from mixing with that of the city itself—and when the city was on a war footing, the generators would be kept running as a matter of course in case a quick getaway should be needed. The gadget would point him away from New York for half his trip, and an ordinary magnetic compass would serve to show which way; thereafter, the homing compass would be pointing steadily toward Scranton.

The second advantage was light. Argus had no moon—but it had the hundred eyes of the nearby blue-white giant suns of the cluster, and beyond

296

them the diffuse light of the rest of the cluster, throughout this half of the year. The aggregate sky glow was almost twice as bright as Earthly moonlight— more than good enough to read by, and to cast sharp shadows, though not quite enough to trigger the color sensitivity of the human eye.

Most important of all, Chris knew pine woods and mountains. He had grown up among them.

He traveled light, carrying with him only a small pack containing two tins of field rations, a canteen and a change of clothing. The "fresh" clothes were those he had been wearing when he had first been transferred to New York; it had taken considerable courage to ask the City Fathers if they were still in storage, despite his knowledge that the machines never told what they knew unless asked. The request left behind a clue, but that really didn't matter; once Sgt. Anderson realized Chris was missing, he could be in little doubt about where he had gone.

By dawn he was almost over the crest of the range. By noon he had found himself a cave on the other side from which a small, ice-cold stream issued. He went very cautiously in this, as deep as he could go on his hands and knees, looking for old bones, droppings, bedding or any other sign that some local animal lived there. He found none, as he had expected; few animals care to make a home directly beside running water—it is too damp at night, and it attracts too many potential enemies. Then he ate for the first time and went to sleep.

He awoke at dusk, refilled his canteen from the stream, and began the long scramble down the other side of the range. The route he took was necessarily more than a little devious, but thanks to the two compasses he was never in any doubt about his bearings, for more than a few minutes at a time. Long before midnight, he caught his first glimpse of Scranton, glowing dully in the valley like a scatter of dewdrops in a spider's web. By dawn, he had buried his pack along with the New York clothes—by now more than a little dirty and torn—and was shambling cheerfully across the cleared perimeter of Scranton, toward the same street by which he had boarded the town willy-nilly so long ago. There were many differences this time, not the least of which was his possession of the necessary device for getting through the edge of the spindizzy field.

He was spotted at once, of course, and two guards came trotting out to meet him, redeyed and yawning; obviously, it was near the end of their trick.

"Whatcha doin' out here?"

"Went to pick mushrooms," Chris said, with what he hoped was an idiotic grin. "Didn't find any. Funny kind of woods they got here."

One of the sleepy guards looked him over but apparently saw nothing but the issue clothing and Chris's obvious youth. He cussed Chris out more or less routinely and said:

"Where ya work?"

"Soaking pits."

The two guards exchanged glances. The soaking pits were deep, electrically heated holes in which steel ingots were cooled, gently and slowly. Occasionally they had to be cleaned, but it wasn't economical to turn the heat off. The men who did the job were lowered into the pits in asbestos suits for four minutes at a time, which was the period it took for their insulating wooden shoes to burst into flame; then they were hauled out, given new shoes, and lowered into the pit again— and this went on for a full working day. Nobody but the mentally deficient could safely be assigned to such an inferno.

"Awright, feeb, get back on the job. And don't come out here no more, get me? You're lucky we didn't shoot you."

Chris ducked his head, grinned, and ran. A minute later, he was twisting and dodging through the shabby streets. Despite his confidence, he was a little surprised at how well he remembered them.

The hidey hole among the crates was still there, too, exactly as he and Frad had last left it, even to the stub of candle. Chris ate his other tin of field rations, and sat down in the darkness to wait.

He did not have to wait long, though the time *seemed* endless. About an hour after the end of the work day, he heard the sounds of someone threading the labyrinth with sure steps; and then the light of the flash came darting in upon him.

"Hi, Frad," he said. "I'm glad to see you. Or I will be, once you get that light out of my eyes."

The spoor of the flashlight beam swung toward the ceiling. "Is that you, Chris?" Frad's voice said. "Yep, I see it is. But you must have grown a foot."

"I guess I have. I'm sorry I didn't get here sooner."

The big man sat down with a grunt. "Never thought you'd make it at all—it was just a hunch, once I heard who it was we were up against. I hope you're not trying to switch sides, like those other three idiots."

"Are they still alive?" Chris said with sudden fear.

"Yep. As of an hour ago. But I wouldn't put any money on them lasting. Frank is getting wilder by the day—I used to think I understood him, but not any more. Is that what you're here for—to try and sneak those kids out? You can't do it."

"No," Chris said. "Or, anyhow, not exactly. And I'm not trying to switch sides, either. But we were wondering why you let your city manager get you into this mess. Our City Fathers say he's gone off his rocker, and if the machines can see it, you ought to be able to. In fact, you just said you did."

"I've heard about those machines of yours," Frad said slowly. "Do they really run the city, the way the stories say?"

"They run most of it. They don't boss it, though; the Mayor does that."

"Amalfi. Hmm. To tell you the truth, Chris, everybody knows that Frank's lost control. But there's nothing we can do about it. Suppose we threw him out—not that it'd be easy—where'd we go from there? We'd still be in the same mess."

"You wouldn't be at war with my town any more," Chris suggested.

"No, and that'd be a gain, as far as it went. But we'd still be in the rest of the hole. Just changing a set of names won't put any money in the till, or any bread in our mouths." He paused for a moment and then added bitterly, "I suppose you know we're starving. Not me, personally—Frank feeds his own—but I don't eat very well either when I have to look at the faces I meet on the streets. Frank's big play against Amalfi is crazy, sure—but except for that we've got *no* hope."

Chris was silent. It was what he had expected to find, but that made the problem no easier.

"But you haven't answered my question," Frad said. "What are you up to? Just collecting information? Maybe I should have kept my mouth shut."

"I'm trying to promote a revolution," Chris said. It sounded embarrassingly pompous, but he couldn't think of any other way to put it. He was also trying to avoid saying anything which would be an outright lie, but from this point onward that was going to be increasingly difficult. "The Mayor says you must have flunked your contracts because you don't have any machines to judge them. Evidently that happens a lot of times to small cities that don't have computer control. And the City Fathers say you *could* have done this job."

"Now wait a minute. Let's take this one step at a time. Suppose we got rid of Frank and patched things up with Amalfi. Could we get some help from your City Fathers on reorganizing the job?"

Now the guesswork had to begin, to be followed rapidly by the outright lying. "Sure you could. But we'd have to have our people back first—Piggy Kingston-Throop and the two women."

Frad made a quick gesture of dismissal in the dim light. "I'd do that for a starter, not as part of a deal. But look, Chris, this is a complicated business. Your city landed here to do the job we defaulted on. If we do it after all, then somebody doesn't get paid. Not a likely deal for Amalfi to make."

"Mayor Amalfi isn't offering any deal yet. But Frad, you know what our contract with Argus is like. Half of it is to do the job you didn't do, sure. But the other half of it is to get rid of Scranton. If you turn into a decent town instead of a bindlestiff, we'll get that part of the money—and it's the bigger part, now. Naturally the Mayor'd rather do it by finagling than by fighting—if we fight, we'll need all the money and more just to pay for the damages, both of us. Isn't that logical?"

"Hmm. I guess it is. But if you want to keep *me* reasonable, you'd better lay off that word 'bindlestiff.' It's true enough, but it makes me mad all the same. Either we treat as equals, or we don't treat."

"I'm sorry," Chris said. "I don't know a lot about this kind of thing. The Mayor would have sent somebody else if he'd had anybody who could have gotten in. But there wasn't anyone but me."

"Okay. I'm edgy, that's all. But there's one thing more, and that's the colonists. They're not going to trust us just because we've gotten rid of Frank. *They* don't know that he's the problem, and they'll have no better reason to trust the next city manager. If we're going to get back the mining part of the contract, Amalfi will have to guarantee it. Would he do that?"

Chris was already in far deeper waters than his conscience could possibly justify. He knew abruptly that he could push no farther into the untrue and the unknown.

"I don't know, Frad. I never asked, and he didn't say. I suppose he'd have to ask the City Fathers for an opinion first—and *nobody* knows what they might say."

Frad squatted and thought about it, smacking one fist repeatedly into the other palm. After a moment, he seemed about to ask another question, but it never got out.

"Well," he muttered finally, "every deal has one carrot in it. I guess we take the chance. You'll have to stay here, Chris. I can knock Barney's and Huggins' heads together easy enough, but Frank's something else again. When the shooting really starts, he might turn out to be a lot faster than I am—and besides, he won't care what else he hits. If I manage to dump him I'll come back for you soon enough—but you'd better stay out of sight until it's over."

Chris had expected nothing else, but the prospect of again missing all the excitement, while he simply sat and waited, disappointed him all the same. However, it also reminded him of something.

"I'll stay here. But, Frad, if it doesn't look as if it's working, don't wait till it's hopeless. Let me know and I'll try to get help."

"Well . . . all right. But better not to have any outsiders visible if it's going to stick. If anybody in this town sees New York's finger in this even people who hate Frank'll be on his side again. We're all a little crazy around here lately."

He stood up, his face somber, and picked up the flashlight.

"I hope you've got the straight goods," he said. "I don't like to do this. Frank trusts me—I guess I'm the last man he does trust. And for some reason I always liked him, even though I knew he was a louse from the very beginning. Some guys hit you that way. It's not going to be fun, stabbing him in the back. He's got it coming sure—but all the same I wouldn't do it if I didn't trust you more."

He swung to the exit into the labyrinth. Chris swallowed and said: "Thanks, Frad. Good luck."

"Sit tight. I'll see you."

Of necessity, Chris did not stay in the hole every minute of the day, but even so he found that he quickly lost track of the passage of time. He ate when he seemed to need to—though most of the food had been removed from the hide-out, Frad had missed one compact cache—and slept as much as possible. That was not very much, however, for now that he was inactive he found himself a prey to more and more anxiety and tension, made worse by his total ignorance of what was going on outside.

Finally he was convinced that the deadline had passed. After all, all possibility of sleep vanished; from minute to minute he awaited the noises of battle joined, or the deepening drone which would mean that Scranton was carrying him off again. The close confines of the hole made the tension even more nightmarish. At the first faint sound in the labyrinth, he jumped convulsively, and would have started like a hare had there been any place to run to.

In the uncertain light of the flash, Frad looked ghastly: he had several days' growth of beard and was haggard with sleeplessness. In addition, he had a beautiful black eye.

"Come on out," he said tersely. "The job's mostly done."

Chris followed Frad out into the half-light of the warehouse, which seemed brilliant after the stuffy inkiness of the hole, and thence into the intolerable brilliance of late-afternoon sunlight.

"What happened to Frank Lutz?" he said breathlessly.

Frad stared straight ahead, and when he replied, his voice was totally devoid of expression.

"We got rid of him. The subject is closed."

Chris shied off from it hastily. "What happens now?"

"There's still a little mopping up to do, and we could use some help. If you called your friends now, we could let them in—as long as Amalfi doesn't send a whole boarding squad."

"No, just two men."

Frad nodded. "Two good men in full armor should flatten things out in a day or so at the most." He hailed a passing Tin Cab. As it settled obediently beside them, Chris saw that there were several inarguable bullet holes in it. How old they were was of course impossible to know, but it was Chris's guess that they hadn't been there for as much as a week. "I'll get you to the radio and you can take it from there. Then it'll be time to get the deal drawn up."

And that would be the moment that Chris had been dreading above all others—the moment when he would have to talk to Anderson and Amalfi, and tell them what he had done, what he had started, what he had committed them to.

There was no doubt in his mind as to how he felt about it. He was scared.

"Come on, hop in," Frad said. "What are you waiting for?"

CHAPTER TWELVE: An Interview With Amalfi

The city was still administered, with due regard for tradition, from City Hall, but its control room was in the mast of the Empire State Building. It was here that Amalfi received them all—Chris, Frad, and Sgts. Anderson and Dulany—for he had been occupying it around the clock while the alert had been on, as officially it still was.

It was a marvelous place, jammed to the ceilings with screens, lights, meters, automatic charts, and scores of devices Chris could not even put a name to; but Chris was more interested in the Mayor. Since he was at the moment talking to Frad, Chris had plenty of opportunity to study him.

The fabulous Amalfi had turned out to be a complete surprise. Chris could not say any more just what kind of man he had pictured in his mind. Something more stalwart, lean and conventionally heroic, perhaps—but certainly not a short barrel-shaped man with a bull neck, a totally bald head and hands so huge that they looked as though they could crush rocks. The oddest touch of all was the cigar, held in the powerful fingers with almost feminine delicacy, and drawn on with invariable relish. Nobody else in the city smoked—*nobody* else—because there was no place in it to grow tobacco. The cigar, then, was more than a badge of office; it was a symbol of the wealth of the city, like the snow imported from the mountains by the Roman emperors, and Amalfi treated it like a treasure, not a habit. When he was thinking, he had an odd way of holding it up and looking at it, as though everything that was going on in his head was concentrated in its glowing coal.

He was saying to Frad: "The arrangements with the machinery are cumbersome, but not difficult in principle. We can lend you our Brood assembly until she replicates herself; then you reset the daughter machine, feed her scrap, and out come City Fathers to the number that you'll need—probably about a third as many as we carry, and it'll take maybe ten years. You can use the time feeding them data, because in the beginning they'll be idiots except for the computation function.

"In the meantime we'll refigure your job problem on our own machines. Since we'll trust the answer, and since Chris says you're a man of your word, that means that of course we'll underwrite your contract with Argidae."

"Many thanks," Frad said.

"Not necessary," Amalfi rumbled. "For value received. In fact we got more than we're paying for—we learned something from you. Which brings us to our drastic friend Mr. deFord." He swung on Chris, who tried unsuccessfully to swallow his heart. "I suppose you're aware, Chris, that this is D-day for you: your eighteenth birthday."

"Yes, sir. I sure am."

"Well, I've got a job for you if you want it. I've been studying it ever since it was first mentioned to me, and all I can say is, it serves you right."

Chris swallowed again. The Mayor studied the cigar judiciously.

"It calls for a very odd combination of skills and character traits. Taking the latter first, it needs initiative, boldness, imagination, a willingness to improvise and take short-cuts, and an ability to see the whole of a complex situation at a glance. But at the same time, it needs conservative instincts, so that even the boldest ideas and acts tend to be those that save men, materials, time, money. What class of jobs does that make you think of so far?"

"MILITARY GENERAL OFFICERS," the City Fathers promptly announced.

"I wasn't talking to you," Amalfi growled. He was plainly irritated, but it seemed to Chris an old irritation, almost a routine one. "Chris?"

"Well, sir, they're right, of course. I might even have thought of it myself, though I can't swear to it. At least all the great generals follow that pattern."

"Okay. As for the skills, a lot of them are required, but only one is cardinal. The man has got to be a first-class cultural morphologist."

Chris recognized the term, from his force feeding in Spengler. It denoted a scholar who could look at any culture at any stage in its development, relate to it all other cultures at similar stages, and come up with specific predictions of how these people would react to a given proposal or event. It surely wouldn't be a skill a general would ever be likely to have a use for, even if he had the time to develop it.

"You've got the character traits, that's plain to see—including the predisposition toward the skill. Most Okies have that, but in nowhere near the degree you seem to. The skill itself, of course, can only emerge with time and practice . . . but you'll have lots of time. The City Fathers say five years' probation.

"As for the city, we never had such a job on the roster before, but a study of Scranton and some more successful towns convinces us that we need it. Will you take it?"

Chris's head was whirling with a wild, humming mixture of pride and bafflement. "Excuse me, Mr. Mayor—but just what is it?"

"City manager."

Chris stared at Sgt. Anderson, but his guardian looked as stunned as Chris felt. After a moment, however, he winked solemnly. Chris could not speak; but at last he managed to nod his head. It was all the management he was capable of, right now.

"Good. The City Fathers predicted you would, so you were started on the drugs in your first meal of today. Welcome to citizenship, Mr. deFord."

Even at this moment, however, a part of Chris's mind seemed curiously detached. He was thinking of the original reason he had wanted long life: in the hope that some day, somehow, he might yet get back home. It had never occurred to him that by the time that happened, there would be nothing left back there that he could call his own. Even now, Earth was unthinkably remote, not only in space, but in his heart.

His definition of "home" had changed. He had won long life; but with it, new ties and new obligations; not an eternal childhood on Earth, but a life for the stars.

He wrenched his attention back to the control room. "What about Piggy?" he said curiously. "I talked to him on the way back. He seems to have learned a lot."

"Too late," Amalfi said, his voice inflexibly stern. "He wrote his own ticket. It's a passenger ticket. He's got boldness and initiative, all right—all of it of the wrong kind, totally untempered by judgment or imagination. The same kind of pitfall will always lie ahead of you, Chris; that, too, is an aspect of the job. It'd be wise not to forget it."

Chris nodded again, but the warning could not dampen his spirits now; for this was for some reason the highest moment of them all—the moment when Frad Haskins, the new city manager of Scranton, shook his hand and said huskily:

"Colleague, let's talk business."

JOHN DALMAS

He's done it all!

John Dalmas has just about done it all—parachute infantryman, army medic, stevedore, merchant seaman, logger, smokejumper, administrative forester, farm worker, creamery worker, technical writer, free-lance editor—and his experience is reflected in his writing. His marvelous sense of nature and wilderness combined with his high-tech world view involves the reader with his very real characters. For lovers of fast-paced action-adventures!

THE REGIMENT
The planet Tyss is so poor that it has only one resource: its fighting men. Each year three regiments are sent forth into the galaxy. And once a regiment is constituted, it never recruits again: as casualties mount the regiment becomes a battalion ... a company ... a platoon ... a squad ... and then there are none. But after the last man of *this* regiment has flung himself into battle, the Federation of Worlds will never be the same!

THE WHITE REGIMENT
All the Confederation of Worlds wanted was a little peace. So they applied their personnel selection technology to war and picked the greatest potential warriors out of their planets-wide database of psych profiles. And they hired the finest mercenaries in the galaxy to train the first test regiment—they hired the legendary black warriors of Tyss to create the first ever White Regiment.

THE KALIF'S WAR
The White Regiment had driven back the soldiers of the Kharganik empire, but the Kalif was certain that

he could succeed in bringing the true faith of the Prophet of Kargh to the Confederation—even if he had to bombard the infidels' planets with nuclear weapons to do it! But first he would have to thwart a conspiracy in his own ranks that was planning to replace him with a more tractable figurehead . . .

FANGLITH
Fanglith was a near-mythical world to which criminals and misfits had been exiled long ago. The planet becomes all too real to Larn and Deneen when they track their parents there, and find themselves in the middle of the Age of Chivalry on a world that will one day be known as Earth.

RETURN TO FANGLITH
The oppressive Empire of Human Worlds, temporarily filed in *Fanglith*, has struck back and resubjugated its colony planets. Larn and Deneen must again flee their home. Their final object is to reach a rebel base—but the first stop is Fanglith!

THE LIZARD WAR
A thousand years after World War III and Earth lies supine beneath the heel of a gang of alien sociopaths who like to torture whole populations for sport. But while the 16th century level of technology the aliens found was relatively easy to squelch, the mystic warrior sects that had evolved in the meantime weren't. . . .

THE LANTERN OF GOD
They were pleasure droids, designed for maximum esthetic sensibility and appeal, abandoned on a deserted planet after catastrophic systems failure on their transport ship. After 2000 years undisturbed, "real" humans arrive on the scene—and 2000 thousand years of droid freedom is about to come to a sharp and bloody end.

THE REALITY MATRIX

Is the existence we call life on Earth for real, or is it a game? Might Earth be an artificial construct designed by a group of higher beings? Is everything an illusion? Everything is—except the Reality Matrix. And what if self-appointed "Lords of Chaos" place a chaos generator in the matrix, just to see what will happen? Answer: The slow destruction of our world.

THE GENERAL'S PRESIDENT

The stock market crash of 1994 makes Black Monday of 1929 look like a minor market adjustment—and the fabric of society is torn beyond repair. The Vice President resigns under a cloud of scandal—and when the military hints that they may let the lynch mobs through anyway, the President resigns as well. So the Generals get to pick a President. But the man they choose turns out to be more of a leader than they bargained for. . . .

Available at your local bookstore. Or you can order any or all of John Dalmas' books with this order form. Just check your choice(s) below and send the combined cover price to: Baen Books, Dept. BA, P.O. Box 1403, Riverdale, NY 10471.

THE REGIMENT • 416 pp. • 72065-1 • $4.95 _____

THE WHITE REGIMENT • 416 pp. • 69880-X •
$3.95 _____

THE KALIF'S WAR • 416 pp. • 72062-7 •
$4.95 _____

FANGLITH • 256 pp. • 55988-5 • $2.95 _____

RETURN TO FANGLITH • 288 pp. • 65343-1 •
$2.95 _____

THE LIZARD WAR • 320 pp. • 69851-6 •
$3.95 _____

THE LANTERN OF GOD • 416 pp. • 69821-4 •
$3.95 _____

THE REALITY MATRIX • 352 pp. • 65583-3 •
$2.95 _____

THE GENERAL'S PRESIDENT • 384 pp. • 65384-9 •
$3.50 _____